Dave stood in the living room,
in the center of the house.
The walls were wiggling
as if they were made of snakes.

A low hiss filled the air, as if the snakes had simultaneously begun to spit their venom, and a putrid stench filled the room. Paula made a retching noise, but managed to hold down the contents of her stomach.

A black spot grew out of the air and expanded into an undulating, billowing mass. As they stared, it spread wispy tentacles. . . . The undulations grew more rapid, like a pounding heart. Then the blackness lowered itself to the floor, forming long, black limbs. A pair of red eyes appeared and more limbs shot out and were sucked back. . . . A clawed arm appeared, vanished. An octopus tentacle thrust forward, waving its suckers, and then it too was gone. The creature then was covered with eyes. A moment later, it had only two again, glowing red orbs the color of flames. . . .

The monster created hundreds of black ropey limbs around its bottom which frantically whipped and squirmed like roots desperately trying to work their way into the floor. Beneath its skin odd shapes were constantly moving, aligning themselves in curves, spirals and wiggly lines. . . .

Then a raspy voice spoke: "Here I am."

Most Pocket Books are available at special quantity discounts for bulk purchases for sales promotions, premiums or fund raising. Special books or book excerpts can also be created to fit specific needs.

For details write the office of the Vice President of Special Markets, Pocket Books, 1230 Avenue of the Americas, New York, New York 10020.

NIGHT SOUNDS

WARNER LEE

POCKET BOOKS

New York   London   Toronto   Sydney   Tokyo   Singapore

This book is a work of fiction. Names, characters, places and
incidents are either products of the author's imagination or are
used fictitiously. Any resemblance to actual events or locales or
persons, living or dead, is entirely coincidental.

An *Original* Publication of POCKET BOOKS

POCKET BOOKS, a division of Simon & Schuster Inc.
1230 Avenue of the Americas, New York, NY 10020

Copyright © 1992 by B. W. Battin

All rights reserved, including the right to reproduce
this book or portions thereof in any form whatsoever.
For information address Pocket Books, 1230 Avenue
of the Americas, New York, NY 10020

ISBN: 0-671-70426-5

First Pocket Books printing March 1992

10 9 8 7 6 5 4 3 2 1

POCKET and colophon are registered trademarks of
Simon & Schuster Inc.

Cover art by Jim Warren

Printed in the U.S.A.

To Sandy,
who makes it all worthwhile

And ye shall know the truth,
    and the truth shall make you free.

—John 8:32

NIGHT SOUNDS

AWAKENING

•1•

Images, strange and disquieting, tumbled through his mind.

He saw himself suspended in blackness, drifting, as if he were a child's balloon, gently being pulled along by an invisible string. Although he could detect no walls, no top or bottom, he sensed there were unseen boundaries here, that he was in a defined place.

Suddenly he was surrounded by shadowy figures. *Come to us,* voices called. *This way.*

He reached out to them. *No, not that way,* other voices warned urgently, *for that way lies your destruction.*

Terrified and confused, he floated on, eschewing all the voices. Several times he nearly bumped into the shapes, but he never came into contact with them. And even though he was close enough to reach out and touch them, he was unable to see them clearly. It was as though he were drifting through a scene in a movie that had deliberately been shot out of focus; he was surrounded by blurry forms. Some of them, he sensed, were hostile, while others were not. Yet he was unable to tell which were which. There was no air here, he realized, and yet he could breathe. The airlessness seemed natural for this place, as if oxygen were unnecessary here.

Where am I? he wondered desperately. He sensed that he knew but was unwilling to admit the truth to himself.

And then one overpowering thought gripped him,

1

squeezed him, as if he were in the grasp of some enormous hand. And he knew terror as he had never known it before, for this was a contest, but one whose rules he did not understand. He was being called upon to choose. And he sensed that *he* was what was at stake here, not just his life, but his center, his essence, his most personal and sacred core.

No! he screamed, but then he realized that, although his lips had moved and his vocal cords had vibrated, he'd made no sound. There *were* no sounds in this airless place. The voices he heard were in his head.

Where am I? he demanded.

Nowhere! came the reply in a chorus of voices.

But that was impossible.

He did not know what was happening or where he was, but he did know he wanted out of here, desperately wanted to escape. Looking in all directions, he frantically searched for an exit. But everywhere it was the same. Just shadows and shapes.

And then it grew darker, too dark to see.

Blackness spread out in all directions. It was like being in a cave so vast that he was unable to discern its ceiling or walls or floor.

And yet while he couldn't see as humans see, his skin had become sensitized, his pores becoming tentacles that felt what was around him, as if his flesh were made up of thousands of eyes that could "touch" something merely by looking at it.

He saw/felt a face in front of him. Although he was unable to tell whether it was attached to a body, his skin could feel sores all over it. Gathering a mental image of it, he felt flakes of skin, saw some of them fall off, like leaves dropping from a dying tree. He wanted to pull away from the face, from the leper-like flakes, from the blood and the pus that appeared beneath them. But some force compelled him to continue his search of that hideous countenance.

The sensation of seeing/feeling was strongest in his hands, and they felt as if they'd been dipped in fresh blood. Then it seemed as if the blood was puddling, and soon his whole body felt immersed in it, as if he were taking a sanguinary bath. He saw/felt the edges of what he realized were razor-sharp teeth.

The face grinned at him, and it was an expression of pure malice, the smile a torturer gives his victim as he takes the glowing iron from the fire.

He was drifting closer to it. As he did, he realized it was huge, its vile mouth large enough to chew him up like a bite of roast beef—except he would be raw beef, a few more drops of blood to trickle down among the oozing sores on the chin.

Everything within him, every nerve ending, every brain cell, screamed with such intensity that the sound itself should have knocked down the malevolent giant.

And yet there was only silence.

With all his strength he fought to change his direction of movement, to move away from this hideous thing that surely planned to devour him. But he had absolutely no control. He drifted, helpless, toward the waiting mouth.

Which opened.

Choose, the voices said.

Choose, choose, choose, choose.

He could feel other presences around him, swirling and dancing, and he knew that he had to pick one side or the other. The choice was the only thing that could save him.

But what was the choice?

And what if he made it wrong?

From the back of the mouth came a rasping laugh; like all the other sounds in this place, it existed only within his brain. It was a madman's laugh, the laugh of one who would launch nuclear weapons and be delighted that he was ending the world. It was the laugh of soldiers who enjoyed killing and plundering and looting and raping. It was the laugh of evil enjoying what evil did.

He was in the mouth now.

Although there was no air, he choked on the overpowering stench, a smell so vile it could not have been equaled by the opening of a million graves. His sense of smell seemed more acute than it had ever been before, able to identify the various components of the stench, detect the subtlest nuances of odor.

He stopped moving.

All around him were teeth as large as he was. Spires, jagged and pointed.

Choose, the voices chanted.

Choose!

Choose!

The mouth began to close.

And the man chose.

•2•

He came out of the blackness bit by bit. At first his surroundings grew gray, as if the night were slowly giving way to the dawn. The shadowy shapes were gone now, as was the horrible mouth. For a few moments, he was just hanging in a gray nothingness, and then a light appeared, a big glowing circle that spread until it filled his field of vision.

He blinked his eyes, and a room came into focus.

He was in a bed.

A tube was attached to his nose; other tubes were connected to his arms.

Sounds came to him then. People talking about someone who'd just had an operation. Clinks and clanks. A woman's amplified voice said, "Dr. Lord, call extension 227, please."

He tried to lift his head to get a better view of his surroundings, and the pain that shot through his temples was so intense that white lights momentarily danced before his eyes. He waited until the pain subsided, then waited a little more. Finally he tried again, more cautiously this time, and succeeded in lifting his head enough to see two large white objects. It took him a moment to realize they were his legs. They were in casts. One was suspended by a pulley.

Why was he in a hospital? What had happened to him?

But before he could address these questions, a nurse stepped into the room and walked over to his bed. She was middle-aged, chubby, tired-looking—not the sort they made naughty nurse movies about. But when she smiled at him, it was genuine, warm, and there was compassion in her brown eyes.

"I see you've decided to rejoin us," she said. Then before he could ask her all the questions that were circling in his head like hungry vultures, she wheeled and left the room, saying, "I'll tell the doctor you're awake."

A few moments later, another woman was looking down at him. She was younger and prettier than the nurse, but she didn't smile, and her blue eyes, though filled with intelligence, showed little warmth. "I'm Dr. Nelson," she said. "How are you feeling?"

"Well, I might have to withdraw from the Boston Marathon if it's being held within the next few weeks."

She frowned. Apparently Dr. Nelson didn't have much of a sense of humor. "You from Boston?"

"No. I was just making a joke."

"Ummm."

"Where am I?" he asked.

"St. Louis."

"St. Louis?" He'd meant what hospital was he in. It had never occurred to him that he might need to know what city this was. Why the hell was he in St. Louis?

"Do you remember what happened?" the doctor asked.

"What do you mean?"

"The plane crash."

"Plane crash?" But even as he said it, bits and pieces of memory were coming back to him. The jetliner filled nearly to capacity, the plane descending for a routine landing in St. Louis. Then the seatbelt digging into his flesh as his body was lifted violently upward, a momentary sense of weightlessness. A stunned hush falling over the passengers.

Then the screams.

Followed by the ripping of metal.

"Yes," he said, "there was a plane crash."

Dr. Nelson held a clipboard, which she'd been studying. "Can you tell me your name?"

"Dave Guthrie."

"How old are you?"

"Thirty-two."

"Where do you live?"

"Castle Bay, California."

"What's your address?"

"You mean you don't know who I am or where I'm from?"

She smiled resignedly, the way a worn-down parent looks at an unruly child. "We have your identification. We need to find out what you know."

"You mean whether I'm suffering amnesia or anything." He gave her his address.

"Where were you going?"

"New York. For a conference with the writer and the publisher of a children's book I'm illustrating. That's what I do. I'm an illustrator."

"Do you have any next of kin—or anyone else we should notify? The card in your wallet left that line blank."

"I don't have any family," he said. "I'm an only child, and both parents are dead. But I do have a fiancée—in Castle Bay. Jackie Lake. And there's my publisher, who's probably wondering where I am."

"We've heard from Miss Lake."

"How . . . how long have I been here?"

"Five days."

"Five . . ." He hadn't been prepared for that. A day or two maybe, but five days?

"When you first arrived, it was touch and go," she said. "But you've got the doctor's best friend, a very strong will to live."

"It does beat the alternative," he said slowly. Five days? He couldn't believe it.

"I hope you're ready for a good bit of poking and probing," the doctor said. "Now that you're awake, we're going to have to give you a thorough going-over."

Assisted by a red-haired nurse, she checked his blood pressure, took his temperature, had him breathe while she listened through a stethoscope, shined a light in his eyes, checked his casts. By the time the examination was over,

Dave was so exhausted he felt as though he truly had just run the Boston Marathon. Although he wasn't in any great pain, it was obvious that his body had been through a lot—and the pain was most likely being thwarted, at least for the moment, by drugs.

"How badly am I hurt?" he asked.

"Two broken legs along with assorted lumps, bruises, and abrasions," the doctor said. "Nothing vital was damaged."

"But . . . I thought you said I nearly didn't make it."

"You were in shock." She hesitated, as if debating whether to go on, then said, "You were thrown out of the plane. They didn't find you for two hours."

"How many people were hurt?" he asked.

Again the doctor hesitated, her efficient blue eyes meeting his, assessing him. "Did you know anyone on the plane?" she asked.

"No." This time he tried to assess what was going on inside *her* mind, but the blue eyes were those of a poker player, and they told him nothing. "Was anyone . . . was anyone killed?"

She nodded.

"How many?"

"All of them—except for you."

The exhaustion was rushing over him in a wave now. In a moment he would be unable to ask anything else. "I'm the . . . the only . . ."

"The only survivor, yes."

He peered into her eyes, thinking he saw the warm and sensitive person that lay hidden beneath the doctor's businesslike exterior, but a moment later he was sure he'd imagined it. Blackness closed in on him and took him, and the doctor and nurse faded away. Dave Guthrie swirled downward into the world of dreams.

He was in the plane again, and he heard the captain telling everyone to lean forward and put their heads on their knees, clasp their hands beneath their legs. And in the dream Dave Guthrie thought, *Yeah, because it'll make it easier for us to kiss our asses goodbye.*

Then he heard the screams, felt his body tugged first this

way, then that by an incredible force. As if his eyes were camera lenses zooming in for a series of tight close-ups, he studied the horror-stricken faces of the other passengers. He saw the blond woman whose hair was cut shorter than most men wear it. The fat guy with the triple chin who wore a cheap polyester suit. The freckle-faced stewardess. The little girl with the shiny black hair that hung to her waist.

And they were going to die. All of them.

Except him.

Why? his sleeping brain asked. Why me? But the question floated away unanswered.

And horrifying as these images were, there were darker, more terrifying things hanging in the corners of his dozing consciousness. Things he was unable to see clearly.

Choose, voices seemed to say.

Fuzzily he saw a huge, hideous mouth, opening, ready to consume him.

Choose!

DAVE

•1•

Dave Guthrie arrived back in Castle Bay two weeks after the plane crash. During his stay in the hospital, he'd tried to make his peace with what had happened. He hadn't known any of the people on that plane; he couldn't even recall the names of the flight crew, which had been announced shortly after the jet took off from San Francisco. An airplane crashed; 123 strangers died.

Jackie Lake, Dave's fiancée, was waiting when an employee of the small commuter airline that served Castle Bay rolled his wheelchair into the terminal. She was about five-five, blonde, and the word most people used to describe her was cute. Her hair bounced when she walked. She had freckles around her nose, and a few on its turned-up tip. Boys who dated Jackie in school must have automatically become the male half of Castle Bay High's cute couple. Jackie had enough cute for two.

She rushed up to him, then abruptly stopped herself. "I'm sure glad to have you back here in one piece," she said.

"I'll take that hug," Dave said. "Don't worry, I won't break."

She threw her arms around his neck and kissed him.

Jackie had flown to St. Louis as soon as he'd come out of the coma—prior to that the doctors had told her that making the trip would be pointless since he wasn't permitted visitors and would be unaware of them even if he was. She spent the next two days hovering over him like a mom with a sick child and getting in the way of the nurses. But once she was sure Dave would be okay, Jackie began to fret about all the business she was losing while she was away, and Dave had insisted that she return to California. Jackie was a go-getter, a workaholic, a real estate agent whose goal was to earn a million dollars in commissions, which she could invest in properties and make more millions. She was the typical yuppie, Dave supposed.

"Any luggage?" she asked.

"No. It's all gone."

For a second, that seemed to dampen their mood, but then Jackie said, "I saw you on TV."

Countless reporters had interviewed him. He'd been on all the networks. *Time* had run his photo with the caption "Sole Survivor."

"How did I look?" Dave asked.

"A little confused."

"In reality I was a little drugged."

"Are you okay now? I mean do you have any pain or anything like that?"

"A twinge now and then, but generally I'm okay. The left cast will come off in a few weeks. The right one will probably be on longer. Depends on how quick the bones mend."

"You trust me to drive this thing?" Jackie asked, taking hold of the wheelchair.

"Let's go."

She wheeled him through the terminal. It was tiny, a single room with a lone ticket counter. No bar, no restaurant, no newsstand. Luggage was carried in and lined up along the wall by the Coke machine. The airport's official name was Hopewell Field, though locals jokingly called it Castle Bay International.

A bearded man in jeans and a red-and-black checked lumberjack shirt held the door open for them as Jackie rolled Dave out of the building. She opened one of the Oldsmobile's rear doors, and Dave managed to work his way from the chair to the car, although when he was done, he was dripping sweat and his arms and shoulders ached. People in wheelchairs, he realized, had to develop strong upper body muscles.

The airport was on a bluff overlooking the Pacific. The road to Castle Bay twisted and turned and occasionally offered up some spectacular views of the ocean and the town. It was a beautifully clear day, and the Pacific stretched off to the horizon, looking blue and pure.

The ride to town took ten minutes. Located between San Francisco and Eureka, Castle Bay had been passed over by the California growth boom. Both California 1 and U.S. 101, which took turns clinging to the coastline along most of the state's length, swung inland here, so no tourists passed through. No fishermen made the town their home port. There were no paper mills, no silicon chip factories, no defense contractors. Castle Bay was a place that had no economic reason for existing.

It was here simply because people liked it and wanted to be here.

It was a picturesque little town on the coast, with year-round sea breezes, rolling hills, narrow streets lined with weathered clapboard houses. It looked like a New England fishing village without the fishing boats.

The name Castle Bay came from the bluff that rose above the community, a massive granite wall that extended inland for miles. Approaching from the sea, it looked like a foreboding castle, with two towers rising high above its ramparts and merlons and wards. It was an illusion, of course, and it vanished into the gray cliff face as soon as you entered the bay.

The bay itself was enclosed by two fingers of land that curved out to sea. Seen from above, they looked like pincers.

The road from the airport ended at a stop sign. Jackie turned left, onto Humboldt Avenue, the main drag. It was a narrow street that seemed to make its way through town aimlessly, winding between the clapboard buildings as if it had nowhere to go. Nothing was flashy here. Even burger

11

joints and gas stations had inconspicuous signs. Small pink letters in the window of Giorgio's Lounge spelled BAR, and that was the only neon in town.

That was why Dave Guthrie had come here: to live in a quaint, quiet place. Being an illustrator, he had that rare privilege people in his profession shared with writers, the ability to make a living anywhere they pleased.

Jackie was a native. Born here. Went to school here. Would most likely die here. Dave met her the day he walked into Castle Realty and announced that he wanted to buy a home.

The property Jackie found for him was right on the ocean and had one of the few patches of beach on what was otherwise a rocky stretch of coastline. The house was a small two-story place with two bedrooms and only one bathroom. Nothing fancy, but it suited him perfectly. He used one of the bedrooms as his studio, and it was full of easels and drawing tables and supplies. Sometimes he'd move his work out on the small balcony, when he wanted to enjoy the view of the Pacific or needed a little extra inspiration. For someone who lived alone and needed privacy to be creative, the place was ideal.

Jackie pulled into the gravel drive and stopped in front of the attached garage. She got the wheelchair from the trunk and rolled it up to the car, held it while he worked his way out of the car's seat and into the chair's.

The doctors in St. Louis had warned him about being confined to a wheelchair in a place that wasn't designed for one. Like most oceanfront houses, this one was built well off the ground. To get up the wooden stairs to the porch, Dave had to sit backwards on the steps, his casts sticking out in front of him, and use his arms to lift himself from one step to the next. They were made of weathered wood that was full of splinters, as were his palms after two steps. His entire right leg was enclosed in plaster, his left one in just an ankle cast. By the time he was halfway to the top, he was sure the casts weighed a ton each. Perspiration ran down his cheeks, dripped from his chin. There was nothing Jackie could do except carry the wheelchair and look helpless as he moved from step to step. Although he was sure at one point that he wouldn't, he made it to the top.

Back in the chair, he still had to get over the raised threshold but with Jackie hanging on to make sure he didn't kill himself, he managed to jump the front wheels over the hump, then roll the back ones over it. By the time he was in his living room he was exhausted.

"I cleaned all the old stuff out of your refrigerator," Jackie said. "There was some lunch meat in there that had grown into a green fuzzy glob the size of a basketball."

"A basketball?"

"Would you believe a softball? How about a baseball?"

"Oh, my god, I'm engaged to Maxwell Smart."

She laughed. "He was just a secret agent. The real estate business is much more cutthroat."

Jackie had been bringing in his mail. The oak coffee table was piled high with letters and magazines and advertisements. A *Newsweek* had slipped off onto the hardwood floor.

It was good to be home again. Entering this familiar place was like slipping into a pair of faded ratty jeans that fit him just right. He just sort of belonged in those jeans, as he belonged in this friendly room with its throw rugs, stone fireplace, and big picture window looking out on the Pacific. As he studied the ocean, Dave let his artist's eyes lose their focus, and the gulls wheeling over the water became fuzzy snowflakes dancing on a field of blue.

For the first time since the accident, Dave felt he could truly appreciate how lucky he was to be alive.

But 123 others weren't so lucky. He let the thought go. Fate had given him no more say than it had given those whose lives it had claimed.

"I put two steaks in the fridge," Jackie said. "I thought we might fire up the Weber later. If you're not feeling too tired, that is. I can always freeze them."

"Don't you dare freeze them. I'm ravenous."

She studied him a moment, as if making sure he meant it; then she said, "When's your nurse arriving?"

"Tomorrow."

"You and a private nurse. Here all alone. Hmmm." She cocked her head, frowning.

"Ripe with possibilities for hanky panky, isn't it?"

She nodded. "Can I trust you?"

"Absolutely."

"That's what they all say."

"The nurse's name is Ed. And it's not short for Edwina."

Her eyes travelled down to his legs. "With you in that shape, I guess I didn't really have much to worry about, even if the nurse's name *was* Edwina."

"You think I'd let a little thing like two broken legs stop me?"

"Seems to me it might be a little awkward, to say the least."

"I can manage it."

She eyed him doubtfully. "You sure?"

He grinned at her lasciviously. "Why do you think I told the nurse to come tomorrow?"

Jackie shook her head. "I can see being in a plane crash hasn't done anything to disturb your hormone levels."

"Nothing disturbs my hormone levels."

• **2** •

Dave lay in bed that night, feeling content for the first time since the plane crash. Jackie was asleep beside him. Making love hadn't been that difficult. They simply did it with her on top. He was unable to bend his right leg, of course, and the casts were like lead weights, but he hadn't let any of that interfere with his enjoyment. The hormone levels had indeed been up.

Beside him Jackie stirred, mumbled something. Suddenly she sat up. "Have I been asleep?"

"Unless you snore while you're awake."

"I snore? I didn't know—never mind that. What time is it?"

14

"Probably around eleven-thirty."

"Oh, good. I was afraid it might be three in the morning or something. I've got to go."

"Why?"

"You know why. It's a small town. Everyone would know."

Jackie had never spent an entire night with him. The excuse was always the same. Dave said, "But we're grown-ups, consenting adults. It's none of anyone else's business."

"But I grew up here. Everybody knows me." She got out of bed, began putting on her clothes. As she stood in the darkened room, fastening her bra, she was silhouetted against the moonlit rectangle of the window. She looked like a painting, an artist's conception of a woman dressing.

"You can say you had to stay to take care of me. I'll need help in the morning, getting out of bed, getting breakfast."

"I'll come back," she said. "Help you get up, make your breakfast."

"It's a lot easier just to stay."

"Easier for the moment, more complicated in the long run."

"Are people here really that prudish?"

"We've talked about this before."

"We could get married, live in matrimonial bliss."

"We are getting married," she said. "You proposed, and I accepted. Remember?"

"But you said we had to wait a year."

"To be sure."

"I'm sure now."

"I'll be sure if a year from now we still feel the same way. Why rush it? We make love now."

"But I get lonely at night."

"I'm sorry, but you'll just have to pass the time by sleeping." She was dressed now. She came over and kissed him. "I'll see you in the morning."

"What if I have to get up in the middle of the night to go to the bathroom?"

"Do you usually have to go in the middle of the night?"

"Well, not very often."

"How often is not very often?"

"Uh, the last time was about three years ago."

She sighed. "In the morning. The phone's within easy reach. If there's an emergency, call me."

• 3 •

After Jackie had gone, Dave lay in bed, wondering how he'd fallen in love with a woman who wanted an ironclad guarantee that a marriage would work before stepping up to the altar. He understood where she was coming from, he supposed. Although she didn't talk about it much, Dave knew that the divorce of her parents when she was very young had hurt her terribly, left her feeling alone, vulnerable, afraid, and unloved. There had been a vicious custody battle, each parent using her to hurt the other. Jackie had finally wound up with her mother, who remarried, then divorced again in another bitter court battle. Jackie had seen her share of marriages that had gone bad.

For Dave there was nothing to do but wait until the year was up. He didn't want her to marry him unless she was sure. Besides, only eight months of the waiting period remained. A third of it was behind him.

Dave stared at the moonlit window, recalling Jackie's silhouette. He thought about trying to paint it from memory, then dropped the notion. He had more pressing things to do. For one, all the drawings he was taking to New York had been lost in the plane crash. He could redo them, but it would take time, and the publisher and author were waiting.

A shadow appeared on the window.

Dave blinked. All the trees were on the other side of the house, where they wouldn't block the view of the ocean. How could there be a shadow there? It was a silhouette, like Jackie's, except this appeared to be the profile of a man's face, its mouth open, screaming.

He felt the urge to get up and look out the window, see what was causing this, but he couldn't get out of bed, not without a great deal of difficulty. So he lay there, watching the man's silent scream, wondering how the image got there, and feeling progressively more ill at ease.

A gust of wind came up, howled through the eaves.

It was as if he could hear the man screaming.

A drop of perspiration, so icy it left a trail of goosebumps, trickled down his back. The character of the moonlight was changing, he realized. It was dimming, graying. Fog was rolling in off the ocean.

A long misty tendril snaked its way across the window, as if reaching for the screaming man. The instant it touched him, he vanished. Dave Guthrie let out a small gasp.

Tricks of the fog and the moonlight, he told himself. But he wasn't sure he believed it, not deep down where it counted.

The window was blank now, barely discernible in the foggy night.

Suddenly a chill seemed to invade the room. A moment ago, he'd been warm and content. Now he was on the verge of shivering. He pulled up the covers, closed his eyes. Letting shadows on the window scare him was just being childish.

There was nothing outside that window, he told himself. *Nothing.*

Forcing his thoughts to go elsewhere, Dave recalled his old apartment in San Francisco, the face of the super, the names of his neighbors. He remembered the illustrations he'd done there, the fire engines and trains and bulldozers with smiles on their mechanical faces and headlights that were really eyes. A children's book by a woman in Kansas. The book hadn't sold well, but the publisher loved his drawings. It had been his breakthrough.

Nothing there. Nothing.

The San Francisco memories were replaced by the image of his fifth-grade teacher, a stern gray-haired woman whose name he was unable to recall. Then he saw Sarah Goodwell, his first high school crush. He'd been enchanted by her smile, her long red hair, her deep blue eyes. Sarah Goodwell had been unaware of his existence. In her senior year, she got knocked up by a stupid jerk named Calvin something-or-other.

Nothing.

Eventually Dave drifted off to sleep, and his mind was filled with bizarre images. He was in a place of total blackness, and yet he was able to see. He was surrounded by things, shapes. He drifted. He saw a monster, a hideous giant who tried to grab him and eat him, but he managed to get away. And he heard voices chanting *He has chosen; he has chosen; he has chosen. . . .*

THUMP!

Instantly Dave was awake. What was that? He listened intently, hearing only the sounds of waves gently rolling onto the beach. But he'd heard something. A car door slamming? A vehicle hitting a pothole out on the street? No, it had sounded as if it had come from the house. From *within* the house.

His eyes were drawn to the closet. Its door was a dark rectangle, barely discernable in the shadows. As Dave stared at it, a chill slithered through his body, settled in his gut. There was something in that closet. Something evil. Something that wanted to harm him.

And then he was ashamed of himself. He was acting like a little kid, seeing scary faces in the window and thinking there was a monster in the closet. Must be the bogeyman, come to get him.

But, hey, Dave, a little voice way back in the recesses of his consciousness said, *how do you know the kids aren't right? Huh? Tell me that. Isn't it possible kids are more attuned to such things, more sensitive to them? Maybe adults just can't sense what's really there.*

No way, he told that part of himself. He wasn't superstitious, and he didn't believe in goblins or devils or bogeymen. Nonsense. All nonsense.

He half expected another thump to come from the closet, just to prove him wrong. But Dave's world remained silent except for the surf and the other normal night sounds. Clearly something had fallen over in the closet, or pipes had clanked, or the water heater had thunked. It was probably a sound he'd heard a thousand times before, but tonight it had awakened him because he'd grown used to the hospital noises over the past couple of weeks, and the normal clanks and clunks of his own house seemed strange to him.

But he kept looking at the shadowy rectangle that was the closet door. It appeared to be open a crack, for there was a vertical line of darkness along one side. It was total blackness, that line, much darker than the surrounding shadows. And for some reason, Dave couldn't help but think that if he opened the closet door, the blackness would spill out, spread, absorb the light, make the entire room utterly, uncannily dark. It seemed to be more than just an absence of light, as if it were a substance in its own right, a thing . . . or a presence.

Dave turned his head away from the closet. Stop it, he told himself. Just stop it. Why was he suddenly afraid of shadows? He'd never been afraid of the dark—not since he was six or seven anyway. So why was his imagination running wild now?

He didn't know.

But he resolved to make it stop.

He lay there, not looking at the closet or the window, focusing his mind on safe things, childhood memories of birthday parties, bicycle rides, his season in Little League during which he'd played left field for two innings of one game and spent the rest of the time on the bench.

There were no more unusual noises.

After a while he drifted off to sleep.

19

PAULA

• 1 •

"Okay," Paula Bjornson told her fourth-period English class, "pass your reports to the front of the room." There was a rustle of papers as the students complied. After Paula collected the book reports, she sat down at her desk and surveyed the well-scrubbed, mainly middle-class, white, Protestant faces that stared back at her.

"Anyone who didn't hand in a report?" she asked.

The kids exchanged glances, and the room became unnaturally silent. Paula waited. Finally a hand appeared in the back of the class, raised just high enough to be barely noticeable.

"Andy?" Paula said.

"Yes," the boy said innocently.

"Do you have your hand up?"

He mumbled something incomprehensible.

Paula hesitated, not wanting to embarrass the boy in front of his classmates, but there was no way she could let pass Andy's failure to do assigned work. "You'd better come up here, so I can hear you," she said.

The seventh-grader made his way sheepishly to the front of the room, where he stood before her with wide, innocent eyes, his hair sticking up in a springy light-brown cowlick, his round cheeks slightly freckled. His shirt was wrinkled, and the laces of his athletic shoes were untied. He looked like a Norman Rockwell creation, full of boyish purity of

20

heart and all but dripping Americana. All that was missing was a baseball bat on his shoulder with a worn fielder's glove dangling from it.

"Did you have something you wanted to tell me?" Paula asked.

"I don't have my book report," Andy Stanwell said. He was shifting his weight from one foot to the other. Like most junior high kids, he was all energy, constantly in motion.

"Why not?"

"I . . . uh, this morning, before I left for school, I put it in my mom's station wagon, but my dad took it today because he needed to pick up some stuff that wouldn't fit in his car, and the book report was on the back seat."

"I see," Paula Bjornson said.

"So is it okay that I don't have it?"

"What book did you read?"

"The Three Musketeers."

"The book or Cliff's Notes?"

The boy looked shocked. Teachers clearly weren't supposed to know about Cliff's Notes. "No, I read the book. Honest."

"What was it about?"

"Swordfighting and stuff. It was really neat."

Although the boy was looking her in the eye and appeared about as deceitful as Mother Theresa, Paula Bjornson knew he was lying. It wasn't just that she'd been a teacher for five years. She'd always known when people were lying. As a girl, she could tell when other kids were making up stories and even when adults were being untruthful. She'd known there was no Santa Claus, no Easter bunny, long before her parents had owned up to these deceptions. She'd known when her mom told white lies to spare her feelings. She'd known when salespeople stretched the truth.

"I'll check with your parents," she said. "They'll confirm what you've told me, and I'll take the book report a day late. How's that?"

Judging by Andy Stanwell's expression, it was the worst suggestion he'd ever heard. "Uh . . . well, my dad won't be back tonight."

"Your mother can talk to me."

"Uh . . ." He stared at her, his mouth open, his mind working furiously. But he'd already given himself away, and he knew it.

"Why did you make up that story?" she asked.

He looked at the floor, shuffled his feet. "Because I didn't do it."

"The book report?"

He nodded. The rest of the class was transfixed, the room absolutely silent.

"Why not?"

He shrugged.

"It's not fair if I make everyone else have a book report for today, then let you bring one in later, is it?"

He shook his head.

"Here's what I'm going to do. I'll let you submit it, but I'll knock you down one grade for each day you're late. If you wait too long, the best you can get will be an *F,* and you won't even need to bother. How much of the book have you read?"

"About . . . uh, half." He was telling the truth.

"If you finish the other half tonight and do a good job on the report, you can get a *B.*"

"Half a book? In one night?"

"Better start reading as soon as you get home." Snickers came from various parts of the room.

"But . . . but I gotta play baseball."

"Up to you."

He studied her face, as if trying to read her innermost thoughts. Did she mean it? Would she really give him an *F?* Didn't she understand how important baseball was? Paula gave him her stern teacher look, and he nodded. "I'll start reading as soon as I get home," he said.

The bell rang, and the kids thundered out of the room like a herd of stampeding animals. Andy, clearly happy to get away, joined them. Paula started to tell them to slow down and leave in a dignified manner, but by the time she opened her mouth, the room was empty. After a few moments of mayhem in the hall, a fresh batch of young faces began to arrive.

When the bell sounded again, Paula Bjornson began her second-to-last class of the day at Hubert H. Humphrey Junior High School in Anoka Falls, Minnesota.

•2•

When Paula got home, she was exhausted. Though only twenty-seven, she felt ancient after a day with junior high school kids. They were in that stage in which they were beginning to look like teenagers, but still had a lot of the notions and perceptions of little kids. Going into puberty was like being two all over again, except now you were large enough to do some serious damage.

Still, she loved it, loved the kids, loved trying to make them use their minds. If just a few of them grew up to challenge the stuff society spoon-fed them, then she was a success.

She sat down in her old, comfy recliner and leaned back. "Ahhh," she said to the empty room. "It's good to get home."

She lived in an old two-story house that had been divided into four apartments. The place had character: high ceilings, a fireplace, wainscoting on the walls, floors of honest wood, walls that were thick and solid. She'd picked it because, though old and worn, it still retained some of the elegance of its era. To step inside was to sense, however vaguely, the simpler but more elegant days when there were horse-drawn street cars and the milkman came in the morning and doctors made housecalls.

Paula was fascinated with the past, and a part of her had always longed to live in those simpler times. Her antique bookcases all but bulged with the works of Twain and the Brontës and Hardy and Dickens and Conan Doyle.

She was being a silly romantic; she knew that. The past

was filled with brutality and corruption. Human beings were sold into slavery. Despotic rulers committed genocide. Men of God sanctioned the Inquisition.

Although Paula rarely admitted it to herself, one of the reasons she was fascinated with the past was because she was so unhappy with the present.

Not because of her job, which she loved, but because of the rest of her life. She lived by herself, her only companions her books. When she wanted company, it was provided by Sherlock Holmes or Tom Sawyer or David Copperfield. Although men occasionally asked her out, she always turned them down, opting for the safety of her apartment and her books. Never one to call attention to herself, Paula dressed plainly, usually in a white blouse with a plain skirt in navy or brown or gray with a cardigan and flat shoes. She eschewed makeup, and though Scandinavian, she was dark-haired—in Minnesota, land of blonds.

She was slipping into one of her moods again, and she attempted to shift her thoughts away from her loneliness. She plopped into her recliner, the one modern piece of furniture she allowed in the house, because she found its comfort outweighed its aesthetic disharmony. She began to reflect on her day. She immediately thought of the incident with Andy, how she had caught him in a lie and knew it. There was no doubt.

For Paula, the truth simply had a ring to it, a certain purity of sound. Lies were discordant, filled with unpleasant undertones.

She'd been surprised when she discovered no one else could hear the difference.

It was a gift, she supposed, part of her uniquely limited clairvoyance. Although there were times she'd wished she hadn't known the truth, she'd never considered her ability a curse. It had been given to her for a reason, she believed. Her task was to use it wisely.

Again, thoughts of loneliness and depression started to fill her mind, and she recalled the one time her ability had all but wrenched the soul out of her. She quickly tried to push the painful memory away. But it wouldn't go.

It had occurred during her junior year at the University of Minnesota. As a freshman she was as skinny as she'd been in high school, but during her sophomore year she began to gain some much-needed weight, and most of it went to the right places. She hadn't become voluptuous overnight, but at least she was no longer a walking piece of spaghetti. Though hardly brimming with confidence, she could look in the mirror and see she looked like a woman. A few men asked her out, but she always panicked, said no too quickly, and then wondered whether she'd done the right thing.

Then she met Bruce Hansen.

Bruce had the masculine face, curly blond hair, and broad shoulders you saw in magazine ads. But he didn't seem stuck on himself, and he wasn't the smart-alecky jock type. He sat next to her in her English lit class, and he was a good student, intelligent and interested. He liked the same books she did. She was both afraid of him and drawn to him. And when he asked her out, she swallowed her fear and said yes.

On their first two dates, Paula had banished her remaining anxieties, let herself go, and fallen madly in love with him.

On the third date, they'd parked on a deserted stretch of road that followed the Mississippi, kissed—the first time she had kissed a man—and then Bruce had started unbuttoning her blouse. She told him to stop. He told her he loved her.

The words had been dissonant, grating, like notes played out of tune, tones that combined in disagreeable ways, making sounds that caused you to flinch. Paula had never tried to describe it to anyone. To a maestro, she supposed, it would seem like a symphony composed entirely of sour notes. To a child in school, it would probably sound like chalk screeching on the blackboard. And to others, it might seem like a cry of pain, as if the words themselves were being abused. A lie simply sounded wrong, out of tune, off kilter, unpleasant to hear.

And Bruce Hansen had just lied to her. He said he loved her.

Paula was stunned. She was to be another checkmark on his scorecard, another conquest. And that was all.

He told her again that he loved her, that he couldn't understand what was wrong, that having sex was natural for people in love. Again his words had been discordant, jarring. The emotions on which she'd been floating during the first two dates were snatched out from under her, and she felt herself falling, crashing. She was hurt and angry, and suddenly she was furious, desperately in need of some way to show Bruce Hansen exactly what she thought of him. She clawed his face, called him a bastard. He'd been so completely caught off guard, he hadn't even tried to defend himself. He simply stared at her, dumbstruck.

She got out of his car and started walking. He pulled up alongside her, told her to get back in, but she refused. They were well out of the city, on a country road, and it was a cold winter night, the wind howling, picking up the snow on the ground and piling it into drifts. She didn't care. She wasn't getting back into that car.

Finally he drove off and left her there. As she walked along that country road with the snow whipping around her ankles, she was glad it was a winter night, because the icy wind was pure and it cleansed her of the naiveté that had allowed her to fall head-over-heels in love with someone like Bruce.

She was certain that anyone who spotted her would know instantly how unattractive and worthless she was. A person no one could ever truly love.

Tears rolled down her face, freezing before they could fall, crusting her cheeks and chin with ice.

She walked to a small twenty-four-hour restaurant and phoned for a cab. She had learned that her ability to see lies could not protect her, for sometimes the lies did not come until it was too late. Paula had not been out with a man since. She had learned her lesson. She would not risk the pain and humiliation again, even if it meant being lonely for the rest of her life.

The memories left her, and Paula found herself sitting in her favorite chair with tears streaming down her cheeks.

•3•

She made herself a dinner of lamb chops, sliced potatoes sauteed in olive oil, and a salad with homemade Italian dressing. Paula had concluded that, just because she had no one to cook for, didn't mean she had to forgo home cooking and subsist on TV dinners. She washed the dishes, read for a while, then decided to take a bath before going to bed.

Although the linoleum on the floor was new, everything else in the bathroom was probably original to the house. The sink was a pedestal type with faucets that had porcelain handles. The toilet had its tank mounted on the wall, and to flush you had to pull a brass chain. The tub had clawed feet. There was no shower.

She put the stopper in the tub's drain, then turned on the water. As she slipped off her robe, she averted her eyes from the mirror. She didn't like seeing herself naked. With her left hand she tested the water, gave the hot faucet half a turn, then stood back, waiting for the water in the tub to reach the proper temperature. Without thinking, she looked into the mirror, and this time she didn't turn away. A thin, pale woman stared back at her. She had green eyes, and she wore her hair in a Prince Valiant style, relatively short and sensible.

And yet, as she stared at herself, she noted that she went in where a woman should go in, out where a woman should go out. It was surely a body a man could love. But . . .

But could a man love *me?* Paula wondered.

She shook her head, for she knew that was the wrong question. She should ask whether she could ever take the risk of giving her love.

Her reflection was growing foggy as the hot water running into the tub steamed up the mirror. Paula turned off the tap, tested the temperature with a toe, then climbed in, settled into position, and picked up a washcloth.

Abruptly it hit her.

The odor of turpentine. She felt dizzy; the bathroom seemed to be wavering.

And Paula knew it was happening again. There were two facets to her gift. One was the ability to recognize lies. The other was to know when someone needed help. And it always began like this, always the same. The odor was overwhelming, as if only she and it existed in the world. She was only dimly aware of the distant buzzing in her ears.

Suddenly Paula was no longer in the bathtub in Anoka Falls, Minnesota, but on a small beach, looking off toward a rocky coastline. Then she saw a small two-story house, moved toward it. Entering the house by simply sliding through the wall, she saw a man, a guy in his thirties with brown hair and eyes, a handsome face. He was lying in bed, and she sensed but didn't see the danger that had caused her to be drawn here.

And then she did see something, a vague shadowy shape clinging to the man like an evil aura. As she studied it, it seemed to shrink tightly around the man as if claiming him for itself. She sensed the essence of the thing and recoiled in fear. It was vile and filled with hate.

Suddenly she desperately wanted to get out of that place, as far away as possible from the dark thing she'd just encountered, but she seemed unable to withdraw. Unwilling to get too close to the amorphous evil clinging to the man, Paula kept her distance. As she studied his face, the man's need for her help washed over her, although she had no idea how she could possibly assist him.

And then she was back in her bathtub, and although the water was still steaming, Paula was shivering. She didn't understand what had just occurred. Always before when this had happened to her, the person or creature needing help had been no more than a few miles away, and the problem had been obvious. She'd known exactly where to go and exactly what was wrong.

She'd been six years old the first time it happened. A puppy had fallen into a storm drain a block away. She'd been on the lawn in front of her house, and the acrid odor had come over her, followed by lightheadedness, a blurring of her vision, a strange noise in her ears. For a few moments, nothing happened; then she'd seen the puppy, looked into its terrified eyes, felt the fear in its heart, and she'd known where it was. Paula had run to the spot, but when she got there, she was unable to reach down far enough to get the puppy, so she'd rushed to the nearest house and dragged out a woman who pulled the animal to safety. No one had claimed the dog, and her parents let her keep it. She named her Sally, and she and that dog loved each other faithfully until Sally died of natural causes, an old and contented animal.

It had happened to Paula repeatedly throughout her life. She'd known when an injured man was trapped in a car that had run off the road and rolled down an embankment out of sight. She'd known when a five-year-old child was asleep in a burning house, his parents too zonked on drugs to know there was a fire. She'd known where to find a fifteen-year-old girl who'd been abducted by a man planning to rape, then kill her, and she'd made an anonymous call to the police, telling them where to go to rescue the girl. The officers had shown up in the nick of time.

But this latest occurrence of her gift, this trip to the beach, was different.

For one thing, she had no idea where the man was. The coast she'd seen was no Minnesota lake shore; it was an ocean. The Atlantic? The Pacific? The Gulf of Mexico? And how had this come to her from so far away? Paula had no idea what she was supposed to do. An unidentified man living on an unidentified coast needed her help. Who was he? How could she possibly help him? What danger was he in?

A violent shiver shook her as she recalled the dark thing she'd seen. Although she had no idea what it was, it terrified her. If that was what was threatening the sleeping man, there was nothing Paula could do to help him.

The water in the tub had cooled. Paula turned on the hot tap, let it run until the liquid caressing her bare flesh was warm again. Picking up her soap, she began lathering her legs, trying to put the incident out of her mind.

But she was unable to stop seeing the man's face. It was a handsome face, and on some level Paula sensed that he was a nice person. He needed her help. And she was unable to give it. She didn't even know where he was—or who he was. Again she found herself shivering, so she quickly finished her bath, got out of the tub, and began drying herself off.

She was covered with goosebumps.

Although it was nearly summer—school would let out in two weeks—Paula wished she could turn the heater up to full blast. She couldn't, of course; the maintenance man had turned it off weeks ago. But Paula was freezing.

Slowly she realized the chill wasn't in the apartment. It was within her, a deep, pervasive iciness that seemed to reside in her soul.

Paula climbed into bed but couldn't sleep. She kept seeing the sleeping man and the dark, shadowy presence that appeared to be threatening him. Someone needed her help, and she was powerless to give it. And back in the deepest reaches of her subconscious was a primitive part of herself that was glad she was unable to get involved, for it had recognized the dark thing she'd seen, and recoiled in terror.

Paula got out her electric blanket, turned it up to barbecue and slipped back into bed. It took hours for her to feel warm.

ED

• 1 •

Ed Prawdzik rolled over, and his arm came to rest on something soft. "Nice bumps," he said.

"Bumps?" Andrea said. "You would call my breasts bumps?"

"You get mad when I call them tits."

"I don't get mad. I just point out that you're talking like one of those jerks who uses obscenities to describe all a woman's parts."

"What's obscene about tits? I love tits."

"Why can't you call them breasts?"

"Doesn't sound right."

"It does if you prefer gentle, nonoffensive terms to uncouth ones."

"Uh-oh."

"Uh-oh?"

"Yeah. It means you're leading me into conversational no-man's-land here, and I'm going to find myself with no way out—except maybe total surrender."

Andrea rolled over and hugged him. "You're cute."

"Yeah, I am, aren't I?"

"Oh, pooh," she said, and slugged him playfully in the back.

"Man abuse," he said. "Man abuse."

Andrea didn't respond. The clock on the bed table said it

31

was 6:15 A.M. They'd have to get up soon. Andrea Colmer was an R.N., and she was presently on day shift at Eureka General Hospital. Ed would have to get packed and drive down to Castle Bay, where he'd spend the next few weeks with a guy named Dave Guthrie.

Ed and Andrea lived in an apartment complex in Eureka. They'd met at General, gone out a few times, and somewhere along the line—Ed wasn't sure just where—they'd started living together, a decision he'd never regretted. They'd talked about marriage, but it had never happened, probably because they both liked the idea that there were no ties, that either of them could pull out at any time, and therefore they were together because they wanted to be and for no other reason. Ed could see a few holes in that reasoning, but then they were both happy with things the way they were, so—as the saying went—If it ain't broke, don't fix it.

Ed rolled over so he was facing Andrea, who was hidden beneath the sheet except for a mass of honey blond curls. He wiggled over until his six feet two inches were nestled comfortably against her five feet three inches. "This is the last time we'll be together for a couple of weeks," he said.

"Ummm," Andrea replied.

Ed felt himself stiffening, and he knew Andrea felt it too. He just lay there, not saying anything.

The only male nurse at General, he'd quit his job at the hospital because, no matter how hard he tried, he was unable to please the nursing supervisor. Grace Barclay was a tall, thin, gray-haired woman with an authoritarian personality a lot like that of Nurse Ratched in *One Flew Over the Cuckoo's Nest*. She'd made it clear from the start that she disliked having a man on her staff.

It was the first time Ed had been discriminated against because of his sex, and it taught him what it was like for a lot of women in the workforce. Nothing he could do would satisfy Grace Barclay. He had to be twice as good, work four times as hard as anyone else, and still Barclay was constantly on his ass. When he finally had all he could take, he went to see her, hoping he could make her understand. She told him that if he couldn't cut it, he should get the hell out. He got out.

Sure, he let her win, but he never really saw it as a contest. He went into nursing to help people, not to fight with a domineering woman who saw the profession as a purely female calling. So he went into business for himself. He registered as a temporary live-in, willing to go anywhere in northern California. He didn't make much money. But he was happy.

"Something on your mind?" Andrea asked.

"Who, me?"

"There's something pressing into my left buttock."

"Imagine that."

"I'd say there's something on its mind, even if not on yours."

"Its?"

"Its. Your dick."

"There you go calling my body parts obscene names again."

She rolled over to face him. "What's obscene about that? There's Dick Nixon, Dick Van Dyke, and all those detectives called dicks."

"Some of them are probably pricks."

She rolled her eyes. "You're hopeless."

They made love. Afterward, although they knew better, they drifted off to sleep. Only five or ten minutes, Ed told himself, trying to set his mental alarm clock. You've got to pack; Andrea's got to get to the hospital. Only five or ten minutes. No more.

But the internal alarm clock failed.

What woke Ed was Andrea. She was screaming.

She was sitting up in bed, the sheet having slipped off her large breasts, and she was shaking. She looked up at him, and there was terror in her eyes. She threw her arms around him, squeezed him so hard it was almost painful.

"Andrea . . . what happened?"

"Dream," she said. She was still shaking.

"What dream?"

Andrea believed in dreams. She believed they were a way

33

of seeing things. Like the future, or people in other places. The pictures were distorted sometimes, but the true meaning was always there if you could interpret it. A nightmare meant something bad was going to happen, maybe to you, maybe to someone else, but it *would* happen.

"Falling," she said.

"Who was falling?" When she didn't answer, he said, "That's a pretty common nightmare, falling. You always wake up before you hit the ground and all that."

A violent shiver passed through her. She actually felt cold in Ed's arms. "I'm . . ." She let the word trail off.

"You're what?"

"Scared."

"Nightmares are always scary. All that weird stuff happening."

"This was different."

"Why?"

"Because . . . because . . ."

"Because why?"

"Because this time I *did* hit the bottom."

"No kidding?" A wave of Andrea's chill rolled into his midsection. He'd never heard of that happening to anyone. You always woke up before you hit the bottom. Always.

"I was falling and falling . . . falling . . . from the tower."

"Andrea, it was just a dream, okay? People have nightmares all the time, and nothing happens."

"Falling from the tower . . . in the castle."

"Okay, so this was a medieval dream."

"But in the dream I was you."

"Me?"

"And I hit the bottom. I hit, and I could feel my bones breaking."

"Jesus, Andrea, I can see why it scared you, but you gotta back off from it. It was all that weird shit in your unconscious mind running wild, your id poking through and all that."

"Scared," she whispered. "I'm so scared."

And he held her tightly.

34

•2•

Though awake, Dave Guthrie hadn't opened his eyes yet. There was no hurry, so he simply lay there, letting the last wisps of sleep dissolve away like tendrils of fog being chased by the sun.

Finally he opened his eyes and focused on his dresser, on which there was an alarm clock with oversized red numerals. It was 7:12 A.M. He shifted his gaze to the window. There was no screaming man now, only the sky and the dazzling brightness of the sun reflecting off the Pacific.

His bladder was full, and he eyed the wheelchair, trying to decide whether he should expend the effort to haul himself into it or wait for Jackie, who should be here shortly. While weighing that decision, he let his gaze wander around the room, absently passing over the antique dresser, the wooden rocking chair, a painting he'd done himself—the sea at sunset, the clouds on the horizon pink and purple and breathtaking.

Then he saw the closet door.

It was open.

Last night it had only been ajar.

He recalled the noise, the thunk.

His mind, making deductions, logical connections, informed him that something had been in the closet and left without closing the door. For a few seconds his heart was in his throat as he tried to figure out what it could have been—all his childhood memories screaming that it was the bogeyman, if not something worse. But then rationality cut in, and he realized how ridiculous all this was. The door had been ajar; it could have swung open by itself, because it wasn't hung plumb or because the house shifted slightly in response to cooler nighttime temperatures. Maybe it had been pulled open by a draft. Maybe it had been open all along. It was dark; he could have imagined the vertical shadow at its edge.

And yet uneasiness swirled through him like a winter wind, chilling whatever it came into contact with.

Nothing was in the closet. Don't be stupid.

He recalled the crack along the door's edge, the blackness that had seemed absolute. And he remembered the screaming face in the window and how the image had vanished as a finger of fog snaked over to it, touched it. . . .

And he heard voices, chanting, *Choose, choose, choose*. . . .

Dave Guthrie took a deep breath and put all this nonsense out of his mind. He'd been illustrating so many children's books that he was beginning to revert to childhood—which wasn't as farfetched as it sounded. When he did a children's book, he tried to put himself in the mind of a youngster. Would kids find the smiling dinosaurs friendly and intriguing? Or would they think they were stupid? Grown-ups tended to forget how perceptive kids were. Talk down to them, give them nonsense, and they weren't fooled. So he spent a lot of time trying to get into the mindset of a young child. Maybe he'd done too good a job.

And then Dave realized he was overlooking the most obvious explanation of all. He'd been the only survivor among the more than a hundred passengers on an airliner, and he'd come close to shaking hands with the Grim Reaper himself. An experience like that unnerved you, made you uncomfortably aware of your mortality. He was understandably jittery. In time it would pass. In the meantime, he had to stop getting spooked by every little thing that happened.

The explanation made him feel better. He wasn't going crazy. He'd been through a lot. He needed time to heal—in more ways than just the knitting of his bones.

• 3 •

Jackie arrived about 7:45. She helped him out of bed, which was mainly a matter of holding the lightweight wheelchair steady while he maneuvered himself into it. After Dave had been to the bathroom and was dressed, Jackie went downstairs to make him some breakfast.

Dave was rapidly beginning to hate being confined to a wheelchair. He despised being dependent on someone else, needing help every time he tried to do something. He knew that over the next few weeks—or months—he was going to feel like that a lot, and he knew what he had to do when it happened. Remind himself that he was the lucky one, the one who survived.

Dave Guthrie was born into a middle-class family in Connecticut. His dad was a civil engineer; his mother a full-time mom. An only child, he'd been a little spoiled, but not overly so. He'd been an average student; he'd stayed out of trouble. The worst thing he could recall doing as a child was smashing a home run that not only left the backyard, but went over Mr. Flexner's fence and into the Flexners' bedroom window.

Baseball and drawing had been the things he'd loved best. As a ballplayer, he'd been barely good enough to make the Little League team, and then only as a benchwarmer. He loved baseball; he just wasn't very good at it. His drawing talents, however, served him much better. As a mere sixth-grader, he'd had his sketches displayed at two universities. He drew cartoons for his junior and senior high school newspapers, attracting the interest of his guidance counselor who suggested he apply for art scholarships at a number of universities. He did and won a full scholarship to a little-known but very good fine arts college in Wisconsin.

After graduating, he worked for advertising agencies in Omaha, Denver, and San Francisco before going out on his own.

In short, he'd led an unextraordinary life. He'd succeeded in his career by working hard, eventually realizing the dream of being his own boss. He enjoyed his work, liked his life, and he was generally happy. He'd even received the fifteen minutes of fame Andy Warhol said everyone was entitled to—not for his art, but for being the sole survivor of a catastrophe.

"Breakfast," Jackie said.

Dave turned his wheelchair away from the window. She handed him a tray with his meal on it. Bran flakes, toast, orange juice, and a cup of coffee. "Thanks," he said.

It wasn't his kind of breakfast. He liked bacon and eggs. Lots of cholesterol. But then Jackie was like that. She didn't ask him what he wanted; she gave him what she thought he should have. His mother had been like that too.

After eating about half his breakfast, he said, "Sometimes I wonder why 123 people died and I didn't."

Jackie was sitting on the bed, watching him. "You should just be glad you're the one."

"Yeah, but why should I be? What did I do to deserve it?"

She looked at him as though he were crazy. "Who cares if you deserve it? Just be glad you made it."

"It's not that easy."

Jackie studied him, frowning. She clearly didn't see where he was coming from.

He said, "I feel guilty about it, I guess."

Her frown deepened. "You want to go back, trade places with one of the others?"

"No." But I want you to understand how I feel, he thought.

"Look," Jackie said, "life's full of bad breaks and lucky breaks. If a guy walks in looking for a half-million dollar house, the money all but burning a hole in his pocket, and he walks up to my desk, that's a lucky break for me, a bad break for the other salespeople. But if the same guy walks up to Ted O'Malley's desk, it's a hell of a break for Ted and too bad about me, right? I mean, you should be happy. It was your day for the lucky break."

"And all the other people?"

She shrugged. "It wasn't their day."

Dave stared at the remains of his breakfast, said nothing.

"Come on," Jackie said. "You didn't kill those people. You couldn't have saved them if you'd wanted to. The engines failed, Dave. There was nothing you could do."

"Take my lucky break and run with it?"

"Yeah," Jackie said, "take your lucky break and run with it. Actually, for now, you'll have to hobble."

Dave managed a smile.

"Hey," Jackie said, looking at her watch, "I gotta run. I'm showing a house at nine."

"When will you be back?"

"Don't know. After I show that one, I've got a couple coming in to spend the day, see what's available. Lord knows when I'll get free. You gonna be okay?"

"Sure," Dave said. "Ed the nurse will be here to take care of me. As a matter of fact, you should probably leave the front door unlocked for him. I'm going to wait up here, so I don't have to climb the stairs if I have to go to the bathroom."

Jackie kissed him on the cheek. "Finish your breakfast," she said. Then she dashed from the room.

•4•

The nurse arrived about one. Dave was in his studio, which faced the highway. He saw a red Bronco pull up and a large man get out of it.

"You Ed?" Dave asked, looking down at the man from the second-story window.

"That's me."

"Front door's unlocked. Come on up."

Dave heard the front door open, then footsteps on the stairs, and a moment later the man stepped into the studio. Extending his hand, he stepped over to Dave. "Ed Prawdzik," he said, smiling. "Looks like I'll be your companion for a while."

Dave shook his hand. The nurse was built like a defensive lineman. Broad shoulders, big chest, a lot of weight but all of it muscle. He had a round face, hair that was a mass of tiny curls, and eyes that twinkled when he smiled his slightly lopsided grin. He was one of those people who just seemed to exude warmth and good humor, and Dave instantly liked him, as he suspected most people did.

"For the next few weeks," the nurse said, "I want you to

think of me as your legs. Whatever they used to do, I'll do for you. I'll buy your groceries, wash your dishes, whatever needs to be done."

"I didn't know you'd do all that," Dave said. "Actually, I guess I really didn't know what you'd do."

"Some nurses define the job as just dealing with your medical problems, figure the rest of it's maid's work. I don't see it that way. If I'm here to help, I should help, and that means more than just checking your blood pressure and wheeling you around. Besides, you'll figure I owe you a little extra service when you find out how much I eat." He grinned.

"Bring your stuff in and make yourself at home," Dave said. "I'm afraid all I can offer in the way of accommodations is a cot in the living room."

"Knew that when I took the job," Ed said. "I'll get my stuff. Then we'll talk, iron out some of the details of how we're going to handle things."

The nurse went back to his car, and Dave let his eyes travel absently around the room. Two easels stood to his right, both holding paintings he'd been doing for magazine covers. One showed a group of Boy Scouts having a picnic. The other showed a spectacular mountain scene with parents and two kids standing by the family station wagon, looking at the beauty. The two paintings would be the covers on upcoming issues of *Vacationland West,* a publication put out by a coalition of western state governments, chambers of commerce, tourist bureaus, and the like. To his left were a pair of drawing tables, a paint-spattered wooden supply cabinet, a shelf on which jars containing brushes and thinner were lined up. Tacked to the walls were the watercolors he'd done while developing the pictures for the children's book he was currently illustrating. The smiling dinosaur was green in one, blue in another, brown in a third, its expression running the gamut from delighted to darn near sappy.

Ed reappeared and said, "I've looked the place over, and I've got some suggestions for you. First of all, there's no good way to get you up and down the stairs unless I carry you."

"Carry me? I weigh a hundred-and-seventy pounds."

Ed grinned. "I weigh two-thirty."

Dave nodded. "To tell you the truth, it might be a little embarrassing to have someone carry me."

"There are lots of things that you might feel that way about, but you're just going to have to get over the feeling. I'm a professional, I'm here to help, and you're just going to have to put things like embarrassment aside. Can you do that for me?"

"I can try."

"Good. Now, as I was saying, because getting up and down the stairs is going to be a hassle, I'd suggest you spend most of your time up here. Your work area is up here, along with the bathroom and bedroom. I'll cook your meals and bring them up to you, except for dinner. Dinner you should eat downstairs, and then you should spend the evening in the living room, watching TV or reading, because if you spend all your time up here you're going to have some heavy-duty cabin fever. You'll have it anyway, but there's no reason to make it any worse than necessary. A change of scenery from time to time will help."

"I'll put myself in your hands," Dave said.

"Especially when you go up or down the stairs," Ed said.

"You really going to carry me?"

"Sure am," Ed replied. "Now, to change the subject, my first order of business is going to have to be a trip to the grocery store. You've got a few things in the fridge, but there's nothing I can work with, if you know what I mean. Is there any kind of food you particularly like or dislike?"

"I don't like liver."

Ed made a face. "Me neither."

"Other than that, I only have two requirements: that it be tasty and that there be plenty of it."

Ed beamed. "We're going to get along just fine."

• 5 •

Dave was sitting by the studio window when Ed got back from the grocery. The nurse looked up at him and waved, then set about carrying in about half a dozen bags of groceries. When Ed came upstairs to check on his patient, Dave said, "What's for dinner?"

"Haven't decided yet, but you'll like it. I'm a hell of a cook."

• 6 •

Ed was indeed a hell of a cook. He carried Dave downstairs, lifting him as casually as Dave could pick up a kitten, put him back in his chair, and wheeled him into the dining room. The table had been set, and one chair had been removed, leaving a space into which the nurse rolled Dave's chair.

"Be right back with supper," Ed said and disappeared into the kitchen. He reappeared a few moments later and served a meal of boeuf bourguignon with noodles and green beans almondine, accompanied by rolls and a salad with homemade Italian dressing.

"I can't believe this," Dave said. He tried the beef. "Delicious."

"Hope Italian dressing's okay on the salad," Ed said.

"My favorite," Dave said.

Ed sat down at the trestle dining table, and for a few moments they ate in silence. Dave broke it.

"I haven't eaten like this since . . . well, since my last family Thanksgiving."

"I don't like my patients to get too thin on me," Ed said.

"Thin? It's a wonder they don't all weigh a ton."

Dave ate everything, and when he was done he was

stuffed. Every part of the meal had been prepared with great care. The salad contained chunks of fresh broccoli and cauliflower and the dressing contained a blend of herbs and spices that enhanced the vegetables perfectly.

"I'm not going to want to let you leave," Dave said.

"Save room for dessert."

"You've got to be kidding."

"Just a little ice cream. I'm sure you've got room for that."

Dave found some room.

After they'd eaten, Ed wheeled him into the living room and gave him the remote control for the TV. Then he cleaned up in the kitchen and dining room. When he was done, he sat down on the couch and explained to Dave that he had brought with him some devices that would allow him to perform his bodily functions in the wheelchair, and that Dave was free to use them if he wished. Dave said he'd see. He also said that bathing was going to be a problem because plaster casts had to be kept dry, and that Dave would probably need help.

"And," Ed said, "I brought along one other thing you should know about."

"What's that?"

"It's a little scratcher on a long flexible wire. Made it myself. You can use it to get way down inside those casts and get those places that just itch like crazy."

"Ed," Dave said, "I don't know what I would have done without you."

•7•

In Eureka, Andrea Colmer spent the evening watching television. She didn't like it when Ed took live-in jobs. She missed him. And his presence so filled the apartment that without him it seemed huge and vacant, and her thoughts seemed to echo back to her from a vast emptiness.

This time it was worse than usual, for she'd had the dream. Sure, she knew Ed thought it was silly to believe in dreams, but she couldn't help doing so. The human mind had capabilities we weren't aware of, and what better place for them to show themselves than in the confused images of dreams.

If you could sort through the surreality of dreams, you could find the nuggets of truth.

She'd been Ed, and she'd been falling.

And she'd felt her bones break.

Andrea went to bed with trepidation, afraid she'd have the dream again. She tossed and turned for a while, but she finally drifted off.

• 8 •

At 2:24 A.M., Andrea Colmer woke up screaming.

PLEAS FOR HELP

• 1 •

"After reading these book reports," Paula Bjornson told her second-period class, "I've discovered that most of you people don't know how to write a sentence. I've also got some things to say about your grammar, but I'm not even sure I know where to begin." She held up the book reports as if displaying evidence from a crime.

Paula surveyed the youthful faces that watched her silently. In this day and age, she was lucky if two or three of them showed any interest, any indication that they would be among the handful who became thinkers, readers, people who considered the language a treasure, something to enjoy, something to be preserved as if it were endangered. But then to blame the world or the times was to overlook her own culpability. If it was harder to instill in students an appreciation for language and reading and thinking, then it was up to her to work harder. The failing was hers as much as theirs.

And in fairness to the kids, it was nearly the end of the school year, the time when young minds turned to thoughts of swimming and boating and trips to Disneyland. When you were fourteen, all but twitching with excess energy, less than two weeks from the end of school, and you lived in a climate in which summers were short treasured things, English could indeed be boring.

She gave the class one of her teacher smiles that was only a little implacable. She hoped it communicated, *Okay, I know it's nearly the end of school, but you can't start vacation yet, so let's make the best of the remaining time, what do you say?*

Putting the stack of book reports down on the desk, she said, "Okay, let's review sentences." She could practically see the minds closing around the room, but she plunged ahead. "Becky, what are the two things you need to have a sentence?"

Becky was a tall, gangly, blond girl who was going to be beautiful as soon as she got out of that in-between stage in which she was physically no longer a child but not yet a young woman. She seemed shocked that the teacher had called on her. It was a common reaction. Why did kids always seem dumbfounded to discover they weren't invisible?

Becky said, "Uh, subject and a verb?"

"That's right."

Then Becky did another thing typical of junior high schoolers. She looked shocked that she'd gotten it right.

"Okay," Paula said. "John, give me the simplest sentence you can come up with."

John was a pale kid with light brown hair that hung in his face. "Uh"—kids always began like that—"I will."

"That's right," Paula said. *"I* is the subject, *will* is the verb."

"Sounds like he's getting married," someone in the back of the room said, and the class giggled.

Paula silenced them with a look. "All right, subject and verb. Two parts of speech. Who can tell me some of the other parts of speech?" When no one jumped in, she arbitrarily picked someone. "Sean, what are the other parts of speech?"

Sean's dark hair was cut in a flattop—which was probably explained by his father's being a retired Marine. He was a quiet kid who sat sullenly in the back of the room, giving hostile looks to the other students. He'd been expelled once for smoking on campus. He shrugged, said, "I don't know."

"You can't name one part of speech other than subject and verb?"

"No." He didn't seem the least bit embarrassed. He just seemed bored.

A part of Paula wanted to take this kid aside and make him understand, make his mind work, but it would be one hell of a challenge, and it was also something she couldn't do at this particular moment. She turned to another student. "Pamela, how about you?"

Suddenly Paula's words seemed strangely distant, as if she were hearing a conversation carried from somewhere else in the building by heating ducts.

"Pamela . . . can . . ."

Her speech was bogging down, dropping in pitch, as if played on a phonograph at too slow a speed.

". . . can . . . you . . ."

Getting the words out was like forcing them through quicksand.

". . . you . . . tell . . ."

Paula could see the youthful faces staring at her, but she seemed unable to focus on them.

". . . tell . . . me . . ."

The faces were swirling around her now.

"tell . . . me . . . the . . ."

A sound like surf breaking over rocks filled her ears.

". . . parts . . ."

It grew louder, louder, louder, as if the ocean were inside her head.

". . . of . . ."

The faces spun around her, a blur of white dots, snow-flakes caught in a whirlwind.

". . . speech . . ."

And then the odor hit her, the pungent smell of turpentine. For a moment, Paula felt as though she'd just taken Muhammad Ali's best punch, and then she was swirling downward into blackness. Abruptly she was on the same stretch of beach she'd seen before, heading toward the same weathered two-story house. As she had previously, Paula slipped through the wall. This time there were two men in the house, the one she'd seen before and a big, muscular guy. The smaller man was in a wheelchair, his legs in casts. Paula

47

hadn't seen the casts before, because the man had been in bed. He seemed unaware of her presence, but the big man was looking right at her. Suddenly he spoke to her.

"Help him," he said. "Please help him. You're the only one who can."

"Who are you?" Paula asked. "Where is this place?"

But the man didn't answer.

"How can I help him?" Paula demanded. "What could I possibly do?"

Still the man didn't answer. His eyes were focused on a point beyond her now, and he was frowning, looking puzzled.

Paula was about to speak to him again when an invisible force pulled her through the wall and into a churning mass of grayness. Then she was floating upward, toward an ill-defined brightness, like a diver slowly rising to the water's surface.

•2•

Paula awoke to find herself on the floor. The school nurse and the principal were looking down at her. Someone had put something soft under her head.

"Fire department's on the way," the principal said. He was a tall thin man with gray hair and wire-frame glasses. His name was Frederick Aho.

"Fire department?" Paula asked.

"The paramedics."

"Cancel them," Paula said. "I'm all right now." To prove it, she sat up. The room did a couple of rolls like a ship in a rough sea, then settled down.

"You sure you want us to cancel?" the nurse asked. She was round-faced and what some people called full-figured. Her name was Mary Stromquist.

"Yes. I'll be fine."

Mary nodded at the principal, who went to call off the paramedics. "Has this happened before?" the nurse asked.

Paula chose her words carefully so her answer would be truthful. "I've never fainted before," she said. "It's rather a strange feeling," she added.

The nurse nodded. "It's probably nothing to worry about, I mean sometimes people just faint, no reason. But then who knows, right? It might be a warning. It wouldn't hurt to make a doctor's appointment, have yourself checked out—just as a precaution."

"You're probably right," Paula said. It dawned on her that the classroom was empty. "Where'd the kids go?"

"Mr. Aho took them to the library."

"Good," Paula said.

The principal returned and said, "Judy is cancelling the paramedics and calling in a substitute." Judy was the school secretary.

"A substitute? I'll be all right. I can teach my classes."

"I think you should go home and rest," Aho said.

"And I second that," Mary Stromquist said.

"I guess I'm outvoted."

"If you'd like, I can have Judy give you a ride home."

"I can manage," Paula said. She hoped she was right.

•3•

Paula had no problems driving herself home through the middle-class, midwestern streets of Anoka Falls. A suburb of Minneapolis, Anoka Falls was a community of about sixty-five thousand, a place of straight streets and wooden houses and detached garages. Inside nearly every one of those garages was a snow thrower. Inside half of them were snowmobiles. Inside a quarter of them were campers.

People here were neither poor nor rich. The guys in the thousand-dollar suits who had offices in the upper floors of the IDS Center lived elsewhere. So did the people who cleaned the skyscraper's floors, washed its sinks, scrubbed its toilets. Anoka Falls was a place of union tradesmen, assistant managers, and of course schoolteachers.

Paula's parking place was off an alley that ran behind the building. She left her car next to a detached garage with peeling white paint. The building's owners used it for storage; it was full of old, moldering furniture, and yellow newspapers with headlines like EISENHOWER WINS IN LANDSLIDE.

Paula was glad to get home and lean back in her favorite chair. It had never hit her like that before. Her legs had been knocked out from under her as if she'd been hit with a utility pole. The message hadn't just been transmitted to her; it had washed over like a wave, a huge breaker in which she'd tumbled about helplessly, waiting for it to dash her against the rocks. She'd been out of control, taken over.

"What's happening?" she asked the room.

She felt a tingly emptiness inside, not unlike the sensation that had come over her when at the age of three, she'd wandered away from her mother in a large department store and suddenly had become certain she'd never see her family again. Surrounded by strangers, she'd run this way and that, finding only more strangers, more unfamiliar territory. Confused and terrified, she'd dashed into a rack of clothes, knocking several garments onto the floor. At that moment she'd known she could die in that store, alone, forgotten by her family, by everyone.

Her mother had, of course, found her. But the feeling was the same, the feeling of being alone and in danger and having no control over the events that had swept her up.

Just what was the shadowy presence she'd seen? She shivered. Whatever it was frightened her. Words tumbled through her head. Demon, evil spirit, bogeyman. She wasn't even sure she believed in such things. And yet she was able to recognize the truth, able to know when someone needed help. These abilities were forms of clairvoyance, and if clairvoyance was possible, why not evil? Why not the bogeyman?

The thought hung there.

Another thing she didn't understand was just what it was she was supposed to do for the man. What help could she possibly provide? In the case of the puppy in the storm drain, she found someone with an arm long enough to pull the little guy out. In the case of the kidnapped girl, she'd told the police where to find her. But how could she help the man who lived by the ocean? Exorcising the bogeyman was beyond her abilities.

All these thoughts churned through her mind in a hopeless jumble. She had questions, hundreds of questions, but almost no answers. And even though she had no idea who the man was or where he lived, she was afraid. The fear came from deep within her, from some core part of herself she had no direct contact with, dribbling out constantly, as if there were a leaky faucet inside her from which continuously dripped little globules of dread.

Paula spent the day worrying about things that were beyond her control and posing questions for which she had no answers. Finally, to get her mind off things, she made dinner—leftover roast beef and gravy warmed in the microwave. While she ate, she watched the evening news on the small TV in the kitchen. The news stories faded in and out of her consciousness, without really registering.

Suddenly the TV set got her attention. A man was saying, "This weapons system is absolutely essential to the defense of our nation. Without it, there will be a window of vulnerability—no more than that, a hole, a big hole in our strategic preparedness." It was a congressional hearing into defense spending. The man testifying was a civilian Pentagon official, an assistant secretary of something or the other.

And he was lying.

The words were so dissonant Paula could barely listen to them. They bumped into each other, causing distortion, screechy harmonics that made Paula cringe. Although Paula had no idea what the real reason was for the man's urging the military expenditure, she knew it had nothing to do with defending the nation. Presumably it was a matter of money, and who got it. She turned off the TV set.

People on television lied all the time. Criminals protesting their innocence. Candidates for mayor and governor and president. Guests on talk shows. Hosts of talk shows. The truth on television was sometimes hard to find. She accepted it. People lied. It was the way things were.

But at the moment she just couldn't seem to cope with it.

After eating and washing the dishes, Paula returned to her favorite chair and read, trying to lose herself in an Elmore Leonard novel.

•4•

Paula was a fast reader, and she finished her book about eleven. Then she went to bed.

Knowing that sleep might not come easily, she carefully steered her thoughts away from the man who lived by the ocean and the shadowy presence that threatened him. She concentrated on the mystery she'd just finished, analyzing its structure, the author's writing style. Being a novelist was a dream of hers. In her youth she'd written short stories and made numerous attempts to write a novel, always finding the task too daunting to complete.

It was the way with dreams. They faded as you grew older, and after a while you dismissed them as youthful fantasies. But then, even though she hadn't become a writer, she was doing something she loved, which made her pretty lucky compared to most people.

Suddenly she smelled turpentine.

No, Paula thought, not again.

But the force that grabbed her and swept her away to the familiar beach on a rocky coastline was irresistible. She felt like Dorothy being sucked up into a tornado and carried off to Oz. Paula was as powerless against it as she was against an avalanche or the rising of the tide.

Now, she walked toward the house, entered it by passing through the wall as easily as she could have stepped through a hologram. As before, there were two men here, one in a wheelchair. They were watching television. Everything in the room was crisp, as if she were viewing a picture relayed by satellite.

Paula realized there was a newspaper on the coffee table. She tried to see what its name was, but it was folded so that its name was hidden. The headlines she was able to see gave her no clue. The mayor wanted increased funding for the police department. The Pentagon was asking for more weapons systems.

She tried to read the finer print in the bodies of the local stories, but she couldn't. Shifting her gaze, she took in the room, looking for clues. Whoever had furnished it had taste that was compatible with hers. The room was comfortable, with pieces that were solid-looking, vaguely country style. The floors were wood, and there was a fireplace. A big picture window looked out on the ocean.

Could she look at the sea and know whether she was facing east or west? At sunrise or sunset she could tell, but this was nighttime. Perhaps someone with a better knowledge of the stars and the position of the moon could take one look and say you're facing east or you're obviously so many degrees west. But to her it was just an ocean with moonlight wiggling across its breakers. For all Paula knew it could be the Indian Ocean or the Mediterranean Sea.

Then it occurred to her that the two men were watching television. If she could catch a station break, she'd know where they were. She watched, waited. The two men spoke to each other, words that were distant and distorted. Then the one in the wheelchair used the remote control to switch off the TV set.

"No," she said to him. "Leave it on."

He was unaware of her presence.

Frustrated, she turned to the other one. "Tell me where this is," Paula demanded.

The man frowned, stared at her, stared *through* her.

"I'm here," she said. "Tell me who you are. Tell me where this is."

The man was still frowning, staring in her direction. He spoke, and the words were garbled.

"Slowly," she said. "Speak slowly. Where are you? Who are you?"

"Eddddd Prrrrraaaaazzzzzzzzzzzz . . . iiikkzzkk," came the reply. It sounded like static, like words broadcast in some mode incompatible with the receiver.

"Say it again," she said. "Say it again."

"Ehhh . . ."

Abruptly there was a shadow between Paula and the man, a glob of blackness that seemed to have no substance and yet was impenetrable to light. A coldness washed over her, and although she was not really in that place, not physically, she could feel goosebumps crawling down her arms and legs.

It was the evil thing Paula had seen before. Suddenly a great force seemed to grab her and yank her backward as if she'd just been fired from a catapult. For an instant she felt as if her insides were being pressed against the inner wall of her body by g forces so extreme they might flatten her.

Darkness swirled around her.

Terror stabbed into her like thousands of pinpricks.

And then, cold, shivering uncontrollably, she was back in her own bed.

Paula had just met the bogeyman.

And he was much too powerful to fool around with.

•5•

"Ed Prawdzik."

"What?" Dave asked.

"Ed . . . Ed Prawdzik."

"I could tell it wasn't Kim Basinger," Dave said.

Ed didn't seem to hear him. The nurse was sitting on the couch. He gasped.

"Ed, hey, you with me?"

Slowly Ed's eyes focused on Dave. There was confusion and fear in them. "I . . . I guess I was dreaming," Ed said.

"You kept saying your name."

Ed frowned. "I did?"

"And then you looked kind of stuporous. Are you okay?"

"Yeah, I guess so. I . . . uh, let me think. I was dreaming that someone was asking me my name, and I kept trying to tell them, but they couldn't seem to understand me."

"You sure dozed off in a hurry."

"Yeah," the man said, not seeming to have heard Dave's comment. "And then . . . and then, something scary happened. Something got in the way, made the person asking me my name go away, *forced* the person away. And this thing . . ."

"Yes," Dave prompted.

"It was . . . frightening."

"What was it?"

"Don't know. Can't remember. I had sort of a mini-nightmare, I guess."

Dave put the matter aside, picked up a magazine. But after he read for a few moments, he noticed that Ed was still frowning, still concerned with what had happened.

"You sure you're okay?" Dave asked.

"Yeah, I'm sure. It was just weird, that's all." He, too, picked up a magazine.

HOMECOMING

• 1 •

Terry Oliver drove along the two-lane road, listening to the gentle hum of the BMW's engine and watching the Pacific, which seemed unusually calm today, as if the sunshine were making the water lazy, too contented to produce anything except the gentlest of waves, which lapped almost sleepily against the rocks lining the shore.

Terry Oliver was going home. Not to the place of his birth or the neighborhood in which he'd raced around on his red bicycle with the car radio aerial he'd found out at the dump attached to it, but home to another way of life. A way of life he'd left once and now wanted to reclaim.

You can't go back, he thought. You'll leave in a day or two, a week at the most. A guy wearing an Italian-made suit and driving a BMW doesn't belong here.

But then maybe the car and the clothes were the things that weren't suited to him. In any case, he had to find out. Besides, where else would he go? Home to the father who couldn't possibly understand, who'd consider him a failure? He didn't need that right now. At Falling Star Farm, he could get his head together in ways that would be impossible anywhere else.

The pressures of the job had gotten to him. Made him snappish and irritable, always arguing with Miranda. He'd tried to explain it to her. Silicon chips were a cutthroat business, constant pressure from the Japanese, technologi-

56

cal advancements making a project obsolete even before it could go into production, millions invested in research that could make a fortune or earn back nothing at all. That's what he did. Vice president in charge of research and development. Big house in Silicon Valley with swimming pool and tennis court, membership in exclusive clubs, nice cars, nice clothes. But it was all just hanging by a thread. That was the part Miranda hadn't been able to understand, that it could all go *poof,* just like that.

Miranda left him, taking the kids.

A week later, a yet-to-be-released product his company had pumped millions into developing proved to be inferior to something the Japanese had just come out with.

He started suffering from insomnia. He started drinking heavily and taking pills, uppers when he was down, downers when he was too tense.

Then two days ago, he'd lost his job. Not because of the money wasted when the firm was beat out by the Japanese. But because he'd flipped out in a board meeting. The company had been ready to start production on a nice fat Pentagon contract, making chips to control missiles with nuclear warheads. Terry had stood up, said loudly that they should refuse to make such evil things, that if all the companies in America would do that, there'd be no more missiles and the world would be a much safer place to be.

When another vice president told him to sit down, Terry refused. When the man tugged on Terry's arm in an effort to get him to comply, Terry threatened to kill him.

When the chairman of the board asked Terry to leave, Terry told him to shove it up his ass sideways.

When the CEO flatly ordered Terry to leave, Terry gave him the finger and called him a fascist dictator.

When security was called in, Terry slugged one guard and was dragged out by two others.

"Well," he said, "if you're going to end a career, you might as well do it in style."

Ahead was a fork in the highway, one road continuing to follow the coast, the other heading inland. Terry took the one that went inland. He recalled 1967, when he'd been one of the founding members of the Falling Star Commune. The land had belonged to a girl whose thick straw-colored hair hung an inch or two below her waist. Marla Applegate. The property had been left to her by an aunt, and Marla said it was to be a sanctuary for all those who believed as she did. They were against the Vietnam War. Against the Establishment. For free love. For saving the environment. The list went on, all the usual sixties idealism.

At one time eighty people had lived at the commune. When Terry left, there had been twenty-some-odd. Now he understood there were maybe half a dozen middle-aged hippies whose long hair was turning gray. Relics of another era. God, what had they thought of the Reagan years? Marla Applegate was still here, he'd been told. Growing her own vegetables, raising goats and chickens, scratching out an existence.

The commune was located six miles north of Castle Bay in an enclave of cedar, hemlock, and Douglas fir that was surrounded by California's famed redwood forest. He almost missed the turnoff, a narrow dirt track with grass in the middle. A weathered sign said:

> PRIVATE PROPERTY
> NO HUNTING
> NO WOOD CUTTING

A needle-covered tree branch brushed the side of the BMW. At one time the scratching of the expensive car's finish would have been unthinkable, but now he didn't care. He'd left the commune and returned to the "real" world, where he pursued material possessions and made his once-alienated father proud. Now he was back. He'd had material things aplenty, and they hadn't made him happy. Yanking off his sixty-dollar silk tie, he threw it out the window. Maybe one of the commune's aging flower children would find it, use it for a headband.

From the corner of his eye, Terry thought he caught a glimpse of something moving through the trees to his left. A large . . . something. A black shape. But now he saw nothing but the forest. It was his imagination, he decided. Maybe the shape was just a symbol representing the material world, as if, refusing to let him go, it had come to drag him back to the rat race, kicking and screaming.

Never! he thought, wriggling out of his double-breasted wool coat and hurling it out the window. It caught in the tree branches only two feet from the car.

Rounding a sharp turn in the road, he came to the commune. As it had during his time here, the place consisted of a converted barn in which everyone lived, along with a chicken coop, milking shed, and a fenced livestock area in which cows and goats and chickens wandered around together.

There were no animals there now.

And no dogs came out barking at the stranger who'd just showed up.

The place was quiet. Not just the stillness of the countryside, but totally silent. As if it were long abandoned. But Terry had spoken with an old friend who had told him she'd been here just a week and a half ago, that she'd stopped in to say hi to Marla and the others, and that there were half a dozen people living here. Had they abandoned the commune within the last few days? The notion didn't really make any sense. They'd lived here for years. They were committed to dying as flower children—or flower senior citizens—even if the rest of the world had passed them by.

For a few seconds, Terry just sat in his car, the engine mumbling softly to itself. Finally he switched off the ignition and got out. To his left was a large garden in which spinach and lettuce and beans and other things were growing. It was free of weeds, the plants healthy-looking. Clearly not something abandoned.

But where were the dogs, the other animals?

The former barn that served as living quarters had been painted brightly psychedelic at one time, but now the colors were faded, ghosts of a lifestyle that had all but vanished. By the door was another remnant of a bygone era, an aged

Volkswagen van with peace symbols newly painted on its
rusting sides. On its back doors were the words STOP CONTRA
AID.

Terry stood at the door, reluctant to go in, some inner
sense urging extreme caution, whispering that maybe there
was something wrong here, *really* wrong here, and that
whatever it was was inside, waiting for him, and that
stepping through that door would be like stepping off the
edge of a roof, a one-way trip into some really deep shit.

So Terry stood there, thinking it over. He finally concluded that it didn't make much sense to drive all this way
just to turn around and leave simply because things didn't
feel right. Besides it was possible that something had
happened to the people here, that maybe they'd been
overcome by fumes from a leaky gas connection or something. If so they'd need help, his help.

Terry pushed open the door, stepped inside.

And immediately knew for certain something was wrong.

For the air was filled with the sweet coppery odor of death.

Terry stood just inside the door, letting his eyes adjust to
the darkness. He felt for a light switch, not finding one, and
then he remembered that there had been no electricity in
this place and there probably still wasn't, the utility companies being regarded as part of the fascist Establishment. No
natural gas either, which took care of his thoughts regarding
the possibility of a leaky gas line.

On a small table to his right was a kerosene lamp and a
book of matches. Clearly there was still no electricity here.
His eyes having accustomed themselves to the dimness,
Terry moved forward. The barn was basically a big wooden-
floored dormitory. There were no rooms, not even a bathroom. Beds, a wood stove, a makeshift shower were all out
in the open. Terry recalled that shower. The water came
from a tank on the roof. It had to be hand pumped into the
tank, and it was unheated, like liquid ice cubes on a chilly
morning.

"Hello," Terry said. His voice shattered the silence as if it
were brittle and someone had just smashed it with a rock.

No one answered.

But the smell of death grew stronger.

Resisting the urge to turn and run, Terry moved forward. The beds were scattered around randomly. Some were double beds, some fold-up cots. Some had sheets and blankets, some didn't. An aisle of sorts ran between them. Beams of light from the windows fell into it, reminding Terry of the trail of spotlights Jimmy Durante had walked through at the end of his TV show. His mother had loved that show; she'd watched reruns of it until it disappeared from even the cheesiest of independent TV stations. It was probably back now that there were all those nostalgia channels on cable, but his mother was dead, and Terry didn't know anyone else who would care.

Abruptly he let out a sound that was part moan and part suppressed scream, for he had just come to a rickety-looking double bed that was covered with a brown stain. The adjacent bed was spattered with some of the same stuff, and between the two was a large dark spot on the floor. Blood. And in the quantity one associated with death, terrible death.

Terry stared at it, his heart pounding, his nervous system transmitting little icy impulses of terror throughout his body.

Then he saw something from the corner of his eye, and he turned, slowly, reluctantly, not really wanting to find out whether he'd spotted what he thought he had. A number of pieces of furniture were scattered among the beds, old items that would have been junk anywhere else. Protruding from beneath a dresser with peeling green paint were fingers. Human fingers. In a space too tiny to hold the person to whom they should be attached.

"Oh, God," he whispered. "Get the fuck out of here right now."

But instead of doing that, he decided to find out just exactly what he had discovered. He could be looking at a joke shop trick of some sort, like the infamous plastic puddle of vomit. Something that looked horrible, but was only a practical joke. He reached toward the fingers, then hesitated. He had no intention of touching them.

Looking around for something he could use to slide the fingers out from beneath the dresser, he found a grimy set of high-topped work shoes with a pair of dirty socks stuffed into them, a sandal with no mate, a red neckerchief. Then, in an otherwise empty cabinet, he found a telescoping antenna that had probably come from a portable radio. Extending it, he went back to the spot where he'd seen the fingers.

They were still there. He hadn't imagined them. Curving slightly, as if they were imitating spider legs, getting ready to crawl out from beneath the dresser under their own power. He touched them with the tip of the aerial, then jerked his hand back as if expecting them to leap at him. The fingers didn't budge. Terry eased the aerial under the dresser, slipped the fingers out.

They were attached to a hand.

Which was attached to a wrist.

Which ended in a ragged, bloody hunk of flesh and a stub of bone.

Abruptly Terry Oliver was on his feet, turning, running, hurrying toward the door, wanting out of this place more than he had ever wanted anything in his life, wanting it so much his legs were unable to keep up with his need, and he lost his balance and fell, sliding across the dirty, splintery floor. He came to a stop near the stove, about a foot in front of a set of wooden doors in the floor. The root cellar, where things that had to be kept cool were stored. Both doors were open, flopped back to the sides like a big pair of wooden wings, revealing the steps that led down into the cellar's gloom.

They were stained.

A hunk of bloody flesh clung to a step about halfway down.

The stench of death rose from the place.

His thoughts swirling, Terry struggled to his feet, and in doing so he shifted his position enough to see farther into the cellar. And what he saw froze him, left him staring transfixed into the dank darkness below him.

He was looking at bones.

Some with bits of meat still on them, like corn cobs on which the eater had missed a few random kernels.

He saw a human skull, a clearly recognizable rib cage, a leg bone.

And then he saw, staring hungrily up at him, what had eaten the residents of Falling Star Farm.

Instantly, he turned around, his brain full of desperate and conflicting thoughts. Escape, run, flee, *live!* Destroy it, you have to destroy it, have to, have to, have to, because it's the most evil, vile thing you have ever seen and it can not, not, *not* be allowed to live. He spotted the kerosene lamp, the matches. Then he saw a can of kerosene under the table on which the lamp stood. He grabbed it—a gallon can, nearly full—and began to douse everything in sight with the stuff.

Vile! Disgusting! Have to kill it, have to.

Terry glanced at the open cellar doors, seeing nothing. Why hadn't it come after him? Having emptied the kerosene can, he threw it away, picked up the lantern, lit it with a shaking hand. Okay, he thought, come on up now, and see what it gets you.

As if it had been reading his thoughts, the thing appeared, letting Terry see all of it. And Terry knew that there were things worse than any evil created by man. There were human stupidities, like nuclear weapons; atrocities like war, torture, mass starvation. But now he was seeing pure vileness, total repulsiveness, the physical manifestation of everything unspeakable.

As he watched, it changed form, but the form was unimportant, for in any manifestation it was the essence of repugnance.

He threw the lamp at it.

The thing erupted in flames, the kerosene spreading across the wooden floor until it met the kerosene Terry had poured from the gallon can. There was an enormous *wumpf!* as the interior of the building burst into flames.

The monster just stood there, burning.

Terry ran for the door.

Suddenly the monster was in front of him, blocking his path.

Terry turned, looking for another exit, but there was only fire, orange and hot and hungry for more fuel. He turned again, seeing his way still blocked, the creature advancing on him, preparing to do to him what it had done to the others.

Terry Oliver didn't hesitate. He plunged into the flames.

•2•

After the building had burned to the ground, the creature emerged from the ashes and, unhurt by the blaze, walked into the forest.

Its hunger had been satiated, and it felt good.

For the moment.

•3•

Dave Guthrie slept late that morning. He awoke with a start just before noon, yanked from sleep by a nightmare. In the dream, people had been consumed by some unseen beast. And then the place in which they lived had gone up in flames. As Dave lay there, the dream that moments ago had been vivid enough to wake him began to fade from his memory.

STRANGE OCCURRENCES

•1•

"How's your nurse working out?" Jackie asked.

She and Dave were in his bedroom, Dave in his wheelchair and Jackie sitting on the bed. The room seemed full of the morning's brightness. Waves rolled in from the Pacific, the ocean looking blue and pure, as if it had never been exposed to oil spills or sewage or industrial wastes.

"Ed and I hit it off from the moment we met," Dave said. "You know what he's making for dinner tonight? Linguini with red clam sauce. Last night he made rolled chicken breasts stuffed with chopped ham and olives in a wine sauce. The night before that he made fettucine with crabmeat alfredo. Guy missed his calling. He should have been a chef."

"Maybe you should marry him," Jackie said, a hint of petulance creeping into her voice. Jackie got no particular pleasure from cooking, and the things she made were usually quick and plain.

"Well," Dave said, pointedly eyeing her body, "there are some wifely functions I don't think Ed would be too good at."

Jackie sat there stiffly, not smiling. Her Majesty was not amused. She got like that sometimes. Not exactly irritable, but sort of stony, withdrawn.

She'd been stopping by every other day or so during the week Ed had been here. Dave had suggested several times that she spend the night, but Jackie, no matter what other reasons she might have, wasn't about to sleep with him when someone else was in the house. Dave argued that Ed was a grown-up, an open-minded man of the nineties, but Jackie wasn't about to change her mind. If the first word that came to mind when people thought of Jackie was cute, then the second was uncompromising. When Jackie decided how she wanted to do something, that was the way she did it.

"Been busy?" Dave asked.

She rolled her eyes. "Have I ever. I've spent the last five days—all day and into the evening sometimes—with this couple from Massachusetts. Nothing satisfies them. The house is always too small or too modern or too old-fashioned or too expensive or too far from the ocean. With people like that, it's just not worth it. You put up with fifty-thousand dollars' worth of aggravation to make a ten-thousand-dollar commission—actually on the *chance* you might make the commission."

"You spending today with them?"

"No, they had to fly back to Boston to take care of some business. But in an hour I'm meeting with a guy from Berkeley, a professor from UC. Says he's retiring and wants to live by the ocean, listen to the waves roll in."

"People keep moving in, and Castle Bay will start building subdivisions and malls and all that. It won't be quaint anymore."

Jackie sighed. "People always want to stop growth right after *they* move in." She frowned. "You're not beginning to side with Constance Gresham, are you?"

Constance Gresham was an elderly woman who'd organized the Castle Bay Preservation Society, a group that sought to keep the community the way it was—small and picturesque and unpretentious. Jackie despised Constance Gresham.

"I'm not siding with anyone," Dave said. "Growth and progress have their points, and so does Constance Gresham."

Jackie's expression darkened, suggesting that his saying

anything good about Constance Gresham was an act akin to treason. "Growth doesn't have to destroy the community," she said. "We've got a planning commission to make sure it's done right."

Los Angeles has a planning commission, Dave thought, but he didn't say it.

Jackie glanced at her watch. "Constance Gresham hasn't put me out of work yet, so I'd better get out of here if I ever expect to make any money."

"Wait," Dave said. "Before you go, I have a proposition for you."

"A proposition?" Jackie was standing. She cocked her head.

"In the man-woman sense."

"That kind of a proposition."

Dave said, "You have no doubt realized that Ed will be here for several weeks."

"It had occurred to me."

"But he has to run out from time to time to buy all the goodies he cooks."

Jackie nodded. "You're suggesting a . . ." She searched for the right word.

"A quickie, yes."

"Sounds like something teenagers would do."

"Might be fun."

"What would I tell the O'Banions?"

"The O'Banions?"

"The professor and his wife. Maybe I can tell them I'm going to have to leave them for an hour or so because my boyfriend's free and we're going to have a quickie."

"You're supposed to concoct a plausible excuse."

Jackie shook her head. "You're just going to have to keep your hormones in check until you're well enough for Ed to leave."

"What if they won't cooperate?"

"Be firm."

"That's the trouble. I'm firm most of the time."

"I refuse to dignify that remark by commenting on it,"

Jackie said. She kissed him lightly on the forehead, turned, and walked from the room, leaving the odor of perfume in her wake.

•2•

After Jackie left, Dave wheeled himself into his studio. He'd been redoing the children's book illustrations he'd lost in the plane crash, and all around the room were pictures of stylized animals dressed in human garments and wearing extremely human expressions on their faces. He studied a beleaguered looking dog that wore a topcoat and carried a briefcase. The animal stood at a bus stop. It was supposed to be a working dog.

The pictures were cartoonlike, and they reminded Dave of the Sunday comics. He'd done a strip once. It hadn't been his own creation; rather it was an existing strip whose originators had died, and it was being perpetuated by the copyright holders. Every few weeks a packet arrived in the mail with a storyline he was supposed to follow. He'd done the drawings, mailed them back, and the romantic life of comic strip character Beverly Champion continued on and on, the heroine never aging a day and never quite finding true love, which she continually sought with constant, dripping sincerity. Dave had done it until he couldn't stand it anymore.

He steered his wheelchair toward the easel holding the picture of the dog waiting for the bus. Ed had gone through the studio, rearranging things for a wheelchair-bound artist. Mainly it was a matter of lowering things. The working surfaces of canvases and drawing boards and supplies had to be put within reach. Being in a wheelchair was like having three feet lopped off your height. You could reach the light switches okay, but things like upper kitchen cabinets might as well be in another dimension.

It had taken Ed only a couple of hours to fix everything. He'd foreseen problems before they came up, gotten busy with a hammer and screwdriver. The man was a whiz, no doubt about it.

Abruptly an intense cold closed in around him, as if he'd just rolled the wheelchair into a freezer. Confused, he looked around, seeing nothing out of the ordinary. But the cold was real, as raw and penetrating as if he'd just wheeled himself into the Arctic. He let his breath out, and it was a white stream. His hands were sticking to the chair, freezing to it. He pulled them loose.

Dave shivered.

He was unable to stop shivering.

"Ed!" he called. "Ed!" When Dave closed his mouth, his teeth began chattering.

Gripping its wheels, he tried to move the chair. It seemed frozen in place—maybe *literally* frozen.

"Ed! Help me!" But Dave sensed that his words weren't going anywhere, as if he were in a place that lacked the medium to transmit sound.

Again he tried to move the chair forward, and it still wouldn't budge. Then he gasped, his heart suddenly pounding madly, for a hole had just opened in the floor directly in front of him.

It was a shaft, extending downward, into the earth.

Dave was unable to see the bottom.

A gray smoky haze drifted out of it.

Not real, something inside Dave protested. *A big hole that drops down from the second floor of a house? Think about it. Where's the ground floor? See what I mean? No way, babe. This just plain can't be real.*

But it looked real.

It's all the chemicals that go on your food. They've combined into hallucinogens.

That was it. He had to be hallucinating, had to be. Dave blinked, shook his head.

But when he let out his breath, it was white. And he was freezing, the chill penetrating deeper and deeper. And the hole was still there, inches in front of him, almost beckoning him. It looked like an enormous circular shaft, a mine or a well. He could see the floor joists where it cut through them and farther down he could see earthen sides, a tree root, boulders. It went down and down, the bottom out of sight—if it had a bottom.

It ain't real, none of it.

Dave tried to holler Ed's name again, but his teeth were chattering so badly he was unable to force out the words. And then, rising from the hole, came voices. Barely audible, as if from a long way off. Hundreds, maybe thousands of them, speaking in unison.

He has chosen, they chanted.

He has chosen.

He has chosen.

He is lost.

He is ours.

Ours.

Ours.

Dave sucked in his breath. He was going to attempt to scream for help, and he was going to put everything he had into it.

• 3 •

Ed Prawdzik was sitting at the kitchen table, waiting for the kettle on the stove to start whistling so he could have a cup of tea.

He was happy with the situation here. Dave Guthrie seemed like a nice guy, and he was both cooperative and appreciative. For some people you couldn't do anything right. The food was wrong, his advice was wrong, everything was wrong. Sometimes, he knew, it was people lashing out because of what life had done to them, and he was the only one there to be on the receiving end. Still, it was a lot nicer when his patients were like Dave Guthrie.

The kettle let out a peep, then began whistling in earnest. Ed had a cup and a tea bag waiting. He poured in the steaming water and returned to the table, watching as the liquid darkened, waiting for it to reach just the right color.

A cold breeze blew through the kitchen.

Ed Prawdzik saw his breath. He shivered.

Puzzled, he looked around, seeing no open windows, no possible source for the cold air. And then he realized that this was late May. On the California coast. Where the temperatures were pleasant year round. But the air blowing through the room was New England in January stuff.

As the impossibility of what was happening slowly sunk in, Ed began trembling. Partially because of the cold. And partially due to fear.

A thin layer of ice had formed on his tea, the teabag's string protruding from it as if some invisible tiny person were ice fishing.

The tea kettle screamed.

Ed leaped up, spun around, staring at the stove.

The kettle was boiling wildly, steam squirting out of the whistle, out from under the lid. It rocked and quivered. It seemed about to explode.

Ed just stared, his heart pounding. The world was going crazy. *He* was going crazy. Some part of him that was trying desperately to tame all this by explaining it told him there had been LSD in the tea, put there no doubt by some practical joker at the tea company—or some guy who was mad at his boss. For a brief moment, he clung to that hope, but then it occurred to him that he hadn't drunk any of the tea.

His brain searched frantically for other explanations.

And didn't find any.

The tea kettle hopped two inches into the air, came down on the burner, shooting out clouds of steam and splashing scalding water over the surface of the stove. Got to turn it off, Ed told himself. But his arm refused to obey his command. He was afraid to get too close to the berserk kettle.

But the only way to end this madness was to turn it off. It wouldn't have any effect on the frozen tea in his cup, but at least it would take care of the kettle, which was an immediate danger, while the hot tea turning to ice was not.

Collecting his nerve, Ed Prawdzik stood, moved to the

stove, grabbed the knob. It wouldn't turn. And then he realized why. It was already off.

There was no flame under the screaming, vibrating tea kettle.

Despite the freezing air, beads of perspiration had formed on his forehead. They began trickling down his face. "Jesus Christ," he muttered.

And then it was over. The kettle stopped whistling and stood still. The freezing air warmed. Ed Prawdzik stood there, shaking.

And then he heard Dave Guthrie screaming for him from upstairs.

• 4 •

The hole in the floor shrank down to a little dot, like the aperture of a lens closing, and then it was gone. Dave stared at the spot, listening to his rapid, nervous breathing. The floor looked as it always had. Varnished hardwood. Shiny and unbroken.

Dave heard Ed's footsteps on the stairs. The nurse hurried into the room, and then just stood there, breathing heavily. His eyes were wide, the color gone from his face. He had the expression of a man who'd just seen a nuclear fireball in the distance and knew the world was seconds away from becoming a radioactive cinder.

"What's wrong?" Ed asked between breaths.

"I think maybe I should ask you the same question," Dave said. His voice sounded high and tinny, as if it were coming through the horn of an old gramophone.

"You first," Ed said. "You were hollering for me."

Dave tried to collect his thoughts, wondering how he was going to explain what had just happened without sounding like a lunatic. He said, "You're going to think I'm crazy."

"There might just be a lot of that going around," Ed replied.

"It got cold," Dave said. "Not just cold, but *cold*. And

then there was a hole in the floor, right in front of me. It went down into the earth and seemed bottomless. I heard voices, thousands of them, chanting. The chair wouldn't move. I . . . I called you, but you didn't hear me."

"How many times did you call?"

"I don't remember. Quite a few."

"I only heard you call once. I came right away."

"Yeah," Dave said, "I kinda figured that."

"I don't understand. What made you think I couldn't hear you?"

"I don't know. It just seemed . . . well, that that's how things were. Do you think I've gone off my rocker?"

"No," Ed said.

"Don't humor me. The room's the normal temperature now. There's no hole in the floor. Did something happen to me in that plane crash? I mean, did I mess up my brain somehow?"

"I'm not humoring you," Ed said. "Some weird stuff happened to me too." The big man took a slow breath. "I felt cold too. I had a cup of hot tea. Real hot. I'd just poured it. And it froze."

Dave stared into the nurse's eyes, which were still wide, fear-filled. The craziness, whatever it was, had affected the whole house.

"Then the tea kettle started boiling," the nurse said. "Screaming and jumping around. And . . ." He hesitated. "And the burner wasn't on. There was no flame under the kettle. Now which of us is crazy?"

"What's going on here?" Dave asked.

"Mass hallucination?"

"You believe that?"

"No."

"Me neither."

For a moment, they were silent, each man lost in his own thoughts; then Ed said, "Show me where the hole was."

Dave pointed at the spot. "Right there. Directly in front of me."

Getting down on his hands and knees, Ed felt the floor. "It's cold here," he said. "Like someone had set a tub of ice

73

cream here." He felt around some more. "The coldness, it's going away."

Dave nodded, glad something had been discovered that showed he wasn't ready for the looney bin. Or at least if he was, he'd have some company. He and Ed could play cards and take tranquilizers together, while people in white uniforms kept watch, made sure they didn't do anything to hurt themselves.

"Pentagon death-ray satellite," Ed said. "It's gone amok, and it's firing at us, hitting us with freezer beams and hallucinogenic impulses. You know, one of those twenty-billion-dollar trinkets that never quite work right."

"The trouble is," Dave said, "after what's just happened, that seems like a perfectly rational explanation."

"Maybe we should write Washington and complain."

Dave managed to work up a small smile.

Ed managed to return it.

· 5 ·

A week passed during which no more eerie happenings occurred—unless you counted numerous dimly remembered nightmares.

On the evening of June fifth, Dave Guthrie lay in bed, wondering whether he'd be able to go to sleep. The damn casts were driving him crazy. Not only did they itch, but they were cumbersome, and finding a comfortable sleeping position was difficult. For some reason, he was restless tonight, his mind wanting to ponder this and that, remind him of all the foolish things he'd said in his life. He rolled over again. And still the random flashbacks danced through his mind.

Suddenly he had the feeling of being watched.

Opening his eyes, he studied the portion of the room he could see without moving, seeing nothing out of the ordinary. No one's watching you, he told himself. But the sensation persisted.

Dave slowly raised his head. The moon was hidden behind clouds tonight, so the window was a dim rectangle, barely perceptible. There were no screaming faces there tonight. He looked at the closet. Though barely distinguishable in the shadows, the door seemed to be closed tightly. The room was empty. He was alone.

And yet he felt a prickly sensation at the back of his neck, and some primitive sense was whispering, *You are being watched.* He could almost feel the gaze, as if it were a physical thing that actually touched him.

An icy glob of terror formed in his throat, slid slowly downward and settled in his stomach.

The best way to dispel this nonsense, he decided, was to address it, dispatch it, and be done with it. "You're nothing but my imagination," he said to the room. "So go away and leave me alone."

The feeling of being watched diminished.

Dave scanned the room one more time, then lowered his head, and rolled over onto his stomach, closing his eyes. Go to sleep, he told himself. There's nothing there. Ever since that damn plane crash, you've been acting weird as hell. Now get a grip on yourself.

Minutes passed, stretched into quarter hours, half hours, and then Dave lost all track of time. Finally he began drifting off to sleep.

Scritch!

Dave sat bolt upright in bed. The sound had come from somewhere to his right. He peered into the shadows, seeing nothing.

Scritcha-scritcha-scritcha!

Dave's eyes were drawn to the chest of drawers. It stood there in the shadows, a hulking black shape in the darkness, standing erect like a massive tombstone.

And then he saw a man standing in front of it. He sucked in his breath, his heart pounding madly. He was about to cry out for Ed when he realized he was looking at a wavery image of himself, as if someone had put a fun house mirror in front of the dresser.

But *he* was in bed.

And the other him was not.

And as he stared at the image of himself it began to change. His eyes grew red and began to glow. He smiled, and it was like no grin Dave had ever seen before, for the other him had a mouthful of wicked-looking teeth, long and curved, tapering to needle-sharp points.

And then the image was gone.

Dave lay in bed, trying to make sense out of what he'd just seen. First a bottomless pit had opened up in front of him, then vanished. Now he had appeared in front of himself— except not him, for the image he'd just seen had been a monster Dave Guthrie, a special effects werewolf in a horror flick. But Hollywood's werewolf seemed oddly tame compared to the one his mind had just created.

His mind.

Was there something wrong with it? Why else would he see things that could not be? It's an aftereffect of the plane crash, Dave told himself. It'll stop.

Abruptly he was seized by the certainty that he had made a mistake, a terrible, disastrous error. But he had no idea what it could be. He hadn't made any major decisions lately. He hadn't been confronted with any significant options. The biggest event in his life recently had been the plane crash, and given the choice, he certainly would have opted out of that.

And then he recalled the voices floating up from the seemingly bottomless hole that had appeared in front of his wheelchair. *He has chosen,* they chanted. *He is lost. He is ours.*

But the hole was imaginary. And so were the voices.

And yet the feeling of having made a major blunder persisted.

SCHOOL'S OUT

•1•

The PA system came on, broadcasting the rattle of papers and assorted clunks and clanks to the students and faculty of Hubert H. Humphrey Junior High School in Anoka Falls, Minnesota. Principal Aho cleared his throat. "May I have your attention please? School will be dismissed for the summer at the end of the home room period."

The students in Paula Bjornson's room cheered.

"Hold it!" she said, trying to quell the din. "At the *end* of the period. You still have ten minutes to go."

"You could let us go now," a boy in the back of the room suggested.

"Don't even think about it," Paula told him. "Come on, you've waited nine months. Another ten minutes won't kill you."

"It might," an unseen boy muttered.

"Okay," Paula said. "Do I have everyone's textbook?" When nobody responded, she said, "What about library books? The fines will keep building all summer if you've got books you haven't returned to Mrs. Nordsen in the library. It could be very expensive."

Paula went down the list. "Are your lockers cleaned out? How about your gym lockers? Anyone who forgot to turn in his or her padlock yesterday?" No one responded. Paula wasn't even sure they heard her. Their eyes were on the clock, their minds full of the wonders of summer vacation.

77

"Well," Paula said, "I guess it's just about time for all of us to say good-bye. I've enjoyed having all of you this year. I hope you've learned to think about the English language, to see some of its complexity, its versatility, its beauty. I hope you've learned to appreciate good writing and to enjoy all that books have to offer. And most of all, I hope you've learned some things that will make you think, use your minds."

Paula scanned the fresh young faces, trying to pick out those she might have reached. She saw two . . . three . . . four . . . maybe five. Let there be five, she thought. Five would make it a wonderfully successful year.

She had of course come into teaching hoping to reach them all, to send each and every student out into the world with a love of books and language and thinking critically. But that was beginner's naiveté. Most of them you could never instill such ideals into. They were lost before you ever got them, their minds having been shaped by a world that didn't pride itself on thinking, a world that looked at TV sitcoms and saw real life.

Still, she loved them all. Even those she couldn't reach. The handful she did get through to made it all worthwhile.

The bell rang.

There was a rush for the door.

"Good-bye," Paula called after them. "Enjoy the summer."

A few of the kids spoke to her as they passed her desk.

"'Bye . . ."

"Hope you have a nice summer."

"Maybe I'll see you next year."

"I enjoyed your class."

"I did too. And I learned a lot." That was the one Paula hoped would be number five, a blond girl named Kristin. And Kristin's words had had the clear, pure ring of the truth.

Paula grinned. She couldn't help herself. She knew now for sure she'd gotten through to at least five of them. And, who knew, maybe the others would occasionally recall something she'd told them, something that would cause them to use their intelligence—even if only once in a while.

And then the room was empty. The squeals of the students came from the hall, then from outside the building as well. The sounds grew fewer and fainter, and in almost no time at all, the school was silent.

An empty school, Paula realized, was the emptiest place in the world. It was the contrast, she supposed. When in session, a school was filled with kids who were barely able to control their energy. And with the ring of the bell, all that energy was released. It was gone. And it wouldn't be back for three months.

"Well," Paula said to the empty classroom, "I can stand here all day, or I can get busy and get things in order so I can go on vacation too."

She began cleaning out her desk.

And then a wave of dizziness hit her.

And she smelled turpentine.

• 2 •

Dave Guthrie finished cleaning his brushes, then wheeled himself back to the illustration he'd just completed. It stood at his eye level on one of the easels Ed Prawdzik had modified for use by a wheelchair-bound artist.

It was another hokey creation for *Vacationland West* magazine. A boy stood eye to eye with the carved image of a totem pole, trying to twist his face into an imitation of the one on the pole. The wooden face had an extremely wide mouth, and the boy was pulling his into roughly the same shape with his fingers. In the background the kid's parents and sister studied another totem pole, unaware of junior's antics. Dave sighed. The things one had to do to earn a living.

Although *Vacationland West* would probably be happy with the painting, Dave knew it wasn't his best work. All the strange things that had been happening had unnerved him, made him feel as though he should be constantly looking over his shoulder. Hardly the best environment for being creative.

Rolling over to the french doors that opened onto the balcony, Dave looked out at the slow, steady rain that had been falling all day. He could see the corner of his private patch of beach and the gray rocks lining the shore. They stretched away from him to the north, disappearing after a hundred feet or so into the thickening fog. The drizzle made a gentle patter on the roof. It was the kind of a day in which you could close your eyes and instantly be asleep.

And then Dave heard something that wasn't the rain on the shingles. A barely audible scratching, hissing noise. He wheeled his chair around.

And saw a puddle oozing out from under the closet door. It looked thick and gooey like the original version of *The Blob.* Dave stared at it, transfixed. And then he saw that it wasn't a blob at all. It was made up of hundreds—thousands—of individuals.

Cockroaches.

A sea of them.

Moving toward him.

And Dave realized suddenly that he had to get out of the room before his escape was blocked. He propelled the chair forward with all his strength, heading for the door. The wave of roaches shifted direction, moved to intercept him, almost as if they were all connected and someone were pulling them with a string. The small front wheels of his chair hit them, crushing them, their bodies making cracking, popping sounds. Then the rear wheels were on them too, and still more of them were squashed. The chair's rubber tires were dripping.

Dave thought he could hear the roaches screaming.

But it was just the clicking of their legs on the floor, their bodies knocking together. At least that's what he'd told himself, for the thought of roaches screaming as he crushed them was more than his mind could endure.

He wasn't moving.

The front wheels were jammed up against too many roach carcasses.

And the rear wheels were just spinning, slipping in the crushed roach goo.

Tons of thousands of cockroaches were still alive, swarming onto the chair, moving upward.

Toward him.

And then they were on him, crawling over his clothes, *into* his clothes, thousands of tiny legs prickling his flesh, which shriveled in revulsion. They reached his neck, and Dave frantically brushed them off, but there were just too many of them, and they swarmed over his hands, climbed on his ears, crawled over his eyes and nose and mouth, rushing blindly over his body, bumping into each other, falling off, thousands of prickly feet fighting for purchase.

Brushing them off so desperately he was slapping himself savagely in the face, Dave screamed.

And when he opened his mouth, the roaches scrambled to get inside.

• 3 •

The dizziness passed; the acrid odor disappeared.

Instead of finding herself at the house on the ocean, Paula Bjornson was back in her classroom. For some reason the link had not been made this time. It had started, then . . . well, petered out. She started to sit down, looking beneath her, as she always did. It was a habit she developed after one of the teachers had sat on a thumbtack, presumably placed there by a student. Although it had never happened to Paula, she always remembered to check.

She gasped when she saw what was on the chair.

A cockroach.

No, two. Three.

Paula shook her head. They seemed to be multiplying before her eyes. The three roaches scurried around the chair's seat as if looking for a way to get off. Paula stood there, trembling, feeling as if her stomach were in free fall. How could there be cockroaches on her chair—cockroaches that grew in number as she looked at them?

There were six now, bumping into each other.

And Paula realized suddenly that she'd been wrong in thinking the link had failed to materialize. This *was* the link. Although she had no idea what it meant.

Reaching behind her, she picked up the dictionary she kept on her desk. Holding it over the chair, she waited until the roaches' paths took them all into the center of the chair, then dropped the book. It hit the padded chair seat with a *thlap!* She watched, waited. No roaches came out from under the book. Resisting the urge to simply get the hell out of there, she carefully lifted the edge of the book, seeing nothing. She picked it up.

There were no roaches, squashed or otherwise.

Paula started trembling. What was happening to her? Did this have something to do with the man who lived by the ocean? The only thing she was sure of was that she wanted it to stop.

Leave me alone, she thought. Just leave me alone. I don't know what's happening, and I can't help.

•4•

Suddenly the roaches were gone. He could see his clothes, which a moment ago had been invisible beneath a cloak of tiny bustling bodies. He took a couple of halfhearted swipes at his face, but the prickle of little legs was gone. Nothing was crawling on his face, trying to get into his mouth. Nothing was moving beneath the legs of his trousers. Nothing stirred beneath his shirt.

Grabbing the wheels of his chair, Dave frantically propelled himself forward. He reached the open door. Passed through it. Finally he dared a glance behind him.

There were no roaches.

And no crushed carcasses.

"Oh God," Dave whispered. "Oh God, what's going on here?"

He heard footsteps on the stairs, and then Ed appeared. "You call me?" the nurse asked.

"Um, no, no. . . ." Dave said. "I . . . I needed some stuff I thought I couldn't reach, but I managed to get it by myself."

The nurse studied him. "You sure nothing's wrong?"

"Everything's okay now," Dave said.

Ed eyed him doubtfully, then said, "Well, just holler if you need anything." He headed back downstairs.

And Dave Guthrie wondered whether he was losing his mind. The things he'd been seeing were impossible. They simply couldn't be happening. Therefore, the only explanation was that he'd imagined everything. Maybe he'd even invented the conversation with Ed during which the nurse had told him about the tea kettle.

Dave wheeled into his bedroom, uncertain whether he had a firm grip on reality. He toyed with the logic that if he was still sane enough to realize that he might be insane, then he was still okay—for the moment. But after a few minutes of this, Dave simply pushed everything from his mind and tried not to think at all.

The dreary weather seemed to have seeped into the house, filling him with its raw dampness.

•5•

Ed Prawdzik was in the kitchen, slicing some radishes for the salad he was serving with the veal scallopini tonight. Ed was the sort of guy who was delighted with life's pleasures. And one of the greatest joys of all was cooking—turning the readily-available things you found at the grocery store into culinary delights.

Andrea said he'd make someone a wonderful wife.

Which reminded him that he should call her. They had an

understanding that she shouldn't call him when he was living with a patient, because it was unprofessional having your girlfriend calling you up.

The last few times he'd called her, she'd been worried sick—all because of that silly dream she'd had. Ed hadn't told her about the kettle or the things Dave had seen. If he had, Andrea might have driven down from Eureka and dragged him from the house.

Nothing to be afraid of, Andrea, he thought.

He glanced at the stove, where the tea kettle sat quietly, and then he recalled how it had hopped around, spewing steam. Ed hadn't tried to analyze that day, for he knew he wouldn't find any answers. Nor had he tried to tell himself it hadn't happened. For it had. No doubt. He'd seen what he'd seen, and telling himself otherwise was pointless.

How about what happened to Dave—or at least what Dave said happened? There, too, Ed had decided to keep an open mind. Something had sure as hell frightened his patient, and the only explanation Ed had was the one Dave had offered.

At least nothing had happened for a while now. Maybe the rest of his stay here would be normal. He sure as hell hoped it would.

There's nothing here can't be explained, Ed told himself. You may not know the explanation, but it's there. Don't let your imagination run away with you. Dave's brain could still be recovering from the plane crash, and that could cause him to see things. As for the kettle . . . well, magicians performed more unbelievable feats than that, and he couldn't explain any of them either. But the answers were out there for a person astute enough to find them. Just because he wasn't that smart didn't mean he should go off half-cocked and conclude something ridiculous like the house was haunted.

There was no such thing as a haunted house.

No such things as ghosts.

Okay, Ed told himself, no more nonsense for the rest of my stay here. Dave and I will get along real well, and I'll make lots of good meals, and Dave will recover, and I'll go back to Andrea, and everything will be just fine.

After he finished making the salad, Ed brought Dave downstairs so he could watch the evening news in the living room. When the nurse switched on the TV set the picture came on, then faded out, then came back. Ed tried another channel and it did the same thing. The picture kept fading in and out.

"Never done that before," Dave said.

Ed tried another channel, and got a picture that was so full of snow it could have come from hundreds of miles away. "Where do these stations come from?" Ed asked.

"Translators on Mattole Hill."

"Could be their problem, not ours. Should I turn it off?"

"No, find the station that comes in best and leave it on. Maybe it'll clear up."

Ed complied, and Dave asked, "What's for dinner?"

"Salad."

"Just salad?" He looked disappointed.

"Well, I was planning on veal scallopini as an accompaniment."

"Yum."

"The way I figure it, a well-fed patient will recover more quickly."

"I think you're right. And even if I don't recover any sooner, at least I'm much happier while I'm confined to this thing." He patted the chair's armrest with his palm.

Ed grinned. "Look at it this way. I get to eat real good while I'm here, and you pay for the groceries."

"It's worth every penny," Dave said.

Ed returned to the kitchen, thinking that he liked Dave Guthrie enough that if they didn't live in different communities they could be friends. Of course Ed always liked patients who appreciated his cooking. There'd been one, guy named Henry Munder, who'd written him at least five times asking for Ed's recipes. Which pleased Ed nearly as much as seeing Henry recover completely and resume a normal life.

He opened the refrigerator, intending to get some lettuce for the salad, and heat rushed over him as if he'd just looked into an oven. Ed stared, not believing his eyes.

The plastic food containers had begun to melt, stretching and collapsing like molten wax, turning the refrigerator's interior into a surreal landscape, like that painting with the melted clocks.

The stench assaulted his nostrils—the combined odors of rotting meat and vegetables, souring milk, growing mold, melting plastic.

He slammed closed the refrigerator door. What he was seeing was simply not possible. There was no mechanism in a refrigerator that could turn it into an oven. He took a step backward, away from the refrigerator that was doing what no refrigerator could. From the corner of his eye, he saw movement, and he spun in that direction, a gasp catching in his throat.

He was looking at a spider, a monster spider, the grand-daddy of all spiders.

It was black and hairy, ferocious-looking.

Its legs were at least a foot across.

Its mandibles were as thick as pencils.

And it was eating a cat.

Slowly sucking out the cat's juices while the animal struggled in the monster's grip.

Ed backed up a step. Then another. No such thing as a cat-eating spider, he told himself. No such thing. Not in South America or Africa or anywhere on the whole damn planet. Cat-eating spiders simply did not exist.

The cat made a low pitiful meow.

Ed could hear the spider's mandibles working, hear it sucking.

His stomach lurched, and he was sure he was going to be sick.

• 6 •

Paula sat in her favorite chair, watching TV. She wasn't terribly fond of television with its sitcoms and soap operas and game shows, but tonight she was hoping the tube would keep her from thinking about things like cockroaches that were multiplying in her chair one moment and gone the next.

Somehow she had become part of a tremendously strong psychic link.

What did it mean?

She had to assume it meant the man who lived by the ocean needed her help, even though she had no idea how she *could* help—even if she knew who he was, which she didn't. That summed it up pretty well.

Until now her abilities had been limited to knowing the truth when she heard it and knowing when someone needed help. Suddenly things weren't that simple, and the new turn of events was scary. She sensed that she—and maybe the man who lived by the ocean too—were caught up in something . . . something momentous and awesome and terrifying.

Paula blinked. A gray tom cat had just walked in front of her. Turning to look at her, it meowed.

"What are you doing here?" she asked the cat, confusion and unease spreading through her.

It stared at her with its green, vertically slitted cat's eyes that looked like marbles, its gaze unyielding, as if waiting to see who would blink first.

"How did you get in here?" Paula asked. And then she realized how foolish it was to ask questions of a cat. What did she expect? That it would say, *Oh, I was just out for a stroll, and the door was open, so I thought I'd stop in and say hi?*

The cat, of course, said nothing. It continued to stare at

her for a moment, then it continued across the room, toward the hearth.

In the shadows by the fireplace, something else moved. And then a dark shape attacked the cat.

For a moment Paula saw nothing but a tangle of legs and bodies, the cat hissing and screeching and clawing. But after a moment the tide of battle turned, and the attacker had the upper hand.

It was an enormous spider, a basketball-sized spider. And it was devouring the gray tom, hair and blood flying in the air, and the room was filled with the cat's terrified shrieks. Then the cat was silent, and the only sound was a wet gurgling. And Paula realized it was the sound of sucking.

She opened her mouth to scream, but her throat was so dry she was unable to make a sound.

•7•

Ed Prawdzik picked up a chair, took a second to build up his courage, then smashed the huge spider.

Instantly it was gone.

And so was the cat.

"Everything okay in there?" Dave called from the living room.

"I . . ." Ed's voice was weak and dry and high-pitched. He tried again. "I knocked over a chair," he said.

For a long moment, he stared at the spot where the spider and cat had been. There was nothing. No blood, no cat, no spider parts, nothing. Then he opened the refrigerator. It was normal again, no longer the subject of a surrealistic painting. There was no odor. Nothing was melted. Chilly air leaked out.

"What the hell?" Ed muttered to himself. "What the hell?"

•8•

Paula stared at the spot where the cat and monstrous spider had been. It was like the disappearing cockroaches. One moment there had been a bloodbath going on before her eyes, and the next, the scene had vanished as if she'd switched it off.

There had been no cat.

There had been no huge spider.

It was the psychic link again.

"What do you want with me?" Paula demanded. "Tell me, dammit! What do you want?"

But the only response was the drone of the TV set, sitcom characters babbling about the foibles of their make-believe lives.

"Leave me alone," Paula said. "Please. Just leave me alone." A tear trickled down her cheek. "I can't help you," she whispered. "I can't."

TALKING IT OVER

• 1 •

"Delicious," Dave said contentedly, having just swallowed his last bite of strawberry shortcake.

"Too bad I had to use store-bought shortcakes," Ed said. "I didn't have time to make them from scratch." They were sitting at the kitchen table, empty glasses and dessert plates in front of them.

"A minor omission," Dave said. "All in all I'd say the chef deserves a resounding cheer."

Ed smiled. "Well, if you absolutely have to cheer, I guess it would be all right."

Dave laughed. Someday he was going to tell people about the nurse who cooked beef burgundy and veal scallopini and linguini with red clam sauce, topping off the meals with homemade desserts, and no one would believe him. A guy like that, they'd say, would be tending rich people and charging a hundred thousand a year.

Ed stood up as though he was going to start picking up the plates, but then he hesitated and sat down again. For a moment he seemed lost in his own thoughts; then his eyes found Dave's. "I think we need to talk," Ed said.

"About what?"

"About all the weird stuff that's been happening."

"You mean like the kettle and the hole in the floor?"

Ed nodded. "And other things, things we haven't told each other about."

90

Dave searched the nurse's face. "You mean other stuff has happened to you?"

"Yeah," Ed said. "And I'd be willing to bet there are some things you haven't told me, too."

Dave considered whether he *wanted* to talk about the things he'd been keeping to himself, and he was surprised to discover he did. Suddenly the details were all but bubbling in their desire to come out.

"This morning," Dave said slowly, "when I called you, I thought the studio was full of cockroaches. The chair's wheels were slipping in them, and they were . . ." He shuddered at the memory. "They were crawling all over me. Thousands of them."

"Why didn't you tell me about it?"

Dave shrugged. "I guess I thought you'd think I was crazy. I was having trouble convincing *myself* that I wasn't crazy. One moment, there I was scared shitless, with every cockroach in town swarming over me, and in the next instant they were gone." He stared into Ed's eyes. "It was *real,* dammit. As real as the ocean or the arm of this chair I'm sitting in. And then it wasn't there anymore, so it couldn't have been real. That means it was in my mind, which in turn means there's something wrong with my mind."

Ed shook his head. "I don't think there's anything wrong with your mind."

"You don't know. You didn't see it."

"I saw the kettle with no flame under it, steaming and hopping around."

"That could be explainable."

"Yeah," Ed said, "you might be able to explain that. But how do you account for a spider the size of a small dog that was eating a cat?"

"A cat?" Dave asked, not liking the image of that even one little bit.

"A cat. Spider was sucking it dry."

"Shit."

"And a moment before that, I opened the refrigerator and it was like an oven inside. All the plastic containers were melting."

Dave looked at the refrigerator. It looked normal, as it always had. "And now?"

"Now it's fine. Nothing's melted, everything's cold."

"And the spider?"

"Vanished."

"Shit," Dave said again.

"What haven't you told me?" the nurse asked.

Dave opened his mouth to answer, but before he could speak, the front door opened, and Jackie called, "Where is everybody?"

"In the kitchen," Ed said, and a moment later Jackie stepped into the room, her blond hair swaying slightly, her friendly real-estate-agent's smile firmly in place.

She studied their faces a moment, then said, "Hey, you guys look downright glum."

Dave and Ed exchanged glances, neither of them sure whether they should tell Jackie what they'd been talking about.

"Talking about me behind my back, huh?" Jackie said good-naturedly.

"No," Dave said. "Of course not. Nothing like that."

"What, then?" Her mood abruptly darkened.

No one answered.

Jackie frowned. "I don't like this. I don't like it at all." Her gaze fixed on Dave. "We're engaged to be married, and you're holding stuff back. You're not being honest with me."

"It's not like that," Dave said. Ed was wisely staying out of it.

"Well, that's certainly how it seems." She looked hurt.

Dave wasn't exactly sure how all this had come about. Jackie was showing a side of herself he'd never seen before, a touchy childish side, he thought. And yet she did have a point. Instead of trusting her, sharing everything with her, he was holding back things he wasn't sure she'd understand. He took a slow breath and said:

"When you came in, Ed and I were talking about the strange things that have been going on here."

"Strange things?" she said, clearly perplexed.

He told her about the cockroaches.

"You had a dream," Jackie said.

"Maybe," Dave replied. "But that's only one of the things that's happened." He told her about the others, including the things that had happened to Ed.

"A cat?" Jackie said. "You've got to be kidding."

"That's what I saw," Ed said. "The spider was bigger than it was."

Jackie, who was still standing, shifted her eyes to Ed. "Do you take drugs?" she asked.

"Drugs?" he said, looking bewildered.

"You know, controlled substances. Drugs." Her expression seemed vaguely accusatory.

"I don't take drugs," Ed said softly.

"But you're a nurse, right? You have access to such things."

"Only if I'm working in a hospital, and then access is strictly controlled."

"We're not on drugs," Dave said.

"Well, guys, I've got to tell you that you're sure as hell acting as though you are."

Dave just stared at her, not understanding her reaction. She'd practically accused Ed of drugging him. Jackie could be quick to draw conclusions and slow to change her mind, but this was uncalled for.

"She might have a point," Ed said.

"She might?" Dave replied, confused.

"This could be drug-induced. Maybe there's a chemical dump nearby, one of those places where hazardous wastes are deposited. Some of that stuff is pretty damned potent. If it got into the water—or even just in the air—it could affect you in some pretty strange ways."

"I don't know of anything like that," Dave said. "Do you?" he asked Jackie.

"There are no industrial plants in the area and no hazardous dumps," she said.

"Could be illegally dumped," Ed suggested.

Jackie shook her head. "There was never anything like that here."

"How about during the war?" Dave asked. "Any secret plants in the area?"

"No."

Dave said, "Maybe there's something in the water, and everybody in town's hallucinating."

"Wheat can do it," Ed said. "There's an organism that can get into it and produce a drug that's a lot like LSD. Maybe we got ahold of some bad bread or some bad flour."

They all looked at each other; then Dave said, "Maybe this is an old Indian burial ground, like in *Poltergeist.*"

"Enough of this," Jackie said firmly. "I think you should get your imaginations under control." And hanging unspoken between the words was something Dave couldn't quite get a handle on. This was affecting Jackie in ways he didn't understand.

"We're only trying to figure out what's going on," Dave said.

"You have to stand up to these . . . these delusions. When you have them, you have to tell yourself they're not real, make them go away. Don't you see? You have to. Because they're fake, because you can't live like that, seeing things that aren't there. It's . . . it's not healthy." She was staring at them intently, her eyes driving home the message.

"Jackie," Dave said softly, "there's a little more going on here than our imaginations. These things are real at the moment we see them—or at least they seem to be. We have absolutely no control over it. Telling a hole in the floor it's not there isn't going to make it go away. Whatever's happening here is more complex than that."

Jackie shook her head. "I think the answer's in you. You just have to reach way down inside and find it."

"Jackie—"

"I've got to go," she said, cutting him off. "I've got some paperwork to catch up on."

"I'll walk you to the—" Dave shook his head. "I'll wheel to the door with you."

"Don't bother," Jackie said. "I can see myself out." She turned and hurried out of the room.

"I'm not sure I understand what went on there," Ed said.

Nor did Dave. He said, "I'm sorry about what she said about drugs."

"No problem. Let's face it—the stuff we were saying was pretty weird."

Dave said, "What if these things keep happening? What do we do?"

"I don't know."

"Neither do I."

They were both quiet a moment; then Ed said, "Do you think this place is haunted?"

"If it is, the ghosts waited a long time to make their presence known."

Leaning over, Ed got the phone book from the small table beneath the wall-mounted phone, flipped through it, and put it back. "Ghostbusters don't have an office here," he said.

They grinned at each other. *See, everything's okay.*

But everything was not okay, and they both knew it, and their smiles immediately began to fade.

• 2 •

Frowning, Jackie drove away from Dave's house. She pulled onto the road, roughly shoved the gearshift into second, stomped on the accelerator. She drove angrily for a few moments; then it occurred to her that she wasn't even sure what she was angry about.

But when she thought about it, she did know. She was angry because all this business with Dave and his nurse was very disquieting. And the reason she was uneasy was because it threatened her plans, her notions of the way things should be. Jackie had been planning to wait another seven-and-a-half months, then marry Dave. Dave had a good, steady income, and she was reasonably certain she could be happy living with him. In a word they were compatible.

But now she had doubts.

Jackie had trouble seeing herself tied to someone who saw holes open up in the floor and imagined himself attacked by a swarm of cockroaches. Her stepfather had imagined crazy things. Oh, he'd seemed normal enough at first. Handsome and charming and gentle. But then he'd begun hearing the voices. Creatures from outer space who could communicate with no one but him.

He'd told Jackie and her mother all about it once. Zhanixx was the leader of a space fleet carrying the survivors of a planet destroyed when its sun exploded. Zhanixx was coming to earth to peacefully integrate with our society. Jackie's stepfather was supposed to be the human ambassador for the aliens when they arrived. He clearly felt quite honored.

Jackie's mother filed for divorce.

Jackie's stepfather fought it, saying Zhanixx had told him to do so, because it wouldn't look right for his ambassador to be divorced. As had her mother's first divorce, it had turned quite nasty, both sides out for blood. She had been eight the first time she'd testified in divorce court, eleven the second time. And in both cases she'd been a pawn, something to be used.

But then that was all behind her, wasn't it? Her mother had been married and divorced again since then, and Jackie, an adult by that time, hadn't cared. She made the car's tires squeal as she turned sharply onto Humboldt Avenue. She was still angry.

The problem was that her mother's second husband had ended up in a mental hospital, still hearing the messages from Zhanixx. As time went on, instead of getting better, he started hearing messages from other extraterrestrials. One was called the Black Master, a Darth Vader type who wanted to enslave the universe. In short, the guy was totally bonkers. He occasionally had to be restrained to keep him from hurting himself or other patients. They put electrodes on him and zapped his brain. They pumped drugs into him until he shuffled around in a perpetual stupor.

And it all began with hearing an imaginary voice from outer space.

As imaginary as Dave's cockroaches.

Jackie stopped at a traffic signal. The town square, known as Cooksie Park, was on her left. On her right was Bradley's Hardware and Marine. Ahead were a handful of traffic signals—Castle Bay residents disliked them, so they were kept to a minimum—and numerous weathered-looking clapboard buildings. A light fog was drifting in off the Pacific.

Damn town's too quaint for its own good, Jackie thought.

Sure, she knew that the look of it—the twisting streets, the wooden buildings, the hills—were what made the community what it was. Still, it could use some industrial development. A couple of medium-size plants would mean hundreds of new jobs, which would create a demand for housing, which would raise property values. And Jackie was ready to cash in. She not only sold real estate, but when a promising bargain came along, she invested in it. Though deeply in debt, Jackie could always get a loan to buy more property, using her existing holdings as collateral. She had to stick to places she could rent out, so she could make the payments on the loans, but despite this limitation she had acquired properties all over Castle Bay. Including three rundown houses in the community's southwest corner, which were rented by people on welfare. This made her a slum lord, she supposed, but Jackie didn't really care. She'd never really been into social consciousness and all that.

The light turned green, and Jackie stepped on the accelerator. She realized there was nothing she could do right now concerning Dave except watch the situation. Which she would do. Very carefully. Although she hadn't changed her mind about Dave—not yet anyway—she had no intention of stepping into something that would make a mess of her life.

If Dave Guthrie was going to start communicating with his own version of Zhanixx, Jackie Lake was moving on.

•3•

The place was as cheerless as a mortuary. Paula and two other people sat in the waiting room of the Anoka Falls Dental Associates, their eyes buried in magazines, nobody speaking, nobody looking around. When Paula looked up from her month-old copy of *U.S. News & World Report,* she got the impression she was in a kindergarten class. Posters on the walls showed stylized toothbrushes proclaiming that they were your pal, the plaque fighter and tooth saver. And then there were teeth—smiling molars no less—letting her know that the dentist was her friend, the guy who'd make the world right if she just trusted him and did what he said.

A frizzy-haired hygienist stepped into the room and said, "Anna Lundquist."

A pale blond woman in her late twenties put down her magazine and stood up.

Offering a dazzling smile, the white-coated hygienist led Anna Lundquist through a door and into the bowels of the building.

Paula put down the magazine and picked up a copy of *Time* that was only two weeks old—new by dentist-office standards. She flipped the pages absently, not really seeing what was on them. After a few moments, she put the magazine down.

For the last week or so, she'd had no further contacts—if that was the right word—from the man who lived by the ocean. Nor had she seen any cockroaches or cat-eating spiders. She had no idea what that meant. Maybe it was over; her help was no longer needed. Or maybe the link had simply broken down somehow, and she would never know who the man was or what had happened to him.

Paula didn't know how she felt about that. If it was over, she supposed she was both relieved and disappointed. Relieved that the images were gone from her life. Disappointed because someone needed her help and she'd been unable to give it. It wasn't that simple, of course. There were other feelings swirling around within her, dimly-sensed emotions she was unable to identify.

Paula's mind presented her with an instant replay of the spider devouring the cat, and she shivered. It hadn't been there. And yet it had. Its plane of existence had briefly overlapped with hers, and for that instant it was real. Then the overlap had come undone, and what had been real was no more.

Did she know what she was talking about?

Paula shook her head. There were things she sensed, not things she knew. Perhaps she sensed them through her psychic abilities. On the other hand, she could just be searching for rational explanations because that's what the human mind did. It disliked things it was unable to understand, so it worked with them until it had come up with something. Primitive societies invented gods to account for day and night, rain, earthquakes, the seasons, whatever was not otherwise explainable. Maybe that's all she was doing, inventing her own sun god or cloud god or god of nightfall to explain away the incomprehensibility. She had used the notion of overlapping dimensions. Maybe she believed in the science-fiction god.

Paula picked up the magazine again, having decided she'd rather fill her mind with stale news than think about cat-eating spiders. She opened it to the story of the plane crash in St. Louis in which all but one of the passengers had died. She didn't want to read about so much death.

Paula almost didn't look at the photo whose caption was "Sole Survivor."

She was about to flip that page too, when she found her eyes being drawn to the photo, and as she focused on it, a chill hit her with the startling suddenness of a plunge into icy water.

"Paula Bjornson," the hygienist said.

Paula was reading the article, only vaguely aware of the white-coated woman standing beside her.

"That must really be interesting," the hygienist said.

Paula still didn't respond.

"Dr. Stoner's ready."

Slowly Paula stood. The hygienist was smiling at her, ready to lead her to the brightly lighted room in which Harold Stoner, DDS, waited.

"I'm taking this magazine," Paula said.

"Uh, well, I guess it would be all right. It looks pretty old."

Paula started toward the door.

"Wait, Ms. Bjornson, your appointment."

"Reschedule me," Paula said.

"You'll have to do that at the desk . . . Uh, Ms. Bjornson . . . ?"

Paula walked out of the building.

INCIDENT AT THE OCEANVIEW
TRAILER PARK

Maude Youngman lay in bed, waiting, knowing it was coming.

Whenever Wendall got home late, it meant he'd been out drinking. And when he'd been drinking, he came home angry. Maude never knew what to do. If she spoke to him, tried to be nice, she'd often as not say something that would set him off. On the other hand, if she just lay there, pretending to be asleep, he might get mad because she was ignoring him.

Life with Wendall was like that.

You never knew what was the right thing to do.

Hearing a car door slam, Maude sat up, looked through the trailer's small window. The sound had come from three trailers away from hers, where Maggie Riverton lived. A man was getting out of a pickup, going in to see Maggie. Maggie's husband, Quentin, was a lineman with the phone company, and he was off in the Salmon Mountains, running new phone lines to a number of small communities. And whenever Quentin was away, Maggie had visitors.

No one had ever mentioned anything about it to Quentin, and no one ever would. People in the Oceanview Trailer Park minded their own business. Like the time Wendall had thrown her out of the trailer, then kicked her while she screamed for him to stop. No one had intervened. It was a private matter, between husband and wife.

There was probably a clause in the rental agreements the residents all signed—Thou shalt not poke thy nose into thy neighbors' business.

Maude had scrubbed the trailer from top to bottom. There wasn't a speck of dust anywhere. She always did that when Wendall was late. A little dust on the top of the refrigerator or a spot of something or another on the stove could set him off. Wendall liked things neat. He kept his tool box neat, his pickup neat, his clothes neat. Maude even ironed his work clothes, though they consisted of jeans and a permanent-press western shirt.

Wendall was a heavy equipment operator for a construction company that built highways. He and Maude had come to Castle Bay about a month ago because it was the closest place with a trailer park to the twenty-mile stretch of state highway that was being widened. Maybe come fall they'd be in Oregon. Or Nevada. Or Arizona. Didn't matter. For Maude, life would be the same. One trailer park was like another. And Wendall . . . well, Wendall never changed.

Fog was starting to roll in off the Pacific, long wispy tendrils reaching into the trailer park like the tentacles of some enormous ghostly sea monster. Something moved in the shadows. Maude squinted, trying to see what it was. The trailers were arranged along a curving strip of asphalt. Partway around the bend was a patch of deep shadows, and that's where she'd seen the movement. Maude shook her head. She must have imagined it, for the thing she'd seen—*thought* she'd seen—was enormous, tall enough to look over the tops of the trailers.

An icy feeling slid down her spine, almost a touch, as if Death had run its finger down the center of her back. Maude shivered, pulled the covers around her.

There was nothing there, she told herself. There were no ten-foot-tall monsters in real life. The real-life monsters were the husbands who came home drunk, angry, ready to use their fists.

A pair of headlights appeared at the entrance to the trailer park, and Maude stiffened, knowing it might be Wendall.

But it wasn't. The car pulled in beside a trailer on the left, a good seventy-five feet away. But momentarily caught in the car's headlights had been something that made Maude suck in her breath. Two small, glowing circles. Like an animal's eyes. In that same shadowy place.

It's a bear, she thought, surprised to find that she was relieved. If she could find the thought of a bear tall enough to look over the roofs of the trailers comforting, what had she thought was there before? She didn't know, but she clung to the notion of a bear. A huge bear, a monster of a bear. Came down from the hills to check out the garbage cans.

A ten-foot-tall bear, Maudie? This ain't Alaska, kid. Who you fooling? But she pushed these thoughts aside. It was a bear, dammit. A bigger-than-usual one to be sure, but a bear nonetheless. She stared out the window for a long time, seeing nothing else.

And then a sound from the boys' bedroom distracted her, a soft childish mutter, full of sleep. It had to be Wendall Junior, who'd talk a blue streak in his sleep sometimes. He was eight. His brother Bobby was six. The boys were Maude Youngman's life. They had come from her body, and they were connected to her in a way no other relative could be—except her own mom, of course.

Maude recalled a conversation she'd had with her mother after receiving a particularly brutal beating from Wendall. She'd been hospitalized with two cracked ribs, one eye swollen shut. Sitting there by the hospital bed, her mother had told her how sorry she was that her little girl had been hurt.

"I'm thinking of leaving him," Maude had said, and dark clouds had gathered in her mom's eyes.

"Don't you say anything like that, Maude," her mother had said. "You've a family to think of. You've got two little boys who need a daddy to provide for them."

Maude was stunned. "But, Mamma, he hurts me, hurts me bad. And I can't take it anymore."

"Marriage isn't like in the storybooks, Maudie. Marriage

is working hard and putting up with things you don't like putting up with. You're a wife now, and it's a wife's job to make her man happy, to keep a nice and decent house for her family, to be there when they need her."

Maude thought this all over. "Mamma," she said, "did Daddy ever hurt you?"

Her mother studied her silently for a moment; then she said, "Those are the details of my marriage, Maudie, and they're none of your business. You should concentrate on your marriage, do everything you can to make it work, to make a good home for little Wendall and Bobby."

And Maude had taken her mother's advice. There had been a number of times she'd doubted the wisdom of that decision, but she'd never tried to leave Wendall. If her mom had advised her to leave, she would have. But she wasn't going to do something that would make both her mother and husband look down on her. She had too much pride for that. Besides, what would she do? Get a job as a waitress? How would she raise her kids while she worked all day, barely earning enough money to get by on? The alternative would be the shame of going on welfare, paying with food stamps at the grocery store while everybody watched, thinking you were a no-account. A tear trickled down her cheek, and she wiped it away. There was nothing to be gained by feeling sorry for herself.

Headlights appeared out the window again, and this time they continued on toward Maude. It was Wendall. She could see the row of lights mounted above the roof of his pickup. It was one of those tall trucks, with big tires and special suspension that held it way up off the ground. It was Wendall's pride and joy, that pickup. Sometimes Maude thought he loved it more than he loved Wendall Junior and Bobby. Maude knew he loved it more than he loved her. She heard the truck's motor grow silent, its door close, the door to the trailer being opened. A moment later Wendall was in the room, bumping into the doorway as he entered.

Maude took a guess, decided it would be better if she pretended to be asleep. She heard him pulling off his clothes.

He sat down roughly on the edge of the bed, not caring whether he woke her up. He reeked of booze. He went into the bathroom, and the light came on. Maude could hear him urinating.

The bathroom light went out. The bedroom light came on.

If anything was going to happen, it would happen now.

"Whatzamatter, Maude, you too good to talk to me when I come home?"

Maude kept her eyes closed, kept pretending. Kept hoping.

"Aw, I'll bet you don't want to talk to me because I'm drunk, that right?" When she didn't respond, he said, "Well, you know what, Maude? I work hard all day to take care of you and the kids, and I want to know where you get off thinking you're too good to talk to me just 'cause I had a few drinks."

Maude decided it was time to take a different tack. She rolled over, opened her eyes, and said, "Oh hi, honey. You have a good time tonight?"

"I need something to eat," he said.

Slipping her legs over the edge of the bed, she said, "Okay, honey, what would you like?"

He looked down at her. Wendall was just sort of an average-looking guy. He had light brown hair, blue eyes, and he was neither tall nor short, neither thin nor fat. He had a smile that was sort of honest and open; to look at him you wouldn't say he was real smart or real dumb.

At this moment, to Maude, he looked dangerous.

It was in his blue eyes, the way they looked like balls of ice, the way all the frustrations of a lifetime seemed trapped in that ice, ready to break free and torment the man, drive him to rage.

"Ham sandwich," Wendall said finally.

Slipping on her light-green robe and pulling it tightly around her, Maude went into the kitchen. Her husband followed her. Switching on the light, she went to the refrigerator. A moment later she knew she was in trouble. There was no ham.

"Would a bologna sandwich be okay?" Maude asked weakly.

"I said ham." Wendall was looking at her with those icy eyes, eyes filled with a dreadful cold, the kind of cold you'd find during the long winter darkness at the North Pole, a cold that seemed endless, capable of engulfing the world and freezing everything in it.

"Isn't any," Maude said.

"Why not?"

"You ate the last of it yesterday, honey. Tomorrow's the day I go for groceries. I'll get some more."

"Why didn't you get it today?"

"I . . . I didn't know you'd be wanting any, or I would have."

"Shit," Wendall muttered. "Man comes home after working his ass off all day, and there isn't anything to eat. What the hell kind of thing is that?"

Maude grabbed a package of assorted lunchmeats. "I've got this," she said, holding it out to him. And as soon as she did it, she realized her mistake.

"Any ham in it?" he demanded.

She shook her head.

"Then I don't want it!" he snapped, swatting the package out of her hand. "What the hell did you offer it to me for?"

"I . . . I . . ." Before she could think of an answer, his fist landed in her face, knocking her back into the still-open refrigerator. She hit a bottle of something, and glass broke. Wendall hit her again. And again.

"Please, Wendall," she said. "Please."

He hit her twice more, then stopped. He just stood there, dressed in his underwear, breathing heavily, looking at her, his eyes full of unidentifiable emotions. Finally, he said, "Maude, why did you make me fly off the handle like that?"

"I'm sorry," she said. She was still partway into the refrigerator. Something cold and wet was seeping into her nightgown and robe. She'd hurt her back where it hit one of the shelves.

"Why do you do it, Maude? Huh? Why do you do it?"

"I . . . I just didn't think, honey. I'm sorry. I am. I really am sorry."

"That's right, Maude. Sometimes I wonder if you'll ever learn to think."

"I'll try harder, honey. I promise. You want me to get dressed and run to the 7-Eleven, get you some ham?"

"Be too late then, Maude. I'll have lost my appetite by then."

"I'll get it tomorrow."

Wendall nodded. "I'm not tired. I'll go get something over at Chaseman's." Chaseman's was a truck stop on the interstate, fifteen miles away.

"I'll fix you something here," Maude said.

Wendall's expression darkened. "I told you I don't want nothing you got here. You had some ham for me, I wouldn't have to go to Chaseman's, but you don't, so I have to go."

"I'm sorry," Maude said. "It's all my fault."

He nodded. It was all her fault.

Wendall got dressed again, gave her an angry look, and left. He wouldn't be home all night probably. Maude thought he had something going with one of the waitresses at Chaseman's, but she wasn't sure. It could be any woman. He might not be going to Chaseman's at all. At least it wasn't Maggie Riverton. She was already taken for the night.

Maude went into the bathroom, looked into the mirror. A tired-looking middle-aged blonde woman stared back at her. I'm wearing out, Maude thought. I'm twenty-seven and I look forty or fifty. But that wasn't why she was looking at herself. She wanted to see how much damage Wendall had done and whether she could hide it with makeup. Split lip appeared to be the only thing. No bruises. No black eye. She'd gotten off easy this time.

Maude heard a noise, sort of half cry, half grunt.

She went into the bedroom, looked out the window. Nothing outside was moving. And then she realized that Wendall's truck was still there. Had something happened to him? Had he cried out? She considered that. And then she remembered the bear—or whatever it was. She'd put it out of her mind, convinced herself she'd been imagining things. But . . . but what? Did she now believe that a ten-foot-tall *something* had just devoured Wendall?

A scream filled the night air.

A sound of pure terror. Spewed from that primal part of a man where ancient animal instinct lives. At least Maude thought the sound had come from a man. All she knew for sure was that it had come from something that had just experienced fear on a level she could hardly imagine. Pulling her robe around her, she rushed to the door, then hesitated. Did she really want to go out there? Her hand hovered over the knob, trembling.

But she had to see about her husband. Although he was mean and a drunk, he was still the only husband she'd ever had, the father of her boys.

"Mom . . ." A child's voice said hesitantly.

Maude turned around, saw Bobby and Wendall Junior in their pajamas, standing by the door to their room, looking at her with wide, questioning eyes. "Go back to bed," she said. "Hurry along now."

But the boys didn't move. "Mom . . ." Wendall Junior said. "What . . . what was that noise?"

"I don't know," Maude said. "Back to bed. Both of you. Right now."

The boys reluctantly complied. Bracing herself, Maude opened the door. The lights had come on in other mobile homes. Her next-door neighbor, Henry Ingram, was standing in the yellow glow spilling from the open door of his trailer, dressed in a blue robe, a pistol hanging from his hand.

Another man came up, a guy who'd just moved into the space on the other side of Ingram. Maude didn't know his name. He was dressed in khaki work clothes, and he looked nervous.

"What the hell's going on?" he asked Ingram.

"I don't know," the other man said.

"It sounded like . . . like something awful happened out here."

Maude started toward them, and Ingram said, "I'd recommend you go back inside, Mrs. Youngman. At least until we find out what's going on out here."

Maude ignored the advice and continued toward him. She'd never understood men. Ingram wanted to protect her from whatever danger might lurk out here, but he wouldn't lift a finger to prevent her husband from killing her. In one instance he figured it was a man's job to protect a woman, and in the other he figured a man should mind his own business. Violence against a woman was bad unless it was done by the husband, in which case it was okay.

"I'm staying," Maude said, to head off any further attempts to send her back to her trailer.

No one argued with her. The fog was thickening, the wisps slipping into the spaces between the trailers, blurring the squares of light from the windows, brushing against Maude's flesh like the cold, clammy fingers of a corpse.

Lefty Fowler showed up, carrying one of those long flashlights like the ones the police used. He was wearing a gun belt with a holster from which the butt of an automatic protruded. Men loved to own guns, loved to get them out. Maybe it made them feel important.

"Where the hell did it come from?" the guy in khaki work clothes asked.

"Over there, I think," Ingram said.

They moved toward the rear of Maude's trailer. The first thing they encountered was Wendall's pickup. It stood there on its high springs with its lights on the roof, looking like something used by NASA for getting around on the moon. There was a gun rack in the rear window, along with a National Rifle Association decal. Wendall claimed to be a hunter, although he'd never bagged a deer in his life. She heard that he killed a cow once, just to shoot something, but she didn't know whether it was true.

"Look at this," Lefty Fowler said.

"Ooo-wee!" Ingram exclaimed. "Wendall's sure gonna be pissed when he sees this." There were long, nasty-looking scratches on the fender of the pickup, as if someone had dragged a garden rake across the shiny black paint. The scratches were deep, all the way to the bare metal.

They moved on, the beam from Fowler's flashlight sweeping right and left, illuminating tall dry weeds left over from last year. The new green ones would grow up among them, and no one would cut them down, because the people who lived here didn't own the property and the people who did own it didn't live here.

Abruptly, they stopped. Lefty Fowler was shining his flashlight on something. "I don't like the looks of that," Ingram said.

Maude stepped around the guy in khaki and looked. In the center of the bright circle of illumination from the flashlight was a place where the weeds had been splashed with something wet and red. Maude tried not to think about what it might mean.

They pressed on, finding more splashes of red. In one spot the weeds were covered with it, as if someone had dumped a gallon of paint on them. "Mrs. Youngman," Ingram said, "I really think you might want to——"

"I'm coming with you," she said as firmly as her shaky nerves would allow.

Ingram didn't argue the point. His voice had been a little higher than usual, a little dry. They resumed pushing their way through the weeds, and then a sound froze them. It wasn't loud, but it was the kind of a noise that could instantly turn your insides to ice. It was like creeping into a dark cave and hearing a low, rumbling growl from the shadows, feeling hot breath on your elbow. You knew you were in deep, deep shit.

This sound was like that low growl, except it was also a hiss. And it was filled with hatred and rage.

And instead of hot breath, the air was suddenly filled with a stench, an odor that was like rotting eggs and putrefying meat and the damp scent of a municipal sewer plant. It was those things, and it was none of them. To Maude it seemed to be the stink of badness—all badness, as if every act of torture and murder and cruelty gave off an evil aroma and all those smells had been concentrated, here, in this place.

Suddenly they all jumped, for something was moving through the weeds about a hundred feet from where they stood. Something huge. Almost reluctantly the flashlight beam made its way to the source of the sound. Maude caught a glimpse of something before it disappeared into the trees. Something. Not a bear. But what? It had indeed been ten feet tall, and it had been covered with scales. And it had a single horn protruding from the top of its head.

Something inside Maude rebelled. *Uh-uh, no way. Ain't no such creature, so you couldn't have seen it. Period. End of report.*

Then why am I standing here trembling? Maude asked herself. She made no attempt to answer the question.

"Jesus!" Ingram whispered.

"Did you see it too?" the guy in khaki asked. "Did you? Did you?" He seemed desperate for someone to tell him he wasn't crazy.

"I saw something," Fowler said.

"Christ," Ingram said, "here we are with two of us armed, and no one got off a shot at it."

No one responded to that. Maude suspected they all knew that whatever the monster was it wasn't the sort of thing you wanted to shoot at. Bullets probably wouldn't hurt it, and they might make it mad.

But no one was going to say that.

"Oh shit," the guy in khaki said. "Oh shit . . . oh . . . oh shit!"

For a second, Maude thought he was talking about what they'd seen, but then the guys had all stepped forward a few feet, and they were staring at something in the weeds. Abruptly Fowler whirled to his left, took two quick steps, and vomited. Maude tried to squeeze between the other two guys, see what was going on. Ingram promptly stepped in front of her.

"You don't want to see this," he said.

"Is it Wendall?" she asked.

He didn't reply.

"Is it?" she demanded.

He nodded. "You don't want to see it, Mrs. Youngman. Please go back to your trailer. Please."

"Is he . . . ?"

"Yes. He's all torn up. Why don't you just go—"

"No. If it's my husband, I have a right to see."

"But—"

"I have to see. Don't you understand? I have to see."

She pushed by him and saw what the others had seen, the sight that had made Fowler throw up. It was barely recognizable as a human being, much less Wendall. It was sort of a soggy red mass, as if some hapless creature had been caught in the blades of a huge food processor. Bare bones shone whitely here and there. One eye was missing, but the other stared sightlessly into the foggy night. Death had frozen that eye in a look that went beyond terror, beyond horror. Maude had no words to describe it.

She searched herself for feelings of loss for this man who had beat her, and found very few. But that open blue eye horrified her. She would see that eye in her nightmares for the rest of her life. She had no understanding of what had happened here. What had that monster been? Why had it done this to Wendall? The questions circled in her brain, unanswered.

Maude Youngman felt as though she'd been snatched from the world she'd always known and plunged into a fantasy place where logic had been replaced by madness. Maybe she'd been sucked into a dream, a dream that had crawled up from the depths of some crazy person's mind. Charles Manson or one of them.

"I'll take you home now," Ingram said.

Maude nodded, let him lead her back toward her trailer.

DREAMS AND DECISIONS

• 1 •

In bed that night Dave Guthrie dreamed.

He was running from something, although he wasn't exactly sure from what. He fled down darkened streets, between buildings, through fields. At last he came to a trailer park, a strange, almost surreal assemblage of metal homes that seemed unnaturally tall, leaning at odd angles, their windows all slightly misshapen. He squeezed beneath a home whose metal skirts had been removed in one place. Peering out from his hiding place, Dave sensed that his pursuer was near. He heard breathing, low and rattling. And then he saw a shape, taller than the surreal trailers, a huge shadow that would kill him if it could find him.

A man emerged from one of the mobile homes, walked toward a pickup. Dave tried to call out to him, warn him, but though his mouth moved he made no sound. Suddenly a scaly arm snaked out of the shadows and grabbed the man, a claw digging into the truck's paint. The man screamed, a terrible, nerve-clanging cry of pure terror. And then he was gone. And there were wet sounds, cracking sounds.

Chewing sounds.

Abruptly the dream changed, as if some unseen controller had punched up a new program. Dave was in his house. His wheelchair and casts still not in evidence, he walked from the kitchen to the living room, and suddenly he knew

113

someone was with him. Behind him. About to touch him. He whirled, putting up his hands, as if to ward off a blow.

No one was there.

And yet the feeling persisted.

Someone was here, in the house with him, watching him. It was more than just a feeling. He knew it as surely as he knew the sun would rise in the morning. Someone was here. Period.

Every nerve in his body tingling with the certainty that an unseen peril was about to strike, he turned a slow circle in the living room, his eyes poking into every shadow, lingering on every possible hiding place. No matter which direction he was facing, the presence seemed to be behind him, its eyes boring into his back. Abruptly he whirled around, finding no one.

Get ahold of yourself, he thought. You're going bonkers, old stick. There's no one here except you. Absolutely no one.

And yet his senses knew better.

He lowered himself onto the couch, concealing his back from the unseen watcher. Eyes bored *through* the couch, poking and probing him, looking into him, seeing his most sacred and private places, knowing his deepest secrets.

"Stop it," he said.

And still he was being examined, a bug under a huge invisible microscope.

"Please," Dave said. "Stop."

He shook his head. His senses had gone haywire. They were receiving false signals, telling him things that couldn't possibly be true. It was simply not physically possible for someone to be here and remain hidden. It could be done electronically, he knew that, but why would anyone put miniature cameras and microphones in his house? He wasn't a spy. He wasn't plotting the overthrow of the government. He had no alimony-hungry ex-wives to sic private detectives on him.

Still, he got up and searched the room, looking under furniture, pulling out drawers, checking lamp shades, even looking up the chimney. If there were any cameras or bugs, they were too well hidden for him to find.

He decided he was going to bed. He would leave the prying eyes here in this part of the house to stare at the walls. He was retreating to the safety of his bedroom. He walked out of the room, started up the stairs.

And the unseen eyes followed.

Like cold fingertips pressing into his back.

But Dave didn't look behind him, for he knew he would see nothing. He brushed his teeth. Went to bed. Closed his eyes. And other eyes watched, hovering above him, never blinking.

Dave sat up. "Go away!" he screamed.

But the invisible eyes paid him no heed.

"Please," he whispered. "I've done nothing to you. Why do you do this to me?"

Abruptly the feeling washed over him that these were benign eyes, that they wanted to help him.

"I don't need any help," he said.

And Dave sensed that he was in grave danger. Slowly he realized that someone—some*thing*?—was communicating with him.

You're in danger, and I'm here to help.

But what danger? Why did he need help?

Dave wasn't sure he got the answer correct. A vague set of perceptions gently came to him, all of them fuzzy, but their essence seemed to be, *Unknown.*

"What's unknown?"

The danger.

"Let me see you," he said.

For a moment there was no reply; then it came. *Can't.*

"Why not?"

Never done it before.

"Show yourself. Let me talk to you."

Don't know how.

"There's got to be a way."

There was no reply for several long moments. Then, *Concentrate on me. Draw me to you.*

Dave hesitated. What if this presence wasn't what it seemed? What if it wanted to harm him? Dave dismissed the notion. The sensation of something benign was practically overwhelming. There wasn't even a hint of evil intent.

"I'm concentrating," Dave said.

And he felt the entity reaching out for him. For a few moments, it seemed as though he were grasping blindly, extending his mind into darkness so total he could get lost in it and never find his way back. Then he was sure there was something in the blackness with him. *This way,* it seemed to say.

As Dave moved toward it, he experienced a barrage of emotions. The entity wasn't the all-powerful, all-seeing thing he'd thought. Rather it was delicate, uncertain. And afraid. Terribly afraid. He moved closer to it.

Closer.

Contact was imminent. He was sure of that. At any moment he would meet the presence that had been watching him. And Dave Guthrie was awed. Not by power, but by sensations he didn't understand. The entity he was approaching was vulnerable, every bit as uncertain and fearful as he was. And yet it would aid him if it could, for that was what it was supposed to do.

It?

Suddenly Dave knew that *it* was the wrong word. He was about to meet *someone.*

There was a wave of heat. The stench of things rotting.

But this wasn't from the person Dave was trying to contact. This was something else. He could feel the other presence, the one he'd been reaching out for, recoil in horror. A gust of foul-smelling wind knocked him off his feet, and he was receding, moving back, away from the one who wanted to help him. No, not just moving. He was being pulled back, yanked back.

Something exploded.

And Dave was awake.

His casts were back, as was the wheelchair, which he could see dimly, beside his bed, just as he'd left it. A cold wind blew into the room. Pieces of something covered the bed, small and hard like gravel. But sharper. He touched his face, felt something wet. The door burst open, the light came on, and Ed rushed into the room.

"You all right?" the nurse asked.

Dave just stared, bewildered. The window was shattered, and a chilly wind blew through the opening with such intensity that it made the edges of the sheets flutter. The bed was covered with tiny pieces of broken glass.

Ed walked over to the window, stared out a moment, then turned to Dave. "There was an unbelievable gust of wind," the nurse said. "I thought it was going to tear the roof off the house." His face was white, his movements jerky.

The wind was still howling, moaning in the eaves like a tormented soul. Abruptly it slacked off, the whine becoming a low murmur, and then it was still, as if nothing had happened at all.

Ed came over to the bed. "Your face, it's covered with tiny little cuts from the flying glass."

Not knowing what to say, Dave simply nodded.

"I'll get my first-aid kit," the nurse said. He hurried out of the room, returning a moment later with a white box. He cleaned Dave's cuts with a strong-smelling chemical, then leaned back like an artist examining a painting. "Bleeding's all stopped," he said. "None of the cuts were deep enough to cause a scar."

"I've never seen a gust of wind like that before," Dave said. "At least not since I've lived here."

"It can happen," Ed said.

Then the two men just stared at each other, their eyes communicating an unspoken question: *Is this more of the strangeness that's been happening here? Part of the madness?*

Ed stood up. "I'll get some fresh bedding and get this glass cleaned up. Is there anything we can use to cover this window for the night?"

"Nothing I know of. I don't have any plywood or anything like that."

Ed rubbed his forehead. "Well, you can either stay here and assume the weather will be quiet for the rest of the night, or we can move your bed into another room."

"I'll just stay here," Dave said. "It looks quiet enough now."

And while Ed was getting the things he'd need to clean up the mess, Dave thought about the dream. It was vague now, growing fainter by the moment, as dreams are wont to do. Still, he knew that he'd been trying to make contact with someone, and at the moment the contact was almost made the window shattered. He struggled to recall other details, but they eluded him.

The window breaking, it seemed to him, was like waking up before something terrible happens in a nightmare. Except this hadn't been a nightmare. He was wanting to contact someone—for some reason. And then the window broke, waking him. The mechanism that interrupted his sleep was external, not something triggered within his own mind. What did it mean?

Did it mean anything?

He didn't know, but the whole episode was making him terribly uneasy. But then, now that he thought about it, uneasy was becoming his normal state. It was as if he were lost in the house of horrors at the carnival. Unable to get out the way he'd come in, he moved along, knowing that the floor ahead was full of air jets, the walls covered with trick mirrors, and that rubber beasties waited overhead to drop down and terrify him.

And he had the feeling he wasn't just passing through the house of horrors. He'd become a permanent resident.

"Jesus," he muttered.

"What's that?" Ed asked, as he returned with cleaning equipment and sheets in hand.

"Nothing," Dave said. "Nothing."

•2•

Paula lay in bed, wide awake, anxiety surging through her as if it were being pushed by a massive pump. She'd been dreaming about the man who lived by the ocean—about

Dave Guthrie. She no longer had to think of him as an unidentified stranger. She knew his name now. She knew where he lived.

She'd dreamed that she and Dave Guthrie had been in some dark, unidentifiable place. Although she could see him, he was aware of her only as an invisible presence.

"Let me see you," he'd said.

And she told him to concentrate, to draw her to him.

He did, and they began moving toward each other. But she was having trouble reaching him, as if unseen forces were trying to hold her back. She fought against them, and ever so slowly she was nearing him, their minds like outstretched fingers, feeling for each other in the dark.

They seemed to be only a couple of feet apart.

Then inches.

Then almost touching.

An explosion sent bits of debris flying around, and the intense wind from the blast blew her backward. And for some reason it was a cold wind, with none of the heat that should have accompanied an explosion. Paula was picked up by it, swirled around, buffeted like a light plane in a severe storm.

And then she realized she was in the presence of something dark and terrifying, something powerful beyond her comprehension. And she heard/felt/sensed its message:

Stay away!

Or else!

Paula's eyes had snapped open at that point, and she was wide awake, an unvoiced scream still lingering in her throat. She could have dismissed it as a nightmare, nothing more, if it hadn't been for the subtle odor lingering in the air.

Turpentine.

The smell told her the nightmare had been more than just a dream. In some way, she had actually been linked to David Guthrie, who still clearly needed her help. Which meant the dark force had been real too. She'd sensed its presence before, of course, but now she was certain that it knew about her as well. And it clearly wanted her to stay away from David Guthrie.

Or else!

Paula shivered. Or else what? What could it do to her? She didn't know, although looking back on the horror movies she'd seen, she could probably come up with some pretty fair guesses. People who annoyed the dark forces often wound up falling out of boats, tumbling from upper-story windows, stepping into the paths of speeding cars. Their deaths were always neatly arranged. Nothing suspicious, but the message, for those who knew enough to interpret it, was always the same.

Don't fool with the dark forces, babe. 'Cause if you do, they're going to mess you up bad.

So what was she going to do? David Guthrie needed her help—even if she didn't know *how* she could help—and she had never ignored a call for aid. It was the responsibility that went along with her gift. It was her destiny to help others when they called out for it.

She recalled the dark presence and shivered.

Although she didn't know what the evil force was, she knew it was too powerful for her to stand against. She had been warned, and she ignored that warning at her peril. Logically there should be no question about it. To try to help David Guthrie would be to endanger herself and probably accomplish nothing.

And yet she was filled with doubts. Did it really matter that she probably wouldn't be able to help? If she was being called on, shouldn't she at least *try?* Wasn't it her duty? She rolled over, buried her face in the pillow. That force, whatever it was, would destroy her. How could that possibly help David Guthrie?

•3•

"Pretty morning," Ed said, handing Dave a tray with waffles and syrup, orange juice, a steaming cup of coffee, and a copy of the twice-weekly *Castle Bay Crier.*

Dave was in his wheelchair by the now glass-less window. Ed was right about the morning. Outside, the sun shone from a cloudless, baby-blue sky, and the Pacific, looking as pristine as the day it was formed, rolled onto the beach in gentle waves. "This smells good," Dave said, taking the tray.

"Drink the orange juice first," Ed said. "If you don't, it'll taste awful on top of the syrup."

Dave drank the orange juice.

"That breakfast is healthier than it looks," Ed said. "A lot of eggs go into waffles, which means a lot of egg yolks, which means a lot of cholesterol. But I make them with all whites. There's less fat in the whites and no cholesterol at all."

Finishing his juice, Dave took a swallow of coffee, then dug into the waffles. "Good," he said with a full mouth.

"Amazing thing," Ed said, looking at the window.

Dave nodded, kept eating. He didn't want to talk about it, didn't want to think about it.

"One hell of a gust of wind." Apparently realizing that Dave wasn't going to discuss last night's mishap, the nurse said, "You got anybody in particular you want to fix that window?"

"No," Dave said. "I've never had to replace any glass before."

"I'll just get a name from the phone book then—whoever can get out here today."

Dave said that would be fine, and Ed went back downstairs.

The waffles were excellent. Anything Ed made was fit for the White House. Dave was sure the man could turn a lowly hamburger into a palate-pleasing pleasure. He polished off the last of the waffles and reached for his coffee, and then, despite his efforts to think about something else—*any*thing else—he found himself considering what had happened last night.

The dream was gone, erased from his memory as if it had been a novel written in disappearing ink. The instant he awoke, the images began fading, and now all that remained was the certainty that he'd been calling out for help.

And of course the window had shattered.

Dave was unable to shake the feeling that the shattering of the glass and the dream were somehow connected. The sound had awakened him, and that seemed to have been its function. But there was more. The wind gust that had shaken the house and caused the damage to the window had been more than just a wind. It seemed . . . well, it seemed to be an expression of some sort, a release of emotions. As if he'd angered the sea.

He thought about that. Yes, anger. But not the sea. Something else.

Dave shook his head. He didn't recall blaspheming against Thor.

So what was he, nuts? A gust of wind was a gust of wind. It was neither the planet sighing in frustration—though he could see why it would—nor the wrath of Thor. And dreams were just thoughts allowed to run wild while the censors of the conscious mind were asleep, which was why they were often disturbing. Without the censors, the brain ran amok.

The *Castle Bay Crier* was still rolled up on the breakfast tray. Dave slipped off the rubber band and unrolled the paper. A story in the upper left corner instantly caught his attention. The headline read: MAN DIES AT TRAILER PARK.

Wendall Youngman, a twenty-eight-year-old highway construction worker, was killed by an unidentifiable animal outside his home at the Oceanview Trailer Park last night, the story said. The body was ripped apart, the police finding seventeen pieces of the body over a fifty-square-foot area. A few witnesses said they'd seen a large animal, but they were unable to identify it. At least one of the witnesses said he thought it had scales, but authorities dismissed that.

Although Dave was uncertain why, the story troubled him. He flipped through the rest of the paper, finding the usual small town news: stories about the chamber of commerce, the Rotary Club, the need for a new jail, plans for the Independence Day parade. Then he spotted another item that made him stop, read it carefully. The old Falling Star Commune on Route 12 had burned down. Authorities were uncertain whether anyone had died in the fire, because the destruction was so complete. It would take weeks to sift through the ashes. Investigators had no idea what had caused the blaze. One immediately puzzling thing was the presence of an expensive car belonging to a Palo Alto man who was apparently missing.

It was like déjà vu.

Dave already knew about the fire.

And about the incident at the trailer park.

But no one had told him about either event. He was sure of that. And the trailer park incident had just occurred last night. No one had had time to mention it to him except Ed, and Ed hadn't said a word about it.

Then it hit him. He had dreamt about both incidents. The trailer park dream had been last night, before the one that was ended by the shattering of the window. Suddenly Dave was shaking. Although the details of the dreams seemed lost to him, he was sure he had experienced them.

What did it mean?

Before he could address that question, his thoughts were interrupted by a gentle *skreek* coming from his right, as if someone were opening the door to the inner sanctum. There was a radio station in San Francisco that played "Inner Sanctum" and other old radio shows on Sunday nights. Sometimes Dave had listened.

His eyes were drawn to his right, to the closet door.

It was slowly, almost imperceptibly opening. Then it stopped, leaving an opening of about a foot.

The closet seemed filled with blackness, as if it were a storage space for shadows.

And within those shadows were two glowing red dots.

The tray tumbled off Dave's lap, coffee spilling on the floor, his cup rolling lazily across the hardwood.

"Never try to contact that woman again," a raspy voice said.

Every fiber in Dave's being was screaming for him to spin the chair around and wheel as fast as he could for the door, call for Ed with all the volume he was able to muster. But his hands were paralyzed, unable to operate the chair. His vocal cords seemed incapable of vibrating, as if they were being squeezed together by an invisible fist.

"If you do," the voice from the closet said, "you'll suffer the consequences."

The closet door slammed.

• 4 •

Paula skipped breakfast. After tossing and turning all night, she had no interest in food. She sat in her favorite chair with a piece of paper in her lap. She picked it up, studied the numbers written on it, and her hand started shaking. She put the number down again.

It was a phone number in California.

David Guthrie's number.

She'd gotten it from information a little while ago, but she hadn't tried calling it. What would she say? Hi, you don't know me, but I've been receiving messages from you? If he didn't hang up right then, there was probably something wrong with him.

Let's face it, she thought, this whole business is unbelievable. Anyone she discussed it with would think she was looney-bin material. Dark forces? Psychic links? Come on, lady, you gotta be kidding.

And yet it was real, this ability of hers to psychically receive calls for help. Her ability had truly saved one puppy and a number of humans. She could truly tell the truth from lies, better than any lie detector. The man she had seen was real. There was actually a David Guthrie. And the dark presence was real too. As real as the man. She had no doubt about that.

But how could she explain it to anyone?

The answer was simple. She couldn't.

But that didn't absolve her of the responsibility of trying to help David Guthrie, did it?

While tossing and turning last night, Paula had tried to

figure out what, if anything, David Guthrie's being the sole survivor of a plane crash might have to do with all this. She'd come up with nothing that made any sense. It seemed that the two events—the plane crash and the psychic link—had occurred too closely together to be a coincidence, and yet there was nothing other than timing to suggest they weren't.

Paula sighed, for she'd just admitted something to herself, one of those things you know but try to keep buried in the simmering depths of your consciousness because you don't want it out in the open where you have to deal with it. Like most of the thoughts we sentence to mental exile, it was simply stated, but oh, so complex in its effect. It was the knowledge that there was absolutely no way she could simply walk away from all this, say: Sorry, David, but your problems aren't my problems, and I'm going back to being a teacher, and I don't want any more psychic links with you because I can't help you, so please leave me alone.

She had been pulled into whatever was happening to David Guthrie.

She could not walk away.

She would be part of whatever happened.

Period.

• 5 •

Paula sat there for two hours before she finally stood up, walked into the kitchen, and dialed David Guthrie's number. She had no idea what she was going to say to him. Perhaps she would hear his voice, and suddenly the words would come spilling out, and they'd all be the right words. On the other hand, maybe she'd hear his voice and just freeze, find herself unable to speak at all. Still, she had to at least try to talk to him, explain as best she could the danger he was in.

Maybe if she did that her job would be done.

Or was that just wishful thinking?

Paula stood by the wall phone, resisting the urge to hang up as the number in California rang once . . . twice. . . .

Letting out a startled gasp, Paula yanked the phone away from her ear. The instrument was buzzing so loudly it was painful. Paula could hear it plainly even though she had dropped the receiver and stepped about ten paces back from it. As she listened, the noise changed, becoming more throaty, rumbling.

Like an animal growl.

Shivers shot through Paula's system like an electrical current. She stared at the growling phone, afraid to go near it. Her terror seemed deeper, more primitive than fear of harm or even death. It was a dread that had its roots in the first few particles that had clumped together millions of years ago to become the universe.

The phone stopped growling.

For a long time, Paula just stared at it. Finally she picked it up—gingerly, for she was afraid it might burn her hand. It didn't. She replaced the receiver.

Now what?

She still could not walk away, even though she was more frightened than she had ever been in her life, more terrified than she'd known it was possible to be. She had to overcome that fear, try again.

No! something inside her screamed. *It will swallow you up, destroy you.*

But she had no choice.

Taking a deep breath, she steadied her nerves, then lifted the receiver. Dialed 1. Then area code 707.

The phone began to whine.

She dialed the next digit.

It began to hiss like a serpent.

Steam squirted from the part of the phone that was attached to the wall.

Paula hung up, then stepped back, trembling. Something didn't want her to complete the call, and it had the power to see she didn't.

"Oh, boy," Paula said, her voice sounding hollow and dry.

She left the kitchen, wanting to put as much distance as possible between herself and the phone. For a while, she just paced, not knowing what she should do. She felt as though she were at the mercy of forces she was unable to comprehend.

She wasn't being allowed to abdicate her responsibility to help David Guthrie.

And she was not being allowed to help.

It made no sense. She felt like screaming, demanding that the forces responsible for all this leave her alone, telling them that she refused to cooperate. But she didn't think she could refuse.

Oh Lord, she thought. Forces? Was she going crazy?

She sat down in her chair. Steady, she told herself, steady. The psychic link is real. You know that, because it's been with you nearly all your life. This is just a new twist. David Guthrie's real, and you have to assume he actually needs help.

And the dark force?

Well, it might be symbolic of the threat that's hanging over Guthrie. It doesn't have to be something out of *The Exorcist*. It could represent an as yet unexplained danger.

What about the phone?

Phones often have problems; it's not unusual. But, deep down inside, she wouldn't buy that, so she tried again. I wasn't allowed to talk to David Guthrie on the phone, Paula decided, because it wasn't the right way for me to help him.

If she wasn't supposed to phone David Guthrie, what was she supposed to do? She shuddered because the answer was obvious. She was supposed to go there. To California.

But she didn't want to. She desperately didn't want to.

And she knew she would.

THE TELEVISION ANTENNA

• 1 •

"From the closet?" Jackie said, eyeing him skeptically.

"Yes, from the closet," Dave said. "It told me I shouldn't contact that woman."

Jackie wheeled about and started toward the closet.

"Don't bother," Dave said. "Ed already checked. There's nothing there."

Jackie stopped, turned to face him. "Exactly."

"You mean there was never anything there."

"Precisely."

"I heard what I heard," Dave said. "I didn't imagine it." He was beginning to doubt the wisdom of telling her about what had happened. He'd done it because if Jackie was going to share his life, then he had no right to withhold things from her. She was entitled to know everything about him, even those things that might make her doubt his grip on reality.

"There was nothing there," Jackie said. "Ed checked. You said so yourself."

"The voice was there."

She gave him an appraising look that seemed to say, *You can't possibly believe that.* She said, "Think about it."

"Jackie, I have thought about it. How could anything be in my closet, staring out at me with glowing eyes? And if there was anything there, how come Ed didn't find it? Where did it go?"

She nodded. "The only explanation is that you imagined it."

"In that case I've been imagining a hell of a lot lately."

"You have, haven't you?"

"What are you suggesting?"

She walked to the window. It was still broken. The man from the glass company hadn't arrived yet. She turned, faced Dave. "Maybe you should see a . . ."

"A shrink? You think I'm nuts?"

"I think you're the survivor of a plane crash in which a whole bunch of people died. That's enough to set anyone's psyche on its ear. And then, you being the kind of guy you are, you're probably suffering all kinds of guilt feelings." The way she said it, Dave could tell she considered herself too strong to fall victim to anything as inconsequential as guilt.

"It's not just me," Dave said. "Ed's seen things too."

Jackie studied him a moment, then said, "Yes, I've wondered about that."

"What do you mean?"

"I mean that maybe Ed's not such a good influence on you."

Influence on him? She sounded like a mother who disapproved of one of his pals. "You think Ed is . . . is putting these notions in my head?"

"Well, isn't it possible?"

"Why would he? It doesn't make any sense."

"After the plane crash and everything, you're vulnerable, susceptible."

"Susceptible? Susceptible to what?"

"His influence."

"What influence?" Dave demanded, exasperated. "You still haven't explained why he'd want to influence me in the first place."

"There are lots of reasons," Jackie said, looking at him levelly. "Sometimes those who care for elderly people and invalids and the like trick their charges into giving them money or leaving them everything. Sometimes the people are even abused."

"You think Ed would do that?"

"Other people in his position have done it."

"Jackie, you're not thinking this through. I'm not rich. I don't have anything worth all the effort."

"You have a home, a good income. People who do these sorts of things don't just go for millions. They're greedy. They get every dollar they can."

"I don't believe it. Ed's not like that at all."

"I'm only saying it's a possibility you should keep your eyes open to."

For several moments, Dave studied this woman he was planning to marry. She was usually upbeat and cute, a pleasant and lively companion. She had a good head on her shoulders, and she was a hard worker. Good qualities all. And yet Dave couldn't help but feel that he'd just seen more of that side of her he hadn't known was there. Though reluctant to call it a dark side, Dave could see that it was mistrustful, closed-minded. And she gave no credence whatever to his story. He'd imagined it. Period. It was the only answer Jackie would accept.

And while Dave's mind was playing tricks on him, Ed was using the situation to further his own greedy goals. Well, if Jackie believed that, she had her own overactive imagination.

Dave hadn't told her about the dreams in which he seemed to know about the man dying at the trailer park and the fire at the commune. He'd planned to. Everything out in the open. No secrets. But considering that Jackie was staring at him, looking very much like someone who'd just learned she was engaged to a lunatic, Dave decided this was not the right time to go into it.

"I've got to run," Jackie said.

"Want to have dinner here?" He started to tout Ed's cooking, then decided that it would probably be best not to mention Ed.

Jackie shook her head. "No. I'm going to be tied up. But thanks for the offer."

And then she was gone. Dave could hear her descending the stairs. The front door opened, closed.

•2•

Ed Prawdzik was in the living room, fiddling with the TV set when Jackie hurried out of the house. Although he hadn't heard everything she and Dave had said, bits and pieces of muffled conversation had drifted down, enough for him to get the tone. Jackie had seemed annoyed about something. Ed generally didn't make quick judgments about people. As he got to know them, he'd either feel friendly toward them or he wouldn't. In Jackie's case, she'd seemed okay at first, but as time went on, Ed sensed aspects of her makeup he didn't care for. Words came to mind like haughty, pushy, selfish.

But then he really didn't know Jackie Lake well enough to draw any significant conclusions. Besides, it was none of his business. His only concern was seeing to Dave Guthrie's needs until Dave was back on his feet. Eventually Dave's casts would come off, Ed would help him through any required physical therapy, and sooner or later Dave would be good as new and Ed would be back with Andrea, waiting for the next job to come along. He and his patients rarely encountered each other after the healing process was over.

So, Ed old buddy, why are you feeling so uneasy? But then the answer to that had nothing to do with Jackie Lake. He was uneasy because in this house pots boiled with no flame under them. Windows shattered in the middle of the night.

Come on, Ed, he told himself. If the place is haunted, it's haunted. You can't make it unhaunted, so you just have to live with it. It's a little unnerving, but no one's been hurt, and most likely no one will be. And someday you'll have some great stories to tell.

Let me tell you about this one place. It was in Castle Bay. Damnedest things kept happening. I know this is going to be hard to believe, but . . .

Ed grinned. As a boy, "his most favoritest thing in the world to do" was sit around the campfire—or in his bedroom or in the backyard—and tell scary stories. And Ed had told the scariest stories of all. Kids rarely slept soundly right after hearing an Ed Prawdzik tale of fright.

Letting the memories of boyish faces illuminated by the flickering orange glow from the campfire fade away, Ed returned his attention to the TV set. The picture had deteriorated so that an old Frankie and Annette movie on channel 48 looked as though it had been filmed in a blizzard. Surfers riding in on the waves only to hit the beach and disappear into a snowdrift. Girls in bikinis looking as though they should have goosebumps the size of golf balls.

Although Ed was no expert, he didn't think the problem was in the set itself. Which left the antenna. He studied the snowy picture on channel 31 for a moment—Geraldo interviewing a nun who'd quit the church and started a computer dating service for lesbians—then switched off the set and went outside, looking up at the roof.

The antenna was one of those weird UHF jobs. A screen with a couple of metal bowties fastened to it. Supported by guy wires, it rose on a ten-foot mast from the peak of the roof. The more he looked at it, the more it reminded him of a huge fly swatter. Ed couldn't see anything wrong with it, but then he was probably too far from it to spot any problems. Ed had seen a pair of binoculars in the living room. He went in and got them, then circled the house, looking at the antenna. And he found the problem. The lead-in wire was no longer connected to the antenna. It had probably been loose, and then the wind that had broken the window in the bedroom had most likely torn it completely off.

No problem, Ed decided. All I have to do is get up there and fix it. Maybe this afternoon.

•3•

"You sure wind did this?" the workman asked. He'd removed the window frame and was fitting a new pane of glass into it. He was a chubby blond guy. The name Jake was stitched above the breast pocket of his khaki shirt.

"Gust was a doozy," Ed said.

"Shook the whole house," Dave added. He and Ed were watching the guy work. Dave wondered what it would be like to have a job like that, someone always standing there watching you while you worked. Jake didn't seem to mind.

"What time was it?" Jake asked.

"About midnight," Dave replied.

"You sure? I was still up then, and I didn't notice any wind."

"Where do you live?" Ed asked.

"A mile or so from here. Wasn't any wind at all."

Ed was standing beside Dave's chair. They exchanged glances. Ed said, "Maybe it came in off the sea, just a big gust, and then the hill steered it away from your location."

Jake looked up from his work. "Never happened before. When it blows in one part of town, it blows everywhere else too."

When he finished repairing the window, Jake made out a bill and asked for immediate payment. Dave wrote him a check, which the repairman eyed suspiciously a moment before pocketing it. Ed showed him out, then returned to the bedroom.

"I found out what's wrong with the TV set," the nurse said. "Wire's disconnected at the antenna. I can see it with binoculars."

"I guess you'd better call someone," Dave said.

"Save your money. I can fix it. You already spent enough on the window."

"I'd hate to ask you to do that," Dave said. "It's not really your job."

"You didn't ask me. I volunteered. Once I get the antenna down, it'll take about a minute to fix. It's really no big deal, and if you call a repairman, he'll charge you seventy-five dollars—more if he didn't get any last night."

"Well, if you want to try it . . ."

"Hey, I've put up lots of antennas. There's nothing to it."

"Be careful up there."

The nurse shrugged. "I'll do it this afternoon sometime. Right now, I've got to cut up some skirt steak and get it marinating."

"No hurry," Dave said. "It would probably take a few days to get a repairman out here, and there's nothing to see on TV anyway." Ed nodded, and Dave said, "What are you making with this meat you're marinating?"

"Fajitas. You ever have *fajitas?"*

Dave said he hadn't.

"You'll like 'em."

"I know."

Ed winked, said, "I like your attitude." And then he was heading downstairs, the steps creaking beneath his weight.

For several minutes, Dave simply sat there in his wheelchair, looking out through his newly repaired window. He studied the breakers as they splashed against the rocks that lined the shore. The sea didn't seem to like the restrictive rocks, and it attacked them. Again and again and again. There was no desperation in the ocean's attack, but rather infinite patience. It could take a thousand years or a million years. It was all the same to the sea. It would continue, relentlessly, for however long it took. And eventually the rock would crumble.

And I'm making absolutely no money sitting here staring out the window, Dave thought. He turned his chair toward the door, intending to roll into the studio and go to work, but a strange feeling settled over him. There was someone in the room with him.

Instantly his eyes shot toward the closet, but this wasn't that kind of feeling. There seemed to be no malice in the presence, and Dave had the feeling he'd been in its company before. Maybe in the dream he seemed unable to clearly remember.

"Who are you?" he asked. And then he felt foolish for talking to an empty room.

And yet the feeling that he wasn't alone intensified. Not only was something in the room, he slowly realized, but within his mind too. Not poking and prodding and invading his privacy. It was more like a telephone connection, a call from a friend.

Dave blinked. Did he believe all this? It was a feeling, nothing more. Why did his conclusions seem so . . . so right?

Who are you? he asked with his mind.

The reply came in the form of vague sensations—a subtle tug in his brain, a hint of gentleness, a nebulous sense of trustworthiness. Although they were meaningless individually, taken together they seemed to suggest that someone wanted to help.

Help me how? Dave asked.

Again Dave felt vague impressions swirling and dancing through his head, but this time he was unable to interpret them.

I don't understand, Dave thought.

And then Dave was alone in the room. Whatever had been with him . . . with him? Suddenly he wasn't sure that was the right way to look at it. And then he recalled that he'd likened the phenomena to a phone call. As though he were being contacted from afar.

"Guthrie, old boy," he muttered, "you're stark raving mad."

But that was the easy way out, wasn't it? Relegate anything peculiar to insanity and be done with it. But deep down inside he knew that wasn't the answer. He knew that something had indeed occurred—even if he didn't know what.

Suddenly Dave realized there was a faint odor in the air. Something strong. Like paint thinner. Then the smell was gone.

Never try to contact that woman again, the raspy voice from the closet had said.

Dave was cold all over. Was that what he'd just done? He wasn't sure. Was the presence that of a woman? Dave was confused.

If you do, the voice from the closet had said, *you'll suffer the consequences.*

The words hung in Dave's brain like a condemned man dangling from the gallows.

Suffer the consequences.

The chill Dave was experiencing grew stronger, penetrating his bones, his innermost places.

•4•

Paula was sitting on the edge of her bed as the dizziness passed and the odor of turpentine faded.

She had seen David Guthrie again, sitting in a wheelchair in a room that had a view of the ocean. And again he'd seemed aware of her presence and tried to communicate with her. He'd realized she wished to help him, and he'd wanted her to explain, which she'd been unable to do. Even David Guthrie didn't know what she was supposed to do. And yet there had to be a way for her to help him; otherwise she wouldn't be linking with him. Her job was to find out what that way was.

Feeling afraid and quite vulnerable, Paula stood, picked up her suitcase. For a few seconds, she simply stood there, the bag dangling from her hand; then she turned and walked out of her apartment. She had a two-thousand-mile drive ahead of her.

PERILOUS JOURNEY

• 1 •

Paula took Interstate 35 south to Des Moines, then headed west on Interstate 80, which would take her all the way to California. At dusk, still in Iowa, she pulled into a small motel surrounded by corn fields.

• 2 •

Edwin Hagan pulled into a parking place at a 7-Eleven outside of Omaha. Climbing out of the battered Buick he was driving, Hagan slipped the .357 into the waist of his pants, made sure it didn't show, then walked into the store.

Hagan was a month out of the Ohio state pen, where he'd been serving three to five for knocking over convenience stores, an activity he resumed the moment he hit the streets. It was what he did. It was his calling, he supposed. The way some people were called to journalism or music or the priesthood. Robbing was just his nature, the way he was meant to be.

There was one other customer in the store, a blond teenage girl in cutoff jeans, showing off her nice legs. She had that fresh, country-girl look. Innocent and wholesome. Right off the farm. She was reading the label on a can of beans, maybe trying to figure out what all that stuff they put in there was, all those unpronounceable words. Watching her made Hagan realize how long it had been since he'd gotten laid. The last time had been before he became a guest of the state of Ohio. He'd nearly picked up a woman at a bar in Illinois a couple of days ago, but her ex-husband had showed up, drunk and itching for a fight. Hagan avoided fights.

He hadn't always. Like a lot of guys, Hagan had gone into the pen looking to show how tough he was, how he wasn't about to take any crap off anybody. That attitude nearly got him killed. He mouthed off to the wrong guy, a honcho in one of the gangs. Two days later a member of that gang came up behind him and buried a shiv in his back.

Hagan wasn't breathing when they got him to the infirmary.

They managed to revive him, and then he was transferred to a hospital in town, where he spent a few weeks in a guarded room. When Hagan returned to the general prison population, he made it a point to keep a low profile. He'd learned his lesson. He had no more trouble.

That was all behind him now. He had the car he'd borrowed from a parking lot in Indiana. And he had the gun he'd bought—at a gun shop—the day after he got out. To buy the gun, he'd used identification he'd stolen from a man he followed out of a bar. As the guy unlocked his car, Hagan hit him with a pipe. So, although the serial number of the weapon was recorded, there was no way the .357 could be traced to him. Guy at the gun shop didn't give a shit. He'd glanced at the driver's license and nodded. Picture didn't even look anything like Hagan, who was blond, six-two, blue-eyed, and weighed 210. Guy he'd taken the license from was dark-haired, about five-ten, brown-eyed, and weighed around 165.

Hagan surveyed the soft drink cooler while he waited for the girl to leave. He hoped she'd go before anyone else arrived. Otherwise he'd look suspicious hanging around. He glanced at the clerk, a thin young guy with acne, pale complexion, veins standing up in ridges on his scrawny arms, a few barely noticeable dark hairs where he was trying to grow a moustache. Kid would be raw meat in the pen.

Hagan took out a six-pack of Cokes, as if he were planning on buying it, moved on to look at the chips. A native Kentuckian, Hagan was the son of a coal miner, one of six children, all of whom had been raised in a rundown house in a rundown town, all of whose occupants had depended on the mine. His two brothers had gone to work in the mine; his three sisters had married miners and started having babies so that someday there'd be still more miners. Hagan sometimes wondered whether lust was a company conspiracy, so there'd always be more bodies to send underground.

Edwin Hagan was not a miner.

Edwin Hagan had never worked a single day in a mine.

And Edwin Hagan never would.

He'd quit school in the tenth grade and hitchhiked to Cleveland just to make sure he never worked in a mine. No way would he ever have that kind of life. You worked your ass off underground all day, came out filthy and tired as hell, went home to your crummy house and your complaining wife and your screaming kids. If you were lucky you could afford a new pickup, a big-screen TV. Wasn't worth it. No way was it worth it.

In Cleveland, he'd worked at so many jobs he couldn't remember them all. He had trouble getting along with bosses, didn't like people telling him what to do. And after a while he began to realize that any kind of work was pretty much like the mines. You spent all day, got hassled by the boss, came out tired, and if you were lucky you could afford the payments on a nice car. You missed a couple of those payments and they took the car away, kept the money you'd paid them. You were screwed any way you turned, the world full of assholes to use you, hassle you, take stuff away.

That's why he'd taken up armed robbery.

You didn't have any boss except yourself. Very few demands on your time. And it was fun; it was a charge, a real frolic. He liked watching the clerks' eyes as he pulled the gun, liked seeing them widen as the fear filled them. At that moment, if he said shit, they'd shit. And then he liked the getaway, peeling out, pushing the pedal to the metal. Yes, sir, it was a real frolic; it really was.

The girl was paying for her purchases.

Taking the Cokes and a bag of potato chips with him, Hagan moved up behind her, as if he were forming a line, and waited. He studied her legs.

"Thanks," the girl said, pocketing her change and picking up the paper bag.

"Have a good day," the clerk said. He, too, studied her legs as she left the store.

Hagan put the Cokes and chips on the counter.

"Will this be all, sir?" the kid asked.

"No," Hagan said, pulling the gun. "I'll also take all the money you got."

He watched, pleased, as the young man's eyes widened, all but shimmered with fright. Sucker had been planning to drink some beer with his buddies in a few hours, and suddenly he didn't know whether he'd be alive a minute from now.

"In a bag," Hagan said. "Hurry it up, or I'll shoot you and do it myself."

The kid hurried, scooping out the bills, putting them in a paper sack.

"I want the big bills too," Hagan said. "The ones under the part that lifts out."

"There's . . . there's none," the kid said. "I have to put them in a safe—through a slot. I don't have the key. Only the manager has a key." To prove the point he lifted out the inner portion of the cash drawer, showing Hagan there was nothing underneath.

"I believe you," Hagan said. "I mean, I *have* robbed these stores before."

The boy started to smile, as if maybe it was a joke and he was supposed to laugh.

Hagan glanced toward the entrance to the store. No one was coming. "How much you got in your wallet?" he asked the clerk.

"Five, maybe ten bucks," the clerk said.

"Toss it into the bag. I'm curious to see if you were telling me the truth."

The kid fumbled with his back pocket, finally got the wallet, dropped it in the bag. "There's no more money in the place, except what's in the safe," he said. "I swear. There isn't."

"I believe you," Hagan said, and shot the kid in the chest.

The impact of the .357 round hitting him drove him back against the wall. Hagan shot him twice more before he could drop. The kid stared at him with large disbelieving eyes, and then he keeled over onto the floor, blood leaking from the holes in his chest and neck. Hagan always killed the clerks now. He'd done so in every armed robbery he'd committed since getting out of the pen. It left no employee to identify him, get his license number, testify in court. But Hagan wasn't sure whether he did it for that reason or because he enjoyed it.

He paused to look at the dead or dying clerk, then headed for the door. As he was getting into his car, a van pulled in, parked beside him. A chunky bald guy got out, glanced at Hagan, headed for the store. Hagan shot him in the back, hurried over to the spot where the man lay on the concrete, and put a round into his head.

He floored the Buick, burning rubber as he pulled onto the street and headed west, thinking maybe he'd drive straight through to Denver, spend some time there, see the sights.

• 3 •

Hagan had driven about ten miles when he started thinking about a woman. At first he thought he was just horny, but then he realized that he wasn't feeling aroused. And the woman who kept popping into his head was always the same, as if he were remembering her. But he'd never seen her before. She wasn't bad looking, although she was a little too thin. Nice shape. Nice dark hair. He was sure she was a stranger.

Suddenly anger was bubbling in his gut.

He hated this woman. But he wasn't sure why. He tried to reason it out, determine why he should be so mad at someone he couldn't remember, but the effort gave him a headache.

"Shit," he muttered. "Stop thinking about some damn woman you don't even know."

Instead he thought about the kid in the store, his wide eyes, the look on his face when Hagan blew the bastard away. Before long he'd have to stop and see how much money he'd taken—and see whether the clerk had told him the truth about how much was in his wallet. Hagan reached over to switch on the radio, then remembered that it didn't work. He'd have to steal a better car next time.

He began to whistle, pleased with himself.

And then he was seeing the woman again. Rage, hot and pulsating, gushed through him like a flash flood. He wanted to find that woman, hurt her.

He *needed* to hurt her, the way a junkie needed a fix. The desire, the craving, grabbed him, shook him, slapped him like an angry adversary.

Ahead was an exit, and Hagan began slowing. The woman was behind him, back the way he had come. If he went back he would find her. And finding her was all that mattered.

And just how the hell did he know where the woman was? Posing the question made his head hurt again. Ever since that time in the pen when he damn near died—or maybe he *did* die, at least for a few moments—Hagan had known things he shouldn't know, felt things he shouldn't feel, as if there were two of him, the main him and a secondary him, both of them in his mind, both of them telling him what to do, how to think.

But then that was a nutty idea, wasn't it?

There was only one Edwin Hagan. What he thought of as a secondary self was just another facet of him. It certainly never encouraged him to do anything it wasn't his nature to do. Like hurting this woman. Both facets of Edwin Hagan's personality thought that idea was just fine.

Hagan took the exit, crossed over the interstate, got back on, heading east. Before long he spotted the exit he'd used to get onto the freeway, and he began to slow again. It would be fun to drive by the convenience store, see what was happening, just an innocent passerby. The urge to find the woman pulled at him. As did the urge to see the store.

The urge to see the store won. It would only take a moment, and it was something he had never done before. He took the exit. The store's parking area was full of police cars, their lights flashing. The man Hagan had shot outside was a lump under a white sheet. There were about half a dozen cops hanging around outside; none of them looked at him. He went back to the interstate on a street two blocks down. As he reached it, the desire to find the woman became irresistible. He sped onto the freeway.

As he drove into Iowa, it occurred to him that this was very peculiar, to have this horrendous need to hurt a woman he didn't know. But thinking about that confused him, and he quickly figured out that it was easier to let himself go, give into the urge that was drawing him eastward.

He would find her.

He would kill her.

And he would enjoy it.

•4•

Paula's room was stuffy from being closed up all day, and she immediately switched on the window air conditioner, which made a couple of loud clunks, then began spewing warm air. After a moment, the stream of air began to cool, but it was going to be a while before the room was tolerable. She decided to get something to eat while the air conditioner made the place liveable.

The motel was one of those mom-and-pop operations that

143

seemed to be disappearing as chains came to dominate the
motel business. Paula customarily picked places like this.
They were usually tidy and less expensive than chains. And
they had interesting names. This one was called the Pull
Inn. A bit of Americana, Paula supposed. A motel with a
hokey name surrounded by Iowa cornfields.

As she got into her car, she noticed that the place was
being expanded. The wooden skeleton of five or six new
rooms stood at the west end of the building, along with piles
of wafer board and other building supplies. This place at
least seemed to be withstanding the onslaught from Motel
Six and Holiday Inn.

The nearest town was a mile away, a place called Carswell,
the name proudly displayed on the water tower. The community boasted one restaurant, a drug store, a grocery, a
feed store, two gas stations, and a farm equipment dealer-
ship whose lot was filled with mammoth machines the
purpose of which Paula could only guess at. The restaurant
was called Clyde's Cafe. Paula parked between two pickups
in the side lot and went in.

Paula had her choice of a table, a booth, or the counter.
She chose a booth. The place was baseball-cap city, she
noted. Except instead of the Cubs or the Twins, these caps
bore the logos of Caterpillar, John Deere, and Acco Feeds.
Most of the men in the place wore one, even while they ate.
The menu offered things like country-fried steak, pork
chops, and "homemade" meatloaf with tomato gravy. She
ordered a hot roast beef sandwich. For dessert she had a
slice of apple pie that was so good Granny could have made
it. She ate the meal leisurely, giving the air conditioner time
to cool her motel room.

When she drove back to the motel, it was dark, the night
hot and muggy. Huge red letters spelling out MOTEL flashed
on and off. Below that, in nonflashing turquoise, the sign
said PULL IN. Paula wondered whether the people who
crafted these things out of neon were required to take
courses in gaudiness and bad taste. But then that was their
function, wasn't it, to stand out, be visually blaring, so
people would notice them.

She was in room number twelve. She parked her white Honda hatchback outside the door, pulling the room key from her pocket as she got out of the car. She had taken two steps toward the door when someone grabbed her from behind, clamped a hand over her mouth, and whispered, "Don't make a sound, or I'll kill you."

And Paula, who always recognized the truth when she heard it, knew the man was not issuing hollow threats.

• 5 •

Paula's mind reeled, a part of her saying she should resist, try to call for help, another part saying she should cooperate, not make him angry. Still dragging her from behind, he was taking her away from the lighted part of the motel, toward the construction area.

Into the shadows.

He said, "If I take my hand off your mouth, will you keep quiet?" Then, before she could collect her wits enough to speak, he answered his own question. "Of course you will. Because you know what will happen if you don't, don't you?" He removed his hand. Paula remained silent. She wasn't sure her dry throat could have managed a scream, and even if it could the man would clamp his hand over her mouth again after the first peep. Paula could feel his strength. She was at his mercy.

The cold certainty settled over her that she would not get out of this unscathed. Something bad was going to happen to her. She could even die tonight. She promptly buried the thought. She didn't want to think that.

He pushed her down so that she was sitting on a pile of lumber. By the lights of the motel, she could dimly make out her attacker now. He was tall, heavyset, probably in his mid- or late twenties.

Paula's breath was coming in short, urgent gasps. She could feel the furious beat of her heart, as if somewhere inside her a drummer had gone berserk.

145

"Take your clothes off," the man commanded.

Paula just sat there, unable to move.

"I said get undressed."

"Please," Paula whispered, finding her voice.

"Hey, come on, honey," the man said. "This doesn't have to be so bad. I'm really a pretty nice guy. You show me a good time, and then you'll just go back to your room and everything will be okay. I won't hurt you. I promise."

Paula shuddered. It was a lie. *Everything will be okay, I won't hurt you.* The words had been discordant, garbled, grating. Lies. Total lies. And that meant that he would harm her, no matter what she did. And then she realized the rest of his words had been a lie as well. *I'm really a pretty nice guy.* He wasn't.

She had to collect her thoughts, think about what to do. And she had to do something, or this man would . . . would what? Because of her unique abilities, Paula could get a pretty good idea of what he had in mind just by asking him.

She said, "Are you going to kill me?"

"No," the man said. "Not if you're nice and do what I tell you."

The words had been so dissonant Paula had wanted to cover her ears to shut out the horrible grating sound.

"Take off your clothes," he said. "I'm not going to ask you again."

"Please don't do this," she said. "Please."

He slapped her, hard, and she tumbled backward off the pile of lumber. Instantly he was on her, pushing her face into the dirt and twisting her arm behind her, the pain all but unbearable. She tried to cry out but all she could do was grunt, and her mouth filled up with dirt. Finally, just as she thought her arm would break, he let her go.

"Now get undressed," he said. "I won't ask you again."

She sat up. Her left arm ached; she was barely able to move it. With her right hand, she began unbuttoning her shirt, going as slowly as she dared, trying to give her other arm a chance to become useful again. She undid the second button, the third. . . .

And with her other hand, she began to feel around for

something she could use as a weapon. She realized her chances of overpowering someone considerably heavier and stronger than she was were pretty slim, but he was going to kill her anyway, so she had to try. Again she considered screaming and decided that he could kick her or slap her into silence too quickly for her to take the risk. She had to find some way to subdue him—even if only for a second or two. It would be time enough to run, cry out for help.

The man made an impatient grunt.

Paula said, "I'll . . . I'll show you a good time, okay? You don't want to rush it, do you? It's better if you make it last, isn't it?"

The man said nothing.

A car pulled into the motel, its headlights poking into the shadows but not quite reaching her. The man glanced at the car, looked back at her. Paula thought he'd smiled. She pulled off her shirt, dropped it on the ground. And her hand touched a board, a two-by-four from the feel of it. She pulled it, moving it about half an inch. It was about five feet long, Paula guessed. It was the only weapon she was going to get a chance to find.

"Let's . . . let's go to my room," she said. "You don't want to do it here in the dirt, do you?" She was buying time, hoping she'd get the chance to use the two-by-four.

"Shut up," he said. "We're doing it here."

She debated which garment to remove next, finally deciding on her jeans. As she slipped them off, another car pulled into the motel. As he had before, the man turned to look. It was the only chance Paula was likely to get, and she took it. Standing up, she picked up the two-by-four, raised it.

The man's gaze shifted back to her just as she was swinging the board. He stepped back to get out of the way, but he was too late. The two-by-four hit him in the face. He grunted, staggered back. And Paula leaped toward him, swinging the board with all her strength. It hit him in the knees, knocking his legs out from under him. She raised it again. Some angry, vengeful part of her was taking control, telling her to hit this . . . this creature again and again, pound him until there was nothing left. But the urge was shortlived, for neither violence nor revenge was part of her nature. Dropping the two-by-four, Paula ran.

"Help me!" she shouted, but the words were barely audible. She needed all her breath for running and had none left over for yelling.

And then the man had her from behind, his hands stopping her as though she were a dog that had just raced to the end of its chain. His fingers dug painfully into her shoulders, and she knew he was going to kill her.

Suddenly a light was in her face.

And then a man shouted, "Move away from the woman and put your hands on your head."

For a moment they just stood there, the man holding her, Paula knowing her rescuers had arrived but unable to see them through the glare of what she assumed was a spotlight. Then the man said, "Can't let you go."

"Move away from her!" Paula's unseen rescuers shouted. "This is the police."

"Gotta kill you," the man said. He sounded distant, distracted, as if unaware of the policeman, lost to everything except the voices of whatever madness was driving him.

"Let go of her! Now!" the police officer shouted.

"Left my gun in the car," the man muttered. "Didn't want to make that much noise. Didn't think I'd need it for killing a woman."

"I'm not going to warn you again!"

"No," the man mumbled. "Gotta kill her."

"Last chance, mister—if you don't want to get shot."

Paula heard the scream of sirens, the sound of tires squealing as cars braked hard. Reinforcements had arrived.

"Gotta kill her," the man said. "Gotta."

Car doors slammed, shoe soles pounded on the earth. Paula stared into the glare, still unable to see.

"Gotta." Suddenly the man's hands closed on her throat. Powerful hands. Squeezing. Crushing.

Paula struggled for breath, but none would come.

Pain shot through her neck, spread into her shoulders, traveled down her arms.

I'm dying, Paula thought. I'm dying, and I'm helpless to

do anything about it. She tried to kick her attacker and found she lacked the strength to move her legs.

Suddenly she was surrounded by bodies, pulling, shoving, struggling. The hands were pried off her throat. Cool evening air, sweet and smelling of farmland, passed through her windpipe and into her lungs. Wonderful, wonderful air. Her lungs sucked in more of it, greedily.

"You all right, ma'am?"

Paula tried to focus on the man who'd spoken to her. He was a burly policeman with a moon face, a gray uniform. She tried to say yes, she thought she'd be okay, but her throbbing throat seemed incapable of producing sound.

"Ma'am?" the policeman said.

Paula was still incapable of answering.

"Ma'am, do you need an ambulance?"

Paula started to shake her head, but then everything went blurry. Suddenly she felt weightless, as if she were floating. She was only vaguely aware of the policeman's strong hands catching her, a distant voice saying something about an ambulance.

WESTWARD HO

• 1 •

"Man's name is Edwin Hagan," the gray-uniformed deputy sheriff said. He'd been among Paula's rescuers last night, the one with the moon face. "The name mean anything to you?"

Paula shook her head. "I've never seen him before." She was dressed, sitting on the edge of her hospital bed. The doctors had kept her overnight for observation. She felt fine this morning, ready to resume her journey. She had already told the officer her version of what happened last night.

"Hagan's a parole violator out of Ohio," the deputy said. "He's also a suspect in a couple of convenience store robberies in which the clerks were shot to death. They're running ballistics checks on the gun we found in his car." He studied her with eyes that seemed small in his large fleshy face. It wasn't an unintelligent face, but it clearly belonged to someone from the countryside, a farmer or a tractor salesman or the owner of the feed store. Or a rural deputy sheriff. It was the face of a man content with his lot in life, Paula supposed.

"Car he was driving was stolen," the deputy said.

"I thought he was going to kill me."

"Did he say why?"

"No. He said, 'Gotta kill her.' He said it two or three times but he never said why he had this . . . this compulsion."

150

The deputy nodded, pulled a small notebook from his breast pocket, examined a page.

"Thank you for coming to my rescue," Paula said. "I think . . . if you hadn't shown up when you did . . ." She shrugged. "Anyway, thank you."

The policeman gave her an aw-shucks, slightly embarrassed look. "That's what the county pays me for, to help when I can."

"Well, last night you sure helped me."

"Part of your thanks should go to Jase McConnell, the owner of the motel. Helen—his wife—was handling the desk, but she didn't see or hear a thing. Old Jase, he was sound asleep in his recliner with the TV going. I think Jase has slept through just about every TV show he's ever tried to watch. Kinda makes you wonder why he bought that big-screen, stereo TV set, since all he ever does is sleep in front of it." The deputy chuckled, shook his head. "Anyhow, old Jase says he suddenly woke up because he was certain someone needed his help. He doesn't know how he knew; he just knew. And he knew he was supposed to go to the window. When he did, he saw this man dragging you back toward the new addition he's building, and he called us."

"He knew I needed help," Paula said softly.

"Isn't that something? I've heard of things like that happening, but this is the first time I've ever run into it. It's like he received a mental message from you in his sleep."

"Yes," Paula said. She knew about mentally received pleas for help. But until now she'd always been the one whose help was sought, never the one needing it. Was Jase McConnell, like her, a receiver of such messages? Or was her ability a two-way thing that enabled her to send as well as receive?

The deputy said, "I guess, if you're in a job like mine, sooner or later you see just about everything."

"I guess you do," Paula said.

"I think our business is about finished," the deputy said. "I've got a complaint form I'll need you to sign. Then, if you like, I can give you a ride back to your motel."

Paula signed the form, and the officer delivered her to the motel room she'd paid for and never used. She checked out, drove to the interstate, and considered going east, back to Minnesota. Resisting that urge, she headed toward Omaha. The events of last night had scared her, made her wish for the security of familiar surroundings, but they hadn't changed the circumstances that had made her decide to go to California. David Guthrie still needed her help—even if she still had no idea how she was supposed to provide it.

"Westward ho," she said.

•2•

As Paula drove, she tried to come to terms with what had happened last night. She recalled the man's hands on her throat, squeezing, the world swirling away from her as she plunged into darkness. Not just darkness. Death's firm and unrelenting grasp. She shivered. It was beginning to sink in that she was only here, breathing, driving through this sunny Iowa morning, by the slimmest of margins. Had the police arrived a minute or two later, she could be lying on a slab with a tag on her toe and a sheet over her face.

The image hung before her eyes, as haunting and real as a bad memory. She felt the hardness of the slab, the cold of the refrigerator in which she was being stored, and despite the cheery morning sunshine, she shivered.

Dead. She had come within a whisker of being dead.

Ahead was a rest area. Paula pulled into it, slipped into a parking space. Then she rested her head on the steering wheel and cried. She wanted the image of the dead Paula on the slab to go away. She wanted to stop feeling the chill, the hardness of the cold surface on which she lay. But these things refused to go away, and Paula gave in to her emotions, sobbing as her body shook so violently she was sure she was rocking the car.

After a half hour, the tears stopped. When Paula raised

her head, she saw a man walking a golden retriever in the rest stop's grassy area. He glanced surreptitiously at her, apparently concerned about the bawling woman in the white car, but uncertain whether he should approach her. Paula tried to work up a smile. The man smiled back and went on his way, the dog darting this way and that with its nose to the ground, sampling all the exciting odors.

For a moment, Paula found herself wishing she could trade places with the dog—let others take care of her, run around sniffing things, lead a simple, untroubled life—but the urge quickly faded.

She resolved to put last night behind her. It was over, and she was all right. The man who'd attacked her was in jail. He had had lots of charges to face: parole violations, the attack on her, maybe even murder and robbery. He would be in jail a long time. He couldn't hurt her. She would never see him again. Paula repeated those last few thoughts. Again and again. Until she truly believed them, deep down where it counted. Then she leaned her head back against the seat and closed her eyes.

A stranger had attacked her for no apparent reason.

The owner of the motel had received her plea for help.

What did it all mean?

She didn't know, but she couldn't help thinking that all the things that were happening in her life might be connected. Too much was occurring at once. But the connections, if they existed, eluded her. She felt as though all control had been taken from her. She seemed to be on this trip because she'd decided to take it, but she sensed that the option had never really been hers.

"I could just pull out of here and go home," she said.

But she wasn't sure she believed it.

Forces were propelling her westward, forces she wasn't sure she could resist.

"Nonsense," she said.

Paula drove out of the rest area. Signs with arrows said Omaha, Des Moines. She was free to go either way she chose. But the way she chose was west.

•3•

Ed Prawdzik lowered the TV antenna to the roof.

He hadn't done the job until now because it turned out Dave didn't have a ladder. This morning Ed had bought one at a hardware store, a nice lightweight aluminum one that would easily extend to the roof of the two-story house. But now that he had the antenna down, Ed had a new problem. The lead-in wire was shot, which meant he'd have to wait to fix the antenna until he was able to buy some.

Leaving the antenna where it was, he stood. It was a clear morning with a gentle sea breeze. Ed could see the trail of smoke from a ship's stacks on the horizon, and he could smell the ocean. Gulls circled overhead, making their distinctive cries. Ed took in a deep breath.

And then the house started shaking.

Ed flattened himself on the roof, held on to the ridge with both hands. The house seemed to be vibrating. An earthquake? Ed wondered. But the vibrations continued unabated, and an earthquake, despite its destructive force, lasted only seconds.

And then a black cloud began rising from the roof, as if it were seeping out of the shingles themselves. For a moment, Ed thought something inside had exploded, setting the house on fire, but then he realized that he wasn't smelling smoke. And the roof wasn't hot.

The black cloud continued to rise, billowing around him, enclosing him.

It had the musty smell of a damp cellar.

The house was still vibrating, as if it stood above some huge engine that was thrumming way down in the ground, something powerful enough to drive an aircraft carrier—or maybe a dozen aircraft carriers.

And then it stopped.

And the black mist began to thin.

In a moment it was gone.

What the hell? Ed thought. *What the hell?* This house was the craziest place he'd ever seen. And for the first time, he considered leaving, getting away from whatever was going on here. He shook his head. He wouldn't do that. For one thing, he'd made a commitment, and that was something Ed Prawdzik took very seriously. He had never walked out on a patient, not even when they were tyrannical in their demands, and he wouldn't do it now.

Just because he couldn't explain what was going on here didn't mean he should run from it. Primitives ran from lightning, from fire, from anything they didn't understand. Ed figured humankind had come a way since then, and he didn't intend to turn tail just because things got a little weird.

A little weird?

Okay, a lot weird. But he was staying.

"So there," he said to the roof. The roof gave no indication that it had heard him.

Ed made his way to the ladder and climbed down, grateful to have his feet on solid ground again.

•4•

Paula spent the day driving west on the interstate, the land becoming drier and browner as she crossed Nebraska. After what seemed like a lifetime, she passed into Wyoming. By dusk she was in the mountains. She checked into a small motel.

Putting her suitcase on the bed, Paula sat down beside it. She was exhausted. The incident last night had drained her. Although she'd tried to push it into a dark corner of her mind, and even partially succeeded, her whole system seemed to know that she had come terribly close to being murdered last night. The knowledge slithered through every pore, trickled through her marrow, clung to every neuron like sticky tar. It was something she wanted to clean off but couldn't. And it sapped her energy as if someone had pulled her stopper.

Paula lay back, closed her eyes, instantly drifting off.

No, don't! She made herself get up, swim back to wakefulness. She needed a shower to clean off the road grime and sweat. And she needed to eat. But that was it. Shower and eat, then immediately to bed. Sleep for nine, ten hours.

Tomorrow she'd get to western Nevada, maybe even to California itself. She'd have to check the map, figure it out. But not tonight. She could do that over breakfast. It was one of the disadvantages of traveling alone. No one to read the map for you, tell you what the next town was, how far to the state line. Paula sighed. That was one of the disadvantages, but not the big one.

That was loneliness.

Suddenly Paula wanted to cry. Here she was out in the middle of nowhere, alone, on a mission that seemed hopeless, and last night a man had attacked her and would have killed her had it not been for the man at the motel.

First her assailant would have raped her.

She hadn't thought much about that. Not that rape was something she took lightly, but thoughts of death had simply preempted thoughts of anything else. She could recover from rape. Death tended to be permanent.

And the death that man had in mind for her would have been terribly unpleasant. She shuddered. Although she tried not to, she saw the man climbing on top of her, pressing her into the gravelly earth, forcing her legs apart.

She shook her head, made the image go away.

And then the tears came again, hot and torrential.

Alone and miserable, Paula Bjornson sat on the bed at a motel the name of which she hadn't noted, near a town in Wyoming she'd never heard of. At that moment, she was sure she was the loneliest person in the world.

Finally the tears stopped. Although she hadn't known it was possible, Paula felt even more exhausted than she had when she arrived. She had to hunt for the strength to get up and undress, make her way into the bathroom. The shower stall was made of ceramic tiles—most showers she saw in motels these days were fiberglass or plastic or something like that. The tiles were in good repair. No mildew grew on the grout, lurked darkly in the corners. Paula turned on the water, found the right temperature, stepped under the spray. The warm water felt wonderful, as if it were washing away her tiredness and sorrow, sending them swirling down the drain.

Paula closed her eyes, let the water's cleansing warmth transport her into a safe, dreamy place in which there were no crazed killers, no man in California crying out for her help. And then she amended that last part. David Guthrie wasn't crying out for anyone's help. He didn't seem to know he was in danger.

Paula broke out in goosebumps.

At first she thought the water had turned cold, but it still sprayed out hot and steamy. The air was what had turned cold. And Paula didn't understand that, for the enclosure should be warmed by the water. She was surrounded by hot mist.

And then a chill breeze blew through the shower stall, clearing away the steam. Paula began to shiver.

Suddenly the breeze became a wind, as bitterly frosty as as a January snowstorm in Minnesota. Confused, Paula stood there in what should have been a hot shower, watching her flesh turn blue.

The shower stall door flew open.

Wind whipped through the bathroom, tearing away the shower's steam in long wispy threads. Towels fluttered like flags in the breeze.

Paula stepped out of the shower, moved toward the door.

The wind was holding her back.

The toilet seat was flapping up and down, up and down, as if a bizarre white mouth were snapping at her.

She reached for the door. The air was like pudding, so thick she was barely able to push her arms into it. Her fingers found the knob, slipped over it. And she was blown backward, slamming into the wall.

Paula screamed.

But the wind was screaming louder.

Paula slid down to the floor. Water was being sucked from the shower, freezing, falling as hail. White nuggets were bouncing off her head, her bare shoulders, piling up on the floor. She crawled through them, leaving a trail like a slug. Paula was shivering so much the whole room seemed to vibrate.

She inched her way to the door, reached for the knob.

And the wind stopped.

The hail that covered the floor like a layer of white gravel vanished.

The temperature warmed.

Paula lay there, shaking, trying to make her confused brain function, give her a rational explanation. The steam shrank back into the shower stall as if sucked in by a huge pair of lungs. The stall door swung closed. Abruptly everything was normal again. The room warm, the shower hissing, the air misty. Paula still just lay there, certain she lacked the strength to move.

What happened? she wondered.

But her brain was still incapable of even a ridiculous suggestion. It seemed paralyzed, numb.

Finally she sat up, surprised she had the strength. She waited a moment, then slowly got to her feet. Although she still had no explanation for what had happened, she had come through it in one piece. She pushed open the shower door, intending to turn off the water. Instead she gasped, stepped back. The wall of the shower was covered with some kind of greenish brown slime that seemed to be oozing from the tiles. It smelled like mildew mixed with rotting milk.

Paula stared at it, transfixed.

The slime began to change, pulling apart in some places, congealing in others, running in small rivulets, forming lumpy strands that seemed to pulsate.

Run! a part of her was screaming. *Get out!*

But Paula was unable to move.

The slime began forming itself into letters. The first one was an *S,* then a *T.* After a few moments two words clung like brownish-green Jell-O to the wall of the shower stall: STAY AWAY.

The letters began to run, the water from the shower washing them away. In a moment they were gone, as if they'd never existed.

Paula ran from the bathroom.

SUDDEN STOP

• 1 •

"How's that?" Ed asked. He was looking down over the edge of the roof. The afternoon sun was directly behind his head, surrounding it with a yellow-white glow, as if he were the object of a religious painting.

Dave was on the balcony, where he could see both the small TV set he kept in the studio and Ed. Studying the TV screen, he said, "I think it was better before."

"Okay," Ed said. "Let me aim it back the other way a little bit." Ed's head withdrew.

Dave wheeled himself back into the studio. Ed would holler when he needed him. From above came the thumps and thuds of Ed moving around, working with the antenna. The nurse had driven into town this morning to buy new lead-in wire. Dave would never have asked him to do a job like this, but Ed insisted, and when Ed insisted things were usually done his way. Of course Ed only insisted when he wanted to help.

Unlike Jackie, who insisted to get her own way.

Dave sighed. He had no idea where things stood with Jackie. No, that wasn't true. He knew exactly where things stood: The relationship seemed to be disintegrating. Ever since the plane crash . . . but that wasn't true either, was it? Ever since strange things started happening.

What bothered him the most wasn't that Jackie didn't believe him—the things he told her were, after all, rather unbelievable—but that she'd started backing away at the first sign of trouble. She was supposed to care about him enough to want to help him through whatever difficulties might arise. That's what he would have done for her had their roles been reversed.

She hadn't been around for days. Were they still engaged? Would she ever come back? Dave had no idea. When he phoned her, he always got her answering machine, and he'd left messages for her to call him. But she hadn't. He'd known all along that Jackie had a self-centered streak, but he'd overlooked it. Maybe he thought he could change her. Maybe he thought it didn't matter.

Well, it mattered now.

Dave turned all this around in his mind, as he had time after time the past few days, and as always he came up with no firm solution to the problem. Maybe Jackie would never see him again, never even bother to break off the engagement. He'd read her wedding announcement to someone else in the paper and say, "Well, gosh, guess the engagement's off."

Did he want to end the relationship with Jackie?

The question seemed pointless, for if Jackie decided to end it, it was over. And if she came back? Would it just continue as before? Dave didn't think so. He'd seen a side of Jackie that had given him second thoughts.

And if he had come to this point in his thinking, could the relationship ever be put back where it had been? Had so many doubtful things been thought that it would be forever tainted? He was an adult, and adults had to accept that relationships didn't always work out. They fizzled; that was part of life. An intelligent adult had to see the warning signs and avoid a commitment that would lead to disaster.

And yet the thought of losing Jackie made him feel terribly lonely.

I'm tired of living by myself, Dave thought, and it was like a revelation. Until this moment, he hadn't realized that his own company wasn't enough. He needed someone. The knowledge seemed to fill the air, swirl about him in eddies.

He simply hadn't realized he was lonely. But now that he'd admitted it to himself, the truth hung there like a blazing neon sign: DAVE GUTHRIE IS LONELY.

From above him came the sounds of Ed fooling with the antenna, as if a giant were stomping on the roof. The TV set, a 13-inch color portable, sat on a small stand with casters, which he could roll around the studio. It and the larger set downstairs were connected to the same antenna. As Ed worked, the picture turned to snow, came back, wavered, faded again. Finally it returned, strong and clear, and remained that way.

"How's that?" Ed asked a moment later.

Dave wheeled himself out on the balcony, looked up at him. "Real good."

"Should I try aiming the antenna anymore?"

"No, I think you've got it."

"Okay, I'll tighten 'er up right where she is and come on down."

Dave shifted his gaze from the rooftop to the ocean. On the horizon was the white triangle of a sail, someone enjoying the calm waters and sunny day.

• 2 •

The base of the antenna was attached to the ridge of the roof. The mast was supported by three guy wires. Ed was using an adjustable wrench to tighten the antenna's base mount, after which he'd tighten a loose guy wire, and the job would be done. He was sitting on the ridge, one leg on each side of it.

His right foot slipped six inches or so down the roof, as if he'd stepped on something slick. Ed looked at the spot, seeing nothing out of the ordinary, and decided it was probably just a place where the shingle's sandpaper-like surface had been worn smooth. He went back to work.

Ed had never particularly feared heights. He'd hop up on a roof anytime, to look for leaks, fix a gutter, adjust an antenna. To him it was just about like being on the ground. You were careful, you had nothing to worry about.

Ed found his eyes drawn to the edge, to the earth two stories below.

He could kill himself if he fell off this roof. Or break his bones, maybe end up in a wheelchair for the rest of his life. And why the hell was he thinking like this? He'd never fallen off a roof, and as long as he was cautious, everything would be okay.

And yet his eyes clung nervously to the edge.

He shook his head. Come on, he told himself, let's get this job done and go start dinner. The thought of food caused Ed to brighten. He finished tightening the clamp in the base mount, then stood and moved toward the edge of the roof, where the loose guy wire was threaded through a metal eye.

Reaching the spot, he lowered himself to his knees, untwisted the guy wire, pulled it tight, retwisted it. Then he stood up, headed back up the roof because the ladder was on the other side of the house.

His foot slipped again.

This time it so completely lost its purchase that Ed found himself falling. He landed with a tremendous thud, face first, on the roof. He simply lay there, getting his breath back, trying to figure out what had happened. He'd been on this roof before, and there was nothing slick up here, so why did he keep slipping?

The only thing he was certain of was that he wanted off this roof. Now. Before he slipped again.

But he already *was* slipping again.

Sliding slowly backward on his belly.

The shingles not gripping him at all, as if they had been greased.

He reached for the ridge, but found his fingers groping along the shingles, a good foot below it. Then they were eighteen inches below it, then twenty-four, then thirty. He was still sliding. And he shouldn't be. Because lying flat on his belly like this should provide enough friction that it would be hard for someone to pull him off. How could he be slipping like a slow-moving car on an icy slope?

But he was.

And he was gaining speed.

He started to stand, and that only made him slip faster.

Ed glanced behind him, saw the edge getting closer and closer, saw the two-story drop, the earth below, and his brain told him that this couldn't be happening. He was slipping down the roof, unstoppably, and he was going to fall and maybe die, and it simply couldn't be happening.

An old saying popped into his head, something he really didn't need to recall at this particular moment. *It ain't the fall that kills you; it's the sudden stop.*

The sudden stop.

Oh Jesus, the sudden stop.

Ed slipped to the edge, and then his right foot was hanging in space. The roof, he realized suddenly, was like a living thing, as if the shingles were scales on a monster that resented his presence and was slowly evicting him, as if he were a troublesome insect.

He raised himself up on his knees, tried to move upward, but his knees slipped as if they were on banana peels. His legs slid over the edge, then his belly. He grabbed the gutter, held on, his whole body swinging below him. He heard Dave calling to him, screaming something, but he didn't hear the words. All Ed's attention was focused on his fingers, which clung to the gutter in a death grip—except in this case it was an avoidance-of-death grip.

He saw Andrea's face, her lovely face, and struggled to hang on so he could see her again, hold her again. But his fingers were ever-so-slowly slipping.

• 3 •

Dave was still on the balcony when a housejarring thud came from the roof. For a few moments, he didn't know what was going on, but then he saw Ed's foot come over the edge, then Ed himself, as if some unseen hand were pushing him off the house. A moment later, Ed was clinging to the gutter, and Dave yelled, "Hang on! I'm calling the fire department! They'll get you down!"

He whipped the chair around, wheeled himself off the balcony with every bit of strength he could muster, his heart pounding furiously. He steered between easels and tables as if they were an obstacle course, banging his cast against something and sending sharp pains shooting up his leg. Ignoring them, he made his way to the phone. Grabbing the receiver, he pushed the button that automatically dialed the police, put the phone to his ear. It was dead. He tried again. Still dead.

The fax machine, which sat next to the phone on the desk, suddenly spat out a piece of paper. At first Dave barely noticed as he frantically pushed buttons on the phone, trying to make it work. But then his eyes shifted to it, almost as if they had no choice, as if the same invisible hand that had pushed Ed down the slope of the roof had ahold of his head and was forcing him to look at the paper. There was a crude, splotchy drawing on it, and Dave sucked in his breath when he realized what he was seeing.

It was a drawing of a man falling. A stick figure tumbling off a roof.

And beneath it, in shaky, distorted letters that could have been made by a young child, were the words: YOU WERE WARNED.

From outside came a scream. It was followed by two heartbeats of silence, then a thud.

For a moment, Dave sat there, stunned, his head filled with the sickly numbing horror that comes when you've just experienced something so terrible your mind is incapable of dealing with it. But then he realized he had to do something. Ed was lying out there, maybe dying in agony. If the phone wouldn't work, then Dave had to find some other way of getting help. If nothing else he could roll out on the balcony, wait for a car to come by, attempt to wave it down. He tried the phone again. This time it worked. When the operator at the police department answered, the words came out of Dave in an incomprehensible jumble, and he had to repeat himself. The operator said help was on the way.

Dave looked at the paper from the fax machine again, and a cold bubble of terror sprang into existence in his belly. Except for a few smudges, the paper was blank. For a long moment, he just stared at it; then he wheeled himself to the balcony.

Ed's body lay on the ground, unmoving. He was face down, one arm out to the side, and looked like someone just sleeping there, a vagrant who'd dozed off in the yard.

"Ed!" Dave screamed.

There was no answer, no movement.

"Ed!" Dave screamed again, hysteria rising in his voice. "Please! If you can hear me, let me know! Please!"

But if Ed could hear him, he wasn't revealing it. Dave spun the chair around, rolled through the studio and into the hall. At the stairs he got out of the chair. It seemed to take forever, but eventually he was in a sitting position on the floor. He folded the chair, pulled it over to the stairs, gave it a push. It slid down half a dozen steps and stopped. Dave followed it, keeping his casts in front of him, using his arms to lower his butt from step to step. When he reached the wheelchair, he gave it another shove. By the time he was at the bottom, he was shaking and covered with sweat. Pausing for a moment to find new reserves of energy, he unfolded the chair and laboriously worked his way into it.

Then Dave was wheeling his way across the living room to the front door. He worked the chair over the threshold and onto the front porch. Ahead of him were more steps, wooden ones that led to the driveway. Dave paused, listening for sirens, not hearing anything but the *shhhhhhhhh!* of the waves rolling gently onto the shore and the distant cries of the gulls.

Dave frantically rolled the chair forward. Someone had to get to Ed quickly. Seconds could be critical. Dave realized too late that he was going too fast, rolling toward the wooden steps like a runaway train that was heading unstoppably for disaster. He grabbed the wheels, tried to pull back on them. They slipped in his grasp, burning his hands, but he held on. Just as its front wheels reached the steps, the chair stopped, his legs hanging over an eight-foot drop.

Dave could feel himself slowly tilting forward, starting to go off the porch, and he poured all his strength into his tired arms, forced them to pull back on the wheels. For a second the forces were balanced, gravity's desire to pull him down and the ability of his arms to resist it momentarily equalized.

Then gravity won.

The chair hit the first step, tipped forward, and Dave felt his shoulder hit something hard, splinters digging into his flesh. And then he was in a dark hole. Falling. Falling. Falling.

•4•

At dusk, two days after the incident at the Wyoming motel, Paula was on Interstate 80 between Sacramento and Oakland. She was exhausted. She'd been unable to sleep that night in Wyoming, and she hadn't slept much at the motel in Nevada, where she'd spent the last night.

At least the Nevada stay had been uneventful.

She'd considered getting out of that motel in Wyoming, getting a room somewhere else, some place that didn't have a bathroom in which cold winds blew through the shower stall and words appeared on tiles in green-brown slime. But she'd stayed where she was, because the horror that had followed her to that motel could easily follow her to another. Nowhere was safe. There were no sanctuaries into which the forces wishing to turn her away from California could not go.

A church?

She hadn't considered that. It was apparent that the forces trying to make her abandon this journey were evil. Maybe they couldn't enter a church—or maybe she'd seen too many old horror movies on TV. In any case, the issue really wasn't worth considering, since she could hardly move into a church. Eventually she would have to return to the outside world, and she would again be vulnerable.

Besides, something was propelling her onward. She was like a sailing vessel at the mercy of a current that moved her steadily, inexorably westward. Yo-ho-ho and a bottle of rum.

I could use a bottle of rum, she thought. Maybe a whole case of rum. Which was silly, for she had little experience with alcohol and usually fell asleep after half a drink. Sleep. That was what she needed. Ahead was a motel, one of the cut-rate chains. Paula considered stopping, and then she passed the exit without even slowing down. Why stop somewhere else, expose herself to another crazed killer or more cold wind and slime—or whatever the next step would be? She was going to press on to Castle Bay, find out what she was supposed to do there, and do it, get it over with.

She left the interstate at Vallejo, took state route 37 to U.S. 101, and headed north.

• 5 •

Dave had been lucky yesterday.

Except for cuts and scrapes, a few bruises, and a number of splinters, he'd come through his tumble down the steps unscathed. No damage to the casts or the mending bones they protected. He and Ed Prawdzik had been taken to Castle Bay's small hospital in the same ambulance. Dave had been kept one day for observation, then released. Ed was in critical condition.

But at least he was alive.

Dave's wheelchair was also unscathed, except for a few scratches. He rolled himself over to the base of the stairs, turned around, headed back toward the fireplace. It was the disabled person's version of pacing, he supposed.

Though not seriously injured, Dave had been forced to call an ambulance to get home from the hospital, since Castle Bay had no taxis. He presumed his medical insurance would pay the bill. He called Jackie when he got home, but she was out showing a house and unavailable. It was late evening now, and he still hadn't been able to reach her. Maybe he should have left a message on her answering machine saying it was urgent, there'd been a serious accident. But he hadn't. He'd just said he needed her and wanted her to call him as soon as possible. Maybe he felt the other way was too much like coercion. He wanted her to come of her own free will. Presumably that was why he hadn't called her from the hospital. He wasn't sure.

The ambulance crew had brought him into the house. But shortly he would have to work his way upstairs. His arms and shoulders ached, but he was confident he would make it.

He'd been trying to get more details about Ed's condition, but the hospital was being stingy with information. The woman he'd spoken to the last time he'd called had politely told him to kiss off.

He'd phoned the agency in Eureka that had arranged for him to hire Ed. The woman he'd spoken to said she'd notify whomever needed notifying and send Dave a replacement—a temporary replacement, he hoped. But then that was just wishful thinking, and Dave knew it. Ed's injuries were serious. The agency said it would be a few days before someone else could be sent down to Castle Bay; would he be okay until then? If not they might be able to get someone from the state department of health and human services to look in on him from time to time. Dave said he'd be fine. He wondered whether it was true.

A voice from the closet had warned him not to reach out to the presence he sensed.

But he had reached out, unthinkingly.

And Ed had fallen from the roof.

That was Dave's punishment.

Dave shook his head. How could he believe that? Not to mention voices from the closet, bottomless pits opening up in the floor, disappearing messages on the fax machine. No wonder his girlfriend had made herself scarce lately. Dave Guthrie had become a downright scary guy. He said some pretty weird shit. And he *believed* the stuff he was saying.

Trying to make sense of everything that had happened

was like trying to find order in chaos. He'd found himself using words like supernatural, poltergeist, demons, evil. But those words really had no meaning for him. They were fanciful, rooted in myth, stories. Fodder for scary books and movies. Throughout his whole life he'd known that the supernatural was hogwash. Period. Fake fortunetellers and mediums, rip-off artists the lot. And now that he was seeing it firsthand, knowing it for reality, his brain seemed unable to cope.

Dave rolled his wheelchair from the fireplace to the base of the stairs, then back again. The ache in his arms was getting worse. Although people who spent their lives in wheelchairs had useless legs, they undoubtedly had arms like a gorilla's. He stopped in front of the TV set. It was working now. Ed Prawdzik might die—or never walk again if he survived—all so Dave could see the "Tonight Show" and sitcoms and soap operas. He glared at the set, as if it were all the TV's fault, and then he put his head into his hands and gave in to despair.

He expected Rod Serling to step forward and tell him that all this made perfect sense because he was, after all, in the Twilight Zone, where fantasy was reality and nightmares were not dreams.

You were warned, the message had said, except he had no proof that he'd ever read that message, that it wasn't the invention of a mind slipping over the abyss, into madness.

Dave kept his face buried in his hands, as if he were afraid to look at his surroundings, afraid to look upon the madness that had engulfed him, afraid he might indeed find himself face to face with Rod Serling.

• 6 •

Dave awoke sitting in his chair, facing the TV set, as if he'd dozed off watching Johnny Carson. Except the set was off, its screen blank. His bladder was full, and he found the laborious task of getting up the stairs and onto the toilet before he could relieve himself daunting.

A car door slammed.

And Dave realized that was probably why he'd awoken. He'd heard a car pull up. Jackie? He glanced at his watch; it was nearly midnight. Jackie never came this late. She was an early riser. Get out there and hussle, make those big bucks. In bed by ten, up at six.

A chill settled over him, for he was suddenly certain that it was someone official, the sheriff or a Castle Bay policeman there to tell him that Ed had just passed away. Since you were his employer, we thought we should let you know. . . .

But then Dave realized that he wasn't family, and they probably wouldn't notify him at all. So it had to be Jackie. Maybe she'd just heard what had happened, which would account for her being so late.

There was a knock on the door.

Jackie didn't knock; she just came in as if she owned the place. But maybe this time she decided to knock for reasons of her own. Or maybe he'd locked the door, and she was unable to get in. As he wheeled himself toward the door, Dave shivered, his arms sprouting goosebumps so big they looked like the heads of mushrooms pushing up into a lawn after a hard rain.

It's just someone at the door, he told himself. Most likely Jackie. What are you afraid of?

He was no more than ten feet from the door when the space in front of him turned dark, as if a raincloud had just materialized there, billowing and undulating, lightning flashing back and forth between the various positions of the mass as if they were at war with one another.

Thunder rumbled from the cloud.

Then a wind—a wet, fetid wind that all but dripped of death—blew out of the cloud, pushed him back. Dave wanted to retch. The wind smelled as though it were blowing across the day-old scene of a bloody battle, a place where the rotting was just beginning and the wetness of death hung heavily in the air.

Something didn't want him to open the door.

His chair rolled back, and he grabbed the wheels, stopped it.

Though terrified and confused, Dave somehow understood that he should resist this force that was blocking his way. He tried to move the chair forward. The wind blew harder, slapping his face with wet droplets. Finding reserves of strength and determination he didn't know he had, Dave inched the chair ahead. More drops hit him, and then he realized they were red, like blood.

Through the cloud he heard the sound of more knocking, then the door being tried. Apparently it wouldn't open. Dave forced the chair forward. An inch, two inches, six inches. The wind buffetted him. His clothes were soaked in red now, as if he were bleeding to death.

He moved forward a foot, then another foot, then another.

He was in the heart of the cloud now, small claps of thunder booming only inches from his ears, lightning sizzling past his eyes. There was so much static electricity here that he could feel his hair standing on end, the strands wiggling, twitching. Logic—if a situation like this could be said to contain any logic—dictated that he should turn around, roll away from this cold, away from the danger. And yet he still muscled the chair forward. Somehow he knew—felt? sensed?—that he had to make it to the door, open it. The blackness roiled angrily around him, furious over his defiance.

Lightning stabbed his cheek, making him cry out.

There was a loud rapping on the door. "Are you all right?" a woman called. Was it Jackie? He couldn't be sure.

Dave forced the chair forward. He was drenched now, red rivulets running from his body, the wind whipping them away. A bolt of lightning hit his right hand, making him let go of his wheelchair on that side. The chair immediately swung to the right. Although Dave's hand was scorched, smoking, there was no pain. He straightened the chair, moved forward again.

At last he reached the door, set the brake on the chair, reached out, grabbed the knob.

The black cloud churning around him shrank into a rotating column like a mini-tornado, and then it rose up, as if being sucked back into the sky from which it had come.

The room was silent, still.

Dave's clothes were dry.

As if nothing had happened.

And yet, on some level, it had happened. It wasn't just in his mind.

An urgent rapping came from the door. Dave opened it, and found himself staring at a thin, dark-haired woman whose brown eyes displayed a lot of the same confusion and terror he was feeling.

"You're David Guthrie," she said. A statement, not a question.

"Yes."

"I'm Paula Bjornson. I . . . I think I'm here to help you."

THE MEETING

• 1 •

"To help me?" Dave asked, bewildered.

"Yes. Can I come in? I've had a long drive, and this explanation's going to take some time."

Dave invited her in, and when she was sitting on the couch, he said, "How can you help me?"

She looked at her hands, whose fingers she was lacing and unlacing nervously. She wasn't wearing a wedding ring. She cleared her throat. "I don't know," she said.

"You don't know how you can help me?"

"No."

"I don't get it."

"That's not surprising. I don't understand it myself. Perhaps I should start at the beginning. I'm from Minnesota, from Anoka Falls. It's a suburb of the Twin Cities. I'm a schoolteacher there." She took in a slow breath, then raised her head, her eyes meeting Dave's. He saw all sorts of things in those warm brown eyes—determination, fear, confusion.

She said, "There's no avoiding it, so I might as well get right to the heart of the whole thing. You probably won't believe me. But . . . I have certain abilities . . . psychic abilities." She studied Dave's eyes intently, apparently looking for some hint of how he'd received that statement. Dave tried to show no reaction. She said, "I was born with these psychic gifts. Now, before you jump to any wrong conclusions, I'm not here to try to make any money. I don't want to sell you anything. I'm here because you need help . . . and because I think I have to give you that help."

"I'm afraid I—"

"Don't understand," she said, completing the sentence for him. "Let me get through this, and you'll at least know as much as I do. Then we can talk, and you can decide whether you believe me or you want to throw me out of the house—or whatever you decide."

"Go on," Dave said. "I won't interrupt."

"I have two gifts," she said. "One is the ability to tell when someone is lying. The other is that I can tell when someone needs help. The second one is the reason I'm here. I've been receiving . . . messages is as good a word as any, I guess. I've been receiving them from you."

"From me?" Dave asked, breaking his promise not to interrupt.

"I've seen you. I've seen this house. I knew you were in a wheelchair before I got here."

Dave just stared at her, recalling how he'd sensed a presence, someone wanting to help, and how he'd reached out for that presence. . . .

You were warned.

"It was you," the man said.

"What?" the woman asked, still exploring his face.

Dave shook his head. He wasn't ready to tell this stranger anything. First he wanted to hear everything she had to say. His mind, still reeling from the storm cloud that had tried to prevent him from opening the door, had been sent into a further spin by Paula Bjornson's words. He felt like a man falling down a dark, bottomless hole into unreality.

"Go on," he said. "Finish your story."

She told him how she'd had her first psychic experience as a child, when she'd known of a puppy that had fallen into a storm sewer. As she went on, detailing other instances of her ability to know when help was needed, Dave studied her. He guessed her to be in her late twenties. She had the air of someone who was reserved and bookish. Though thick and lustrous, her dark hair was cut in a plain, no-nonsense style. She wore no makeup. And she was clearly uncomfortable doing what she was doing.

"So once I knew who you were, I had to come," she said. "You needed my help, and I had to come. It's . . . well, it's the responsibility that goes with my gift." She hesitated, then went on. "I think that something didn't want me to come. The first night I stopped at a motel, and a man tried to kill me." She told him the details of the incident. "The next night, in Wyoming, I was taking a shower, and suddenly a cold wind blew through the bathroom, and then I saw words on the wall of the shower stall. They said 'stay away.'"

She stopped, and for a long moment they just looked at each other. Finally, Paula said, "Do you believe me?"

Dave laughed, a bitter chuckle with no humor in it. "I believe you," he said. "What you've told me is no stranger than the things that have been happening to me."

"Would you like to tell me about them?" she asked. "I only know that you're in danger, and that there's some . . . some *thing* here. I don't know what it is, but it's very powerful, and I know you should be afraid of it."

"It's late," Dave said, looking at his watch. It was nearly two in the morning. They'd been talking for a couple of hours. "I'll tell you my side of all this tomorrow. Do you have a place to stay?"

She shook her head.

"I've got a cot if you'd like to stay here."

"Thank you," she said. "I . . . I think I'm supposed to stay here."

He didn't know what she meant by that, but he was too tired to ask. And he still had to empty his bladder, which felt on the verge of exploding. As Paula went out to bring in her things, Dave began the ordeal of making his way up the stairs backward, lifting his butt from one step to another, his casts held out in front of him. Paula returned before he was halfway up and she assisted him by bringing up his wheelchair.

Dave got into bed, uncertain whether the events of the day would keep him awake as his brain replayed them again and again, or whether he'd be so exhausted nothing could keep him awake.

The exhaustion won.

For a while.

• 2 •

The first hint that something was amiss came in the form of a low vibration that barely penetrated Dave's sleep. It persisted, tugging at his awareness until he acknowledged it. At first he thought it was just another of California's brief earth tremors, nothing to disturb his sleep, but it continued jostling him and eventually he came fully awake.

The room was shaking. He sat up, shedding sleep the way one peels off wet clothes after coming in out of a rainstorm.

A shape was moving slowly past the end of his bed, going from left to right. It was huge, filling all the space between the bed and the wall, a thing of quivering mounds filled with speckles, as if it were made of Jell-O salad. It seemed to have no mouth, no eyes. Another creature darted into the room, a thing that looked like an enormous rat covered with spikes and scales. A piece of the Jell-O creature formed itself into a tentacle, flashed out and grabbed the smaller creature, pulled it in like a fish on a line. The smaller creature emitted a howl of terror, and then it was being held against the side of the Jell-O monster, which rippled and emitted a pink light. The spiked rat let out one final shriek, and then it disappeared, absorbed right through the monster's flesh. For a moment, Dave could see the smaller beast's eyes through the flesh of the monster, but then all traces of it vanished.

I'm having a nightmare, Dave thought.

But he knew he wasn't. This was something else.

Panic seized him. The Jell-O monster could absorb Dave Guthrie as easily as it had absorbed the smaller creature. A gelatinous tentacle could leap out, encircle him, drag him into the mass. Easing the covers back so as not to attract attention to himself, Dave reached for his wheelchair, but his grab was overanxious, and he pushed it away, out of reach. His heart thudding madly, he stared at the chair the way a drowning man would look at a life preserver tossed too far away for him to grab. Help was within sight, but the water would pull him down anyway.

Dave almost rolled out of bed, intending to crawl after the chair, but he thought better of it. It would be like waving a flag in front of the monster, which so far had shown no interest in him. Not to mention that he might injure himself. The casts on his legs made him heavy, awkward. He'd drop like an anvil.

So Dave stayed put, hoping the monster would go about its business and leave him alone.

Why was this happening? Where did these creatures come from? He didn't know. It was as if he'd been chosen to be the butt of some bizarre cosmic joke. Hey, look, old Dave Guthrie survived the plane crash, which means luck was with him that day, so let's balance things out by sending him the monsters. It'll be lots of yuks.

Yuk-yuk. Hee-hee.

Chosen. That word again. Except he'd used it incorrectly. He hadn't *been* chosen; he'd done the choosing. *You have chosen,* he'd been told. What had he chosen? To be invaded by monsters? To live in a world that was like a constant LSD trip, full of horrors and surrealities that simply could not be and yet were?

Ed Prawdzik falls off the roof.

Monsters appear in his room.

Voices speak to him from the shadows.

A woman shows up saying she's here to help.

These things hopped around in his head like contestants in a sack race, tripping and falling and getting hopelessly tangled with each other. Nothing made sense. Dave felt as if he'd followed Alice down her rabbit hole and taken a wrong turn, ended up in Terrorland.

The Jell-O monster reached the wall and passed through it.

Behind it was something else. A black blob, like a hole that moved. As Dave watched the black thing, he felt a revulsion that went beyond anything that could be communicated by his normal senses. This was something he felt at a deep, primitive level, something he could not explain in words. The black blob was vile beyond comprehension. He didn't just believe it; he *felt* it, as if the creature's repulsiveness were touching him, forcing itself into his inner being through his pores.

The blackness, he realized, had a sheen to it. He thought of the shininess of a well-brushed dog's coat, but this was something else. More like the gleam from the deadly body of a black widow spider.

The black hole also vanished into the wall.

It was followed by a man-like creature that stumbled along as if drunk. It was covered with matted brown fur. As it reached the end of the bed, it looked toward Dave with its dimly glowing red eyes and smiled—if you could call it a smile. Its mouth was full of wicked-looking teeth, many of which curved into needle-sharp points. Although the creature was man-sized, its head not much larger than that of a Saint Bernard, it looked as though it could chomp Dave's leg off—or even bite him in half. It growled at him, a low hate-filled grumble, but like the others, it slowly marched across the room and into the wall.

And then the procession was over.

As Dave stared at the spot where the monsters had been, he felt certain that he had brought all this on himself. Although he didn't know what he had done, words that had floated up to him from the depths of an imaginary hole in the floor hung in his mind as accusing as if they'd been written into a grand jury's indictment.

He has chosen. He is ours.

•3•

Dave got up in the morning almost expecting to find that Paula Bjornson had been just another one of those things he saw one moment only to have it disappear the next. But

Paula was still here. Dave was halfway to the bathroom when he smelled coffee perking. Inside the bathroom, he found other evidence of her presence—a toothbrush, a woman's comb, a curling iron.

After he was dressed, she carried his wheelchair downstairs for him. He got himself down the stairs in the usual laborious manner, then rolled into the kitchen. Paula poured him a cup of coffee, asked what he'd like for breakfast.

"How about a cholesterol special?"

She raised an eyebrow. "Which is?"

"Two eggs scrambled, a big sausage patty, and toast with jelly."

"Not good for you," Paula said.

"No, but every now and then your stomach rebels at the thought of any more healthy fiber-laden cereal."

She smiled. It was a nice smile, full of warmth, understanding, gentleness. "I'll join you," she said.

The breakfast was delicious, but halfway through it Dave found himself thinking about Ed Prawdzik and the wonderful meals he'd made, and Dave's appetite vanished. He finished the meal just to be polite to Paula. He'd have to call the hospital again this morning, see whether he could get any information on Ed's condition.

"We have a lot more to talk about, I think," Paula said.

Dave nodded. "You'll find a lot of what I'm going to tell you very hard to believe."

"Harder than what I've told you?"

"Yes—some of it."

"Tell me," Paula said. "I'll know the truth when I hear it."

As he had the night before, Dave found himself studying her. Though a bit on the thin side, she carried herself with an unobtrusive dignity. She had a lovely face, full of warmth and intelligence, a flawless complexion. And yet Dave suspected that many men overlooked her beauty because it was so understated.

"You'd really know it if I tried to deceive you?" he asked.

"Yes," she said. And then she looked a little embarrassed.

"I'm sorry. I'm not trying to intimidate you or anything like that. I didn't ask for my gifts. They were simply given to me. I know the truth. I can't help it." She looked down at her empty breakfast plate. "Sometimes I wish I didn't."

Dave waited to see whether she would say more, but she didn't. He said, "All this began after I came home from the hospital. You know from the article you read that I was in a plane crash and that I was the only survivor."

He told her everything that had happened—voices in the dark, glowing eyes, holes opening up in the floor, the house vibrating, the storm that had enveloped him when he tried to answer the door, the Jell-O monster, Ed Prawdzik's fall, the message that came out of the fax machine.

"Wow," Paula said.

"I guess 'wow' pretty much sums it up."

"Ed sounds like a nice man," Paula said. "I hope he's okay."

"Me, too," Dave said. "Which brings me to another point. I think you're a nice person too, and nice people get hurt around here."

"I have to stay," she said.

"I don't want to see anything like what happened to Ed happen to you. If you stay here, I'm afraid it might."

"I have to stay."

"But why? You don't have to answer every call for help, do you?"

"I think I do," she said.

"Okay, you answered the call, and I told you thanks but no thanks."

"I'm not supposed to leave."

"Says who?"

She frowned. "I . . . I don't know. I just know I'm supposed to stay."

"I advise you to go."

"Are you *telling* me to?" Her eyes found his, held them.

Dave sighed. "No." He didn't really want her to. He didn't want to be alone.

A few silent moments passed; then Dave said, "Maybe we

should both go. Here I am in a house that's haunted or full of poltergeists or something, one person has been seriously injured, I have no idea what's going to happen next, and yet I'm staying here. It really doesn't make much sense, does it?"

It took Paula so long to respond that Dave thought she wasn't going to, but then she said, "I don't think it would do you any good to move away."

"What do you mean?"

Again it took her a long time to answer. Finally she said, "It's not the house. It's . . . you."

"You mean if I left the house, all this would just follow me?"

"Yes, I think it would. I'm sure it would."

"How do you know?"

"I . . . I just know." She looked at him helplessly, clearly at a loss to explain it.

Dave simply shook his head. He was riding along on a wave of unreality, a monster howler that would carry him where it pleased, leaving him nothing to do except hope it wouldn't dash him on the rocks when the ride was over.

"So we're in this together," Dave said softly.

"Yes."

"So, what are we going to do?"

"I don't know," Paula said.

"And you've got no idea how you're supposed to help me."

"No. I . . . I think I'll know what to do when the time comes. I hope I'll know."

For a few moments neither of them spoke; then Paula said, "I'll do the dishes."

She rose, gathering up the plates, and from the living room came the sound of the front door opening.

•4•

As Jackie stepped into the kitchen, her eyes settled on Paula, taking her in, then shifted to Dave. "I just heard what happened," she said. "Myra told me when I got to work this morning." Myra was the real estate firm's secretary.

"I left a message on your answering machine," Dave said.

"You didn't say anything about what had happened, or I would have come right over."

"I said I needed you," Dave said.

Jackie frowned, as if ready to dispute that this was really what he'd said, then apparently changed her mind. "I'm surprised you could get a new nurse so quickly," she said, inclining her head toward Paula.

"Uh, this is Paula Bjornson," Dave said. "But she's not a nurse."

"Oh?"

"She's a schoolteacher from Minnesota."

"Are you old friends?" Jackie asked, giving Paula a thorough once-over.

"No," Dave said.

"I'm here to help," Paula said.

"Help?" Jackie asked.

"You know what's been happening here, don't you?" Paula asked.

"You're not part of this same nonsense, are you?" Jackie asked. "My God, it must be contagious."

Paula looked down, said nothing. Jackie shifted her gaze to Dave, waited.

"She's been receiving messages from me—no, not exactly messages. She knows when people need help, and she knew I needed help, so she came."

Jackie's frown deepened. "What kind of help do you provide, Ms. Borman?"

"Whatever kind of help I can provide," Paula said, not

bothering to correct Jackie's mispronunciation of the name Bjornson.

"And just what kind of help do you think you can provide for Dave?"

"I don't know yet."

"How did you know Dave needed your help?"

"I just knew."

"I see. And if you don't mind my asking, how much do you charge for this service?"

"She doesn't charge anything," Dave said. "She came out here at her own expense because she sensed that someone needed help. It's a . . . a power she has, a psychic ability."

For a long time, Jackie simply stared at him; then she abruptly shifted her eyes to Paula. "Would you mind letting us have a few words in private?"

Paula beat a hasty retreat.

As soon as she was gone, Jackie said, "Exactly what the hell is going on here?"

"Just what we've told you."

"What you've told me is a bunch of nonsense."

Dave shook his head. "It's not." He motioned toward the chair in which Paula had eaten her breakfast. "Sit down, Jackie, so I don't have to look up at you."

Jackie took the chair.

"It's not nonsense," he repeated. "After Ed fell off the roof, I got a message on my fax machine telling me that I'd been warned. In other words, Ed's fall was the consequence of my disobeying them."

"Them? Dave, can you hear yourself?"

"Them, Jackie. The spirits or demons or whatever they are. Them."

Jackie looked at him levelly, apparently choosing her words. "Do you have any idea how crazy all this sounds?"

"Sure."

"Now I want you to think very carefully about what I'm going to tell you. What would you recommend to someone who went around saying things like that?"

"I don't know what you're talking about."

"Yes, you do. You'd tell that person to get help. You'd see

someone on a downward spiral into madness, and you'd talk to him, try to get him to seek some help before it was too late."

"I'm not insane, Jackie. The things going on here are not in my head."

Jackie sighed. "How can you say that?"

"Because I believe it."

She started to say something else, then apparently changed her mind. "About this girl, this Paula whatever-her-last-name-is. She just showed up here this morning or what?"

"Last night."

"Saying she'd received messages from you."

"Not exactly—well, sort of. She said she knew I needed help."

"Sole survivor of a big plane crash, a guy whose name was in the news for days."

"What are you saying?"

"I'm saying she's working a scam. Maybe she was in on this with Ed."

"I don't think she is."

"Then you're not thinking straight. Where is this person staying, by the way?"

"Here."

"Here?"

"Sure, why not?"

"Why not? How can you ask why not?" Jackie demanded. "You're supposed to be engaged to me, and yet you've got a woman living with you."

"She's not living here, she's staying here. Besides, she came to help. What do you want me to do, throw her out?"

"Invite her to leave."

"I can't do that, Jackie. I . . . I don't know how to explain it, but I think I might need her help."

"How can she help you?"

He shook his head. "I don't know, but somehow she's involved, and I believe she's on my side."

For several seconds, Jackie just sat there, studying him. Finally, she said, "I'm breaking off our engagement."

Dave just looked at her, uncertain what to say, uncertain how he felt.

"If you're going to act crazy and refuse to get help—and then have this woman stay with you . . . well, you're not right for me, Dave. I'm sorry." She stood up, almost knocking the chair over.

"Jackie—"

"Don't!" she snapped. "Don't Jackie me." She started toward the door, then stopped, whirled to face him. "Will you go for psychiatric help?"

"Jackie, I don't need—"

"That's the reason I'm so angry with you, Dave. That's the reason I'm so hurt." Her face was red with emotion; a tear trickled down her cheek.

"I'm not crazy, Jackie. Ed saw the things that went on here. It's not just me."

"Ed was crazy too," she said and stormed out of the room. The front door slammed.

• 5 •

A moment later, the front door opened again, and Jackie walked back into the kitchen. "I came back for two reasons," she said. "First I forgot to give you this." She handed him her engagement ring. "The second reason is that your little friend let the air out of my tires. And the tires on Ed Prawdzik's car. Even her own tires. They're all flat."

"I don't believe Paula would do that."

"The ghosts did it, right?"

Dave said nothing.

"Can I use your phone to call a service station?"

"Of course."

She lifted the wall-mounted phone's receiver. "I'm going to get my car fixed and get out of here. Until then, keep her away from me, Dave."

Dave Guthrie remained silent, for he had no idea what to say.

CASTLE BAY: THE MADNESS
SPREADS

•1•

T. J. Diller drove the service truck along Pacific Road, so named because it followed the shoreline. His initials stood for Timothy Jacob, his mother being a devout Christian who named all her children from the Bible, but he'd always hated being called Timothy. Sounded like a pussy name. T. J., on the other hand, sounded like one of those dudes on *Dallas*, somebody with power and connections and class.

It was a pretty morning in Castle Bay. The light fog that had rolled in at dawn was burning off, and the sun was twinkling on the waves, while gulls circled overhead. T. J. thought it would make a pretty picture.

He watched the names on the mailboxes. He was looking for Guthrie. Lady's tires were flat, and he was going to fix them, get her on her way, maybe earn a tip if he was polite and smiled real nice.

Not that the tip would help all that much. He'd quit high school because he'd found it stupid and boring, and because he wanted to get a job so he could buy a nice car, have some nice clothes if he had any money left over. Trouble was the only job he'd been able to find was working at Easley's 76 Station, and that didn't pay him enough to buy a nice car—with or without an occasional tip. He could barely afford to run his ten-year-old Chevy, which he drove without the required liability insurance, because the insurance rates for an eighteen-year-old were out of sight. You want to be rich, you should go into the insurance business. It was like legal robbery.

Ahead was the mailbox he was looking for. D. Guthrie, it said. He pulled into the paved drive, discovering that there were three cars there, all with flat tires. There were also three people. A dark-haired woman and a guy in a wheelchair were watching him from the porch, and another woman, a nice-looking blonde, was waiting in the driveway. T. J. wondered whether the guy in the wheelchair could be making it with the two women, what he liked to call a ménage à twats. Just because the guy's legs were in casts didn't mean he couldn't have any fun. T. J. knew a couple of guys couldn't walk who had several kids. Besides, whenever he saw a man and two women together he liked to think about it. Making it with two women at the same time was one of his dreams, right up there with owning a new car.

The blonde hurried over as T. J. pulled to a stop. "That's the one there," she said. "The Oldsmobile."

"What about the other ones? They're all flat, looks like."

"I'm the one who called you, and that's the only car I'm concerned about," the blonde snapped.

"Yes, ma'am," T. J. said, getting out of the truck. "What happened? You have a run in with some neighborhood kids or something like that?"

"What happened," the blonde said, "is that my tires have been flattened. Your job is to fix them, not ask me questions."

"Yes, ma'am," he said, thinking, Well aren't we just the queen bitch of the west? He got a toolbox from the compartment on the side of the truck, and walked over to the woman's car, then circled it, looking at the four flat tires.

The blonde followed him. "Well?" she asked.

"Got four flat tires."

"I know that," she said exasperatedly. "Can you fix them?"

"Probably. Doesn't look like there's any major damage, like if your tires were slashed with a knife or something like that."

"Good. Would you please do it quickly? I've got some very important appointments to keep."

"I'll fix 'em fast as I can," T. J. said. Jesus, he thought, some of the good-looking ones sure are cold. This one would probably freeze your balls off.

He got a heavy-duty jack from the truck, rolled it under the blonde's car, and raised both rear tires at once. Then he got a portable compressor which ran off the truck's battery, and rolled it over to the car. It thump-thump-thumped into life as he switched it on, then settled down and ran smoothly. After he had compressed enough air to work with, he put some into the tire and looked for the leak. He found it almost at once, a small hissing hole in the treads.

"There it is," he said.

"What caused it?" the blonde asked.

"Ordinarily I'd say a small hole like that's a nail hole, but with all these flat tires here, I guess it was something like an ice pick."

The woman glanced angrily at the other two people, who were staying on the porch, keeping out of her way. T. J. wondered what was going on between them. Maybe the blonde hadn't wanted to go two on one; the suggestion had pissed her off.

"How long will it take to fix it?" the blonde asked.

"Minute or so. It's pretty quick."

"Good."

It would be quick because all he was going to do was plug the hole. You weren't supposed to do that with steel-belted radials; you were supposed to take them off and patch them. But that took a lot longer. And if the plug failed sometime in the future, well, that was life.

He plugged the hole, moved on to the the next tire, plugged it, moved on to the next. But this time, when he put air into the tire, instead of hissing the leak gurgled. He spun the tire around until he found the hole. Stuff was oozing out of it, thick and gooey. And red.

Like blood.

"Shit," T. J. muttered.

"What's wrong?" the blonde asked.

"Your tire, it . . . it looks like it's bleeding."

She looked. "Nonsense. It's just something that's supposed to be there. It's probably part of the tire."

Although T. J. didn't scare easily, although he thought horror movies were stupid, although he'd never believed in bogeymen or monsters beneath the bed, something cold reached into his guts, poking and prodding in places, and he knew it was the icy finger of fear. He hesitated, reluctant to touch the stuff, then wiped some of it off with his finger. He sniffed it, and it had the coppery smell of blood. He tasted it, and it had the metallic flavor of blood too.

"Jesus," he said.

"There's nothing there," the blonde insisted.

"What do you mean there's nothing there? Jesus Christ, lady. How can you not see that red goop coming out of the tire?"

"It's nothing. Do you hear me? It's nothing. Now fix the fucking tire."

T. J. was having a hard time understanding the woman's reaction. Maybe it was just something that looked like blood, or maybe someone had found a way to actually put blood into the tire as a prank, but to deny that there was anything unusual going on here was just plain weird. He wiped the bloody stuff away with a rag, inserted the plug into the special tool, dipped it into vulcanizing compound and jammed it into the hole.

The fourth tire bled too.

After he'd fixed it, he made out a bill, which she paid with her Visa card. No tip. She peeled out as she pulled onto the road, roared out of sight. Might not want to do that with plugs in those radials, he thought, then added *Bitch!*

The other woman came down from the porch, walked over to him. "Would you mind fixing a few more flat tires?" she asked.

"No, ma'am. That's what I'm here for. You in any rush?"

"No," she said softly. "There's no rush."

"In that case, I'll go ahead and take the tires off and put patches on them. Takes longer but it's the right way to do it."

"That'll be fine," she said and rejoined the man in the wheelchair.

At first T. J. hadn't thought the brunette was as pretty as the blonde, but now that he'd given her a second look, he realized she was just as attractive. It just took a little longer to see it, he supposed.

As he was dragging the jack toward the Bronco, which he'd decided to do next, T. J. realized that the icy finger was still poking him in the gut. It made him hesitate, thinking maybe he didn't want to fix any more flat tires here. Maybe there was a reasonable explanation, but even if there was, he didn't know it, and tires that bled were kind of spooky. And he was going to take these tires *off.* What if he found they were *full* of blood? What if he spilled it all over himself?

For several seconds, T. J. Diller just stood there, thinking it over. Then he rolled the jack under the Bronco and began moving its metal handle up and down. If it's there, it's there, he decided. At least I won't pretend I can't see it, the way that fruitcake of a blonde did.

Besides, there were ways you could put blood into a tire. Easiest would be to pump it in through the valve, same way you put the air in. As for the blood itself, it had most likely come from a chicken or some other animal. T. J. found the whole idea disgusting. Anyone who'd do something like that was sick. That was for sure.

There was no blood in any of the remaining flat tires, and the dark-haired woman gave him a five-dollar tip.

Even so, T. J. Diller was just as glad to get out of there.

•2•

Paula felt weighted down by uncertainty as she wheeled Dave back inside. "I'm sorry," she said.

"For what?"

"I've messed things up between you and your fiancée.

"She's not my fiancée anymore."

"But she might be if it wasn't for me. Maybe I was wrong. Maybe I shouldn't stay here. Maybe—"

"No," Dave said. "You didn't do anything. I guess things have been falling apart between Jackie and me ever since the plane crash. It just came to a head now. That's all."

"But, I feel—"

"Don't. I think that, slowly but surely, I've been realizing Jackie isn't the right person for me."

In a way no one else could, Paula knew the things Dave said were true. And she was glad. She wheeled him into the kitchen, where he phoned the hospital while she started on the dishes.

"Damned hospital," he muttered when he hung up. "I've managed to find out that Ed's still alive, but that's only because they say he can't have any visitors, and if he was dead they wouldn't say that, would they?"

"No," Paula said. Then she went back to washing dishes, back to waiting to find out why she was here.

• 3 •

As she drove along the two-lane country road, accompanied by a man she'd known less than an hour, Valerie Weeks tried to sort out the events swimming around in her head. A few hours ago she'd been in her large, expensive home in Eureka. She and Bart had argued. It seemed like their hobby, arguing, they spent so much time doing it. Today's dispute was on a common topic. She'd been angry because Bart spent all his time running the Weeks business empire, and there was no time left over for her, for the things she wanted to do with her husband. As she often did when she was unhappy, Valerie had been drinking martinis. They'd argued about that too.

Valerie had stormed out of the house, screeched out of the driveway in her Mercedes. Then she'd simply driven, not really knowing where she was going. She was just staying away, making him worry about her, showing him how deeply he'd hurt her.

About dusk, she'd spotted the sign for Castle Bay. It was a pretty name, and she'd never been there, so she'd taken the turnoff. Castle Bay had turned out to be a small place with little to offer. Valerie had spotted a bar, stopped for a drink.

And that's where she met Strix.

She'd been sitting at the bar, using the little plastic sword with the olive on it to absentmindedly stir her martini. And Strix came over, sat down next to her. He smiled, letting her know right away that he was going to make a move. He looked Italian, but she couldn't be sure. He was tall, broad-shouldered, with a mass of curly dark hair, eyes that were almost black, and when she looked into those eyes Valerie thought they were bottomless. They caressed her, tempted her, pulled her in. In a way, they *touched* her, for she could feel their gaze as if she were being gently stroked.

Valerie was unable to look away.

She did not go into the bar looking for a man. Sure, she fought with her husband, but she was still Valerie Weeks, and she had an image to uphold. Persons of her station didn't pick up men in bars.

And yet here she was. Driving her Mercedes while Strix sat silently beside her, his presence subtly electrifying, causing odd and compelling stirrings within her.

"What kind of a name is Strix?" she asked, her voice sounding strange and distant. And then she wondered whether she'd asked him that before and found she was unable to remember.

"It's a common name where I come from," he replied, the sound of his voice making her feel weak all by itself.

"Where are you from?" Had she asked him that before?

"Europe," he said.

He had a slight accent, but she was unable to place it. She started to ask him exactly where in Europe he was from, but the words just wouldn't form.

"Turn here," he said.

She did so, unquestioningly. She never even considered

not doing what this man said. He had a presence, a power, and Valerie was floating along on it in an easy, relaxed, pleasant stupor no drug could duplicate. Wow, she'd heard of animal magnetism, but this was ridiculous.

I'm going to have an affair, she thought. I'm going to make it with a guy with a weird name who picked me up at a bar. How's that grab you, Bart old buddy?

She wasn't worried about damaging her reputation. Strix (really was a weird name) was a gentleman, a man of discretion and charm. Her honor was safe in his hands.

Honor. Wow. The word made her want to giggle. She felt like a damsel being swept away by a knight. And she was ready for her knight. Moist and anxious and ready.

"Stop the car," he said gently.

She did. They were in a wooded area, at the end of a dirt road. She hadn't thought her knight would take her to a spot that was probably used by the local high schoolers, but then what did it matter? In some ways this made it more exciting.

She reached for him, and he took her in his arms. He kissed her passionately, a long, lingering kiss that left her tingling all over. Then he slowly moved his mouth to her neck, brushed it with his lips.

"Do you want me?" he asked.

"Yes," she whispered. "Yes, yes."

She didn't cry out when his teeth bit through her flesh.

She moaned as the car was filled with sucking sounds.

When those sounds stopped, Valerie Weeks had been drained of blood.

And the ancient creature sitting beside her in the car bit a huge chunk of flesh from her neck, swallowed it, and went back for another. New noises filled the car, the wet sounds of fresh meat being ripped, chewed. When he was finished, Valerie Weeks' bones gleamed whitely, her remains sitting there behind the wheel as if it were some sort of Halloween gag, a car driven by a skeleton.

Nowhere on her bones was so much as a speck of flesh. Her eye sockets were empty, as were her cranial cavity and mouth. Neither a hair nor a fingernail remained. Her rib cage was nothing but a bunch of curving white slats.

Satisfied that he'd gotten it all, the creature pulled her skeleton from the car and tossed it into the woods. Then he slipped behind the wheel and drove away, licking his lips to get any juices that remained.

• 4 •

Officer Patrick Thorpe of the Castle Bay police department drove slowly along Humboldt Avenue in his cruiser. It had been a pretty calm night so far, not many people out, not many calls to respond to. It was a cool, foggy evening, the mist making the streetlights look as though they had haloes.

Thorpe was glad it was a quiet night. The mood around the police department the past few days had been . . . well, sort of tense, uneasy. For one thing they'd been getting a record number of calls concerning prowlers and wild animals running around. Ordinarily such calls turned out to be raccoons looking into garbage cans or bears that had come down out of the hills. But no bears or 'coons had been discovered. In fact nothing had been discovered.

And then there was the guy at the trailer park.

Something had turned him into ground meat, and nobody had any idea what had done it. Certainly no bear or raccoon could do it. Which left what? Bigfoot? A tyrannosaurus rex? Jesus. No wonder everybody was edgy.

And then there was the fire at that Falling Star place. Nobody'd found any bodies yet, but Thorpe knew they were in there. There was something spooky about that fire, although Thorpe was unable to put his finger on just what made him think so.

But those weren't things Thorpe wanted to think about, so he shifted his thoughts to his wife, Katie, who was seven months pregnant. They were still trying to think of names for the baby. He liked Anne for a girl, Steven for a boy; she liked Sarah and Matthew. Maybe they'd just combine them. Steven Matthew Thorpe or Sarah Anne Thorpe. Compromise. That's how people made marriages last for fifty years, by compromising.

He was still thinking about things like baby names and compromising when he spotted something that brought his attention back to Humboldt Avenue and the misty night in Castle Bay. He'd seen movement in the shadows between the streetlights in the next block.

Something dark.

And big.

He leaned forward, straining his eyes, his hands suddenly gripping the steering wheel as if he were clinging to a ledge for dear life. He saw nothing but the street, wooden buildings, shadows. He slowed as he neared the area in which it had been, shining the cruiser's bright spotlight into the dark places between buildings. Nothing seemed out of order. There were no monsters.

Monsters? Was that what he thought he'd seen?

All of a sudden he wasn't sure exactly what he'd seen. He really hadn't observed its shape. It was just a big black shadow. A moving shadow. Finally he decided that he'd seen an optical illusion, something created by the fog and the streetlights and the movement of the cruiser's headlight beams.

Still he was glad when he was out of that block and into the next one.

Gladder yet when he was out of the neighborhood entirely.

"Control to thirteen," the woman dispatcher said over the radio. Her voice made Thorpe jump.

"Humboldt and Gold," Thorpe said into his microphone. Patrol units were required to answer with their location.

"Signal thirty-nine, ten-oh-two Santa Fe Drive." A signal thirty-nine was a disturbance, which could mean just about anything.

"Thirteen's en route. Can you give me anything about the nature of the thirty-nine?"

"Caller said scary noises."

"Scary noises?"

"Ten-four. That's what she said."

The address was only a couple of blocks away, and Thorpe was driving down the block within a minute of getting the call. He was looking for 1002 when a woman came running out, waving her arms. She was gray-haired and plump with a round face that made her look like the quintessential grandmother. Thorpe could picture her smiling as she offered up a big plate of pancakes in a magazine ad.

She wasn't smiling at the moment. "I'm . . ." She caught her breath. "I'm so glad you're here."

"Yes, ma'am. What seems to be the problem?"

"Didn't you hear it?"

"Hear what?"

"The . . . the noise."

"No, ma'am. I haven't heard anything."

"It . . . it . . . it . . . oh, dear, I don't know how to describe it." She was wringing her hands. "It was . . . well, it was terrible."

Two more people came running up, teenagers, a boy and a girl. "It was beside my house," the girl said excitedly. "It ran between it and the Romeros' house."

"What did?" Thorpe asked.

"I don't know," the boy said. "We just saw a . . . a shape. It was at least as big as a man, and it moved between the houses, toward the backyard."

Into his microphone, Thorpe said, "Seventeen, control. I'll be out in the one-thousand block of Santa Fe. Some of the neighbors say they've seen a thirty-five." Which meant a prowler.

Grabbing his extra-bright police flashlight, Thorpe got out of the car. "Let's take a look," he said.

The grandmotherly woman hurried away, and the teenagers led him toward one of the houses. It was a middle-class neighborhood, three-bedroom homes in which people like schoolteachers and policemen lived. The mist was thickening, brushing against Thorpe's flesh like the gentle touch of a ghost. The girl was quite pretty, with long blond hair and big eyes. The boy was thin, and he wore his dark hair in a stubby ponytail. As they led him between two houses, Thorpe switched on the flashlight. With his other hand he unobtru-

sively unfastened the safety snap of his holster, for a subtle
fear was spreading through him, scuttling along his nerves
like spiders. It was a warm night, and yet he had the urge to
wrap his arms around himself, rub away the goosebumps.

"Jesus," the boy said, "my mom's gonna be pi—gonna be
mad. Look what someone did to her flowers."

Thorpe studied the damage with his flashlight. A bed of
tulips ran the length of the house, and a number of them had
been flattened. Kids could have done it, of course, or a large
dog in pursuit of a cat, but Thorpe didn't think so. For one
thing the impressions in the flower bed's soft, moist soil
were too deep. He followed them. The first few he saw were
just hollows that that could have been made by almost
anything—as long as it was heavy. Then he came to one that
was clearly a footprint. Whatever had left it had three long
forward-facing toes, one that faced rearward. Like a bird.
One with talons a foot long.

"Oh . . ." the girl said, the rest of her sentence trailing off
as if her vocal cords had failed her.

"What . . . what made that?" the boy asked.

Thorpe, who had a cop's hard-nosed skepticism, imagined someone with a big wooden footprint, leaving fake
monster bird tracks as part of some elaborate hoax. He was
turning the image around in his mind, trying to decide what
he believed, when he heard something that damn near made
him wet his pants.

It was a reverberating screech, filled with hate and rage
and things Thorpe could only guess at. It was the high-
pitched shriek of a bloodthirsty predator, and at the same
time it was a low and rumbling growl filled with menace, the
desire—the need—to harm. And it seemed to come from
everywhere at once, surrounding him as if he were standing
in the mouth of whatever had made it.

No human could make such a sound.

Thorpe could not believe any animal made it either.

His mind was furiously trying to understand what it had
just heard, and it latched onto the hoax theory again,
suggesting that the noise had been electronically repro-

duced, using big speakers borrowed from someone's stereo system.

But he didn't believe it.

Something living had made that sound. But what kind of something?

The girl clutched the boy, and she was whimpering.

The boy said, "That's it. That's what we've been hearing. Do you have any idea what it is?"

Yeah, Thorpe thought, a prehistoric flying reptile. Or— and he tried to shut this thought off, but he was too late—something from hell.

Thorpe shined his light in the direction he thought the sound might have come from, seeing nothing but a hedge, a storage shed, the dim shapes of other houses. And then the sound came again. It could have been in the next yard or the next block. It so fully filled the air and overwhelmed the senses that it was impossible to tell.

"I . . ." Thorpe realized his throat was so dry he could barely speak. "I think I'd better get some backup," he said. "So we can cover the neighborhood."

When he got back to his car, he was shivering so violently he could barely hold the microphone.

Three police units spent forty-five minutes scouring the neighborhood. They found nothing. Thorpe was glad. He hadn't wanted to meet whatever had made that sound.

DAVE AND PAULA

• 1 •

Paula took her turn in the bathroom, and when she was finished she stuck her head into Dave's room and said, "Can I do anything for you before I go to bed?"

"Thanks for the offer, but I'm fine," Dave replied. "I've got to learn to do things for myself. I have no right to expect you to take care of me." He was in bed, barely visible in the darkened room.

"I want to help," Paula said. She was in her nightgown and robe; although the garb was hardly revealing, she was ill at ease standing there in her bedclothes. She instinctively pulled the robe tightly closed at the neck.

"I appreciate that, but I can't be dependent on you. I've got to help myself."

"Well, if in a moment of weakness, you feel you need a hand, just holler."

A moment's silence passed; then Dave said, "Well, I guess it is a little hard for me to cook."

"Consider me your cook and bottle washer for the duration, sir," Paula said, saluting. She was instantly embarrassed. She was rarely so . . . so what? She searched for the right word. Bold? Forward? Outspoken? Talkative? Then she realized the term was at ease. For some reason she was just at ease around this man. And the situation was hardly conducive to it. What was happening here?

Dave chuckled. "You salute like a girl."

"Big macho guy like me? You've got to be kidding." What am I doing? Paula wondered. I don't *have* conversations like this.

Again Dave laughed. "I think that's what we need around here, a little nonsense to lighten things up."

"That's me," Paula said, still surprising herself with every word. "Chief cook, bottle washer, and official standup comic." And then embarrassment washed over her in a wave that was really serious, and she was sure she blushed. She was acting like a child.

Dave said, "I'm glad you're here, Paula."

"Thank you," she said meekly and hurried down the stairs.

•2•

Paula sat on the edge of her cot, trying to figure out how she'd allowed herself to be so silly. It simply wasn't like her.

Plick!

The sound had come from across the room somewhere. Although Paula didn't find it threatening, she did find it curious, and her eyes took in the area from which it had come. She scanned the fireplace, the TV set, the magazines on the coffee table, seeing nothing that could explain the noise.

Plick! Plick! Plick!

She found herself looking at the TV set, which was off. Was there an electrical short inside, an arc snapping from one place to another? And if so, was it dangerous?

Plick-plick-plick-plick.

She stared at the TV set. It was a console, about twenty-five inches, made in the style that had been popular a few years ago, a sort of pseudo-early American, as if color TV sets had been manufactured in the time of Ben Franklin. She thought about going over to the set for a closer look, but she didn't move. Paula realized suddenly that she was afraid of the television set, so afraid of it that she wanted to dive under the covers, pull them over her head, and hide from the danger like a little girl.

Plickplickplickplick.

Abruptly something flew at her, grazing her hair and hitting the wall behind her with a loud *thwack!* The object landed on the floor near her feet. She stared at it, trembling, bewildered. And then she realized what it was. A knob from the TV set.

Plick. Plick-plick.

Another knob popped off the set and hurled itself at her head. Paula ducked, and it bounced off the wall, landed in the corner. Paula was on her feet, running for the stairs. The TV set's remote control unit flung itself at her. She deflected it with her hand, kept moving.

Then a picture leaped off the wall, sailed at her. Paula shifted direction, lost her footing, and fell, the painting grazing her shoulder. Before she could think, before she could do anything, magazines leaped from the coffee table and began flapping around like huge moths, their pages rattling and snapping angrily.

The magazines came at her.

Diving at her face.

Flapping in her hair like berserk bats.

Backing away on her hands and knees, Paula shrieked, giving vent to the terror that was spinning around within her like a hurricane. "Help!" she yelled. "Please! Help me!"

• 3 •

After Paula had stopped at the door to his room to say goodnight, Dave lay in bed, thinking about her. He was quite taken with this young woman who seemed such an odd combination of self-doubt and determination. One moment she seemed bashful; the next her wit and intelligence would shine through.

But why was he spending so much time thinking about Paula?

Why, if negotiating the stairs wasn't so difficult, would he be sorely tempted to go down to the living room, see if she was still awake, see if maybe she wanted to talk?

All sorts of feelings were gently bubbling within him, and he was unable to sort them out.

And then Paula cried out for help, her voice high-pitched and desperate, the sound rising up the stairs and slamming into his gut like a battering ram. Instantly Dave was throwing off the covers, reaching for the wheelchair.

A gasp froze in his throat.

For the chair was rolling across the room.

And there was a man in it.

Dave stared, not believing what he was seeing. The man stopped the chair, turned it so that he faced Dave. He was heavyset, dark-haired, wearing a cheap polyester suit, a paisley tie. He was bald, round-faced, double-chinned, and Dave had seen him before.

"Who are you?" Dave asked, his voice a raspy whisper.

The man merely stared at him, the hint of a smile forming on his meaty lips.

"What do you want?" Dave asked.

Still the man said nothing.

And then Dave realized where he had seen him. The man had been on the jet that crashed in St. Louis, killing all the passengers save one.

"You're dead," Dave whispered.

The man made a slight movement of his head. It could have been a nod, a shrug; Dave wasn't sure.

"You're dead," Dave whispered. "Goddammit, you're dead."

And the unspoken continuation of that statement went something like this: Dead people do not appear in bedrooms, roll around in wheelchairs, and therefore what he's doing is impossible, which means he can't be doing it.

But he was doing it, this pudgy man with the paisley tie and the double chin, looking at Dave knowingly, smugly.

"What are you doing to Paula?" Dave demanded.

The man made another one of those impossible-to-interpret head movements.

"What have you done to her?" Dave shouted, suddenly finding his voice. "Tell me!"

Paula screamed again, and Dave started crawling out of bed.

• 4 •

Paula was still on the floor, still on her hands and knees. The magazines had stopped attacking her. Now they lay scattered on the floor, torn and lifeless.

Suddenly Paula heard herself make a sound that started out as a gasp and promptly became a piercing cry of pure terror. The coffee table was up on two of its legs like a rearing horse. It leaped forward, spilling on the floor the few magazines that hadn't flown at her. Then it was still, just sitting there, an inanimate object again. Except it didn't look inanimate. It looked like a lion or a tiger or some other ferocious beast. Stalking its prey.

And the prey was Paula.

The table moved forward, almost imperceptibly. It was about ten feet from her.

Then four.

Then two.

Paula watched it, every muscle in her body taut, ready to jump out of harm's way when the table made its move. Made its move? There was something absurd about matching wits with a table. But then the table really wasn't her adversary, was it? She was up against whatever was controlling it.

The table launched itself at her head. Paula threw herself to the left, and the table slammed into the wall, bounced off, and slid across the floor on its back, one of its legs leaning inward at an angle the manufacturer had never intended. Her heart pounding, Paula watched as the table flopped like an insect on its back, making a loud *thwack-thwack!* as it bounced on the floor.

It flipped onto its side.

Then righted itself onto its three good legs.

It stood there for a moment, looking like an animal with a sticker in one of its paws, then it came at her, awkward on three legs, going *clumpity-clump-clack! Clumpity-clump-clack!*

Paula backed away from it on her hands and knees. It pursued her, cautiously but steadily, biding its time. The prey wasn't going anywhere. No need to get overanxious.

Clumpity-clump-clack!

Paula backed into something, which fell behind her with a loud crash. The fire irons. She'd knocked them over. Without taking her eyes off the table, Paula felt around with her hand until she located a poker. Against a piece of furniture it was probably a pretty puny weapon, but at least it was something.

Clumpity-clump-clack!

Paula kept backing away, unsure where she was going. If she came to a door, maybe she could get through it and close it, locking the table in the living room. The table was about ten feet from her. It maintained that distance as Paula moved away from it, holding the poker out in front of her.

Finally Paula decided that she had to stand up. She was faster and more agile on her feet than on her hands and knees. But she would have to do it slowly, for a sudden movement might cause the table to attack. Was her animal analogy right? Was it safe to treat this piece of furniture pursuing her as if it were a vicious animal? She didn't know, but the behavior of predatory animals was the closest thing in her experience, which made it the only thing she had to go on.

Clumpity-clump-clack!

Paula stopped. So did the table. Slowly, her eyes never leaving the table, Paula sat up, put one hand on the floor, started to rise.

The table leaped at her, choosing the moment when her balance was at its most precarious. Paula tried to duck, but she knew she wasn't going to be quick enough. There was a

flash of light that momentarily blinded her, and then a
crash. Paula was on the floor, uninjured, blinking her eyes in
an effort to make the afterimage from the flash go away.

Slowly her vision returned. The table was by the fireplace,
all but one of its legs broken, its top cracked. And as Paula
stared at it, she realized that whatever had made it seem
alive was gone. It was just wood now, inanimate, broken,
useless.

What had caused the flash?

Why hadn't the table hit her?

But before she could consider these questions, the TV set
came on. It was tuned to a channel with no station, the
screen filled with snow, the speaker hissing at her. And as
Paula watched, the screen began to change colors. First red,
then green, then blue, finally turning a deep black, as if the
screen were really an opening into a place of absolute
darkness.

Letters appeared in the blackness. Red, dripping letters
that spelled out the words GET OUT.

"Paula!" Dave was shouting from upstairs. "Paula! Are
you all right?"

She scrambled to her feet and rushed to the stairs,
climbing them so frantically that she nearly lost her footing
twice. Out of breath, she reached the second floor and
dashed into Dave's room, switching on the light.

He was sprawled on the floor, the wheelchair about five
feet in front of him. "Jesus," he said. "The guy . . . he just
disappeared."

"What happened?" Paula asked, kneeling beside him.

"Are you all right?" he asked, looking up at her, his eyes
full of confusion and worry.

"Yes," she said, "I'm fine. Why are you on the floor?"

"You screamed. I was trying to help you."

"But . . ." She put her hand gently on his shoulder. "But
you couldn't"

"No," he said. "But I had to try."

Paula nodded. "Let me help you up," she said.

"Just roll the chair over to me." He shook his head. "No,

206

don't do that. I'd rather not have anything to do with that chair right now. I think I'd rather be in bed."

He scooted backward until his back was against the bed; then Paula helped him up. He sat on the edge of the bed, looking tired.

"What else happened here?" Paula asked. She hesitated, then sat down beside him.

"You go first," he said. "Why did you scream?"

She told him about the objects that had hurled themselves at her, including the coffee table, and how the TV set had given her a two-word message. "Your coffee table's ruined," she said.

"You're all right," Dave said. "That's all that matters."

Paula realized suddenly that she was holding his hand. Embarrassment, hot and tingly, flooded over her. Here she was, alone in this man's house, and now she was in his bedroom, on his *bed*, holding his hand. But she didn't let go. It was a warm, comfortable feeling to hold his hand, and after what had just happened, she needed all the comfort she could get.

"Something doesn't want you here," Dave said.

"No."

"Maybe—"

"No. I can't leave."

"That's not true," Dave said. "You can. You just don't think you should."

"All right. I don't think I should."

"But you're in danger here."

"So are you."

"But this is my problem. You can run from it. I can't."

"I . . . I think it's my problem too."

"Now, listen, Paula," he said sternly. "You—"

She held up her hand to silence him. "What did you mean when you said the guy just disappeared? What happened here?"

• 5 •

Dave hesitated, reluctant to let Paula change the subject, for he was certain the danger to her was real. What happened to Ed Prawdzik proved that. But then there was no chance Paula would leave, no matter what he said. And there was a part of him that was glad. He told her about the man in the wheelchair.

"And you're certain it was someone from the plane?" Paula asked.

"Yes. He was sitting right across from me in the boarding area, waiting for the same flight."

She considered that. "This is all connected to the plane crash somehow, isn't it?"

"It all started when I got out of the hospital in St. Louis and came back here."

"So it has to be connected somehow."

"But how?" Dave asked. "What could the plane crash have to do with all . . . all this?"

"You were the only survivor."

"There have been other sole survivors," Dave said. "Surely most of them didn't acquire poltergeists—or whatever it is I've got."

"No," Paula said. "Probably not."

Dave sighed. "This isn't getting us anywhere. We're trying to understand things that can't be understood."

"No," Paula said, looking at him earnestly. "There's an explanation. We just have to find it." She tightened her grip on his hand. "We have to exchange ideas, to talk, to try to figure things out. The alternative is to wait passively for whatever happens next. If we can make sense of all this, then maybe we can fight back somehow."

"You're right," Dave said. Then he smiled. "It's funny. I see you as a quiet, basically shy person, and yet here you are with me, a stranger, ready to help me battle we know not what."

"Uh . . ." Paula said, and let the word trail off. She looked embarrassed, uncertain what to say. But she didn't let go of his hand.

Dave said, "I'm sorry if I—"

"It's . . . it's all right," Paula said. "I just don't like talking about myself."

"Why?" Dave asked gently.

Paula shook her head. "If I answer that, I'll be talking about myself."

"I'm sorry."

"Don't apologize. It's just me. It's embarrassing to talk about myself. I can understand that you'd want to. I mean, here I am, a stranger who appears out of nowhere and claims to have psychic powers. You certainly have a right to wonder about someone like that."

"Paula," he said softly, willing her eyes to meet his, "if we're going to be here together, in this thing together, then we need to know about each other."

She nodded. "You're right. I'm being silly. I'm sorry."

"Now *you're* apologizing. I'll tell you what. Let's start off this relationship with a bargain. We both agree that we can be open with each other, and nobody has to apologize. Deal?"

"Deal," she said, smiling bashfully.

Dave was still holding her hand. Their eyes met, and although Dave could see the uncertainty flickering in hers, she made no move to free her hand. Dave wanted to say something the essence of which would be, *I'm attracted to you.* But he was afraid anything he said might shatter the moment.

Finally Paula shifted her gaze away from him, gently freed her hand. Although Dave wasn't sure what was happening between him and this young woman, he sensed that he had to be cautious, for in some ways she was very fragile. And he wondered what had happened to her to make her that way.

"I . . . I'd better go," she said. "We both need to get some sleep." She stood, walked quickly to the door, looking vulnerable and quite uncertain of herself. In the doorway, she hesitated, as if wrestling with a decision. Finally she turned to face him. "Would you mind if I . . . well, never mind. It'll be okay."

"Paula, I thought we were in this together."

"We are."

"And I thought we'd sort of agreed that we have to trust each other, talk to each other."

She nodded. "I was going to ask if it would be okay if I brought the cot up here. I'm . . . I'm afraid to be alone in the living room. I mean, with all the things down there that were . . . were attacking me."

"Of course you can," he said. "I should have suggested it myself. I'm sorry I didn't."

"No apologizing," she said.

"I'm—"

"You were going to apologize for apologizing, weren't you?"

"I'm afraid I was."

She smiled at him, almost as if to say, *Caught ya, didn't I?* Then she hurried downstairs.

THREAT

• 1 •

Dave sat on the bed, his casts stretched out before him. He was thinking about Paula's entry into his life, trying to understand his feelings, when the door through which she had left slowly, quietly, closed, the latch catching with a soft *snick!*

The light went out.

Dave's body jerked as if it were recoiling from the touch of something unthinkably repulsive. Dave blinked, trying to see something, anything, but the room was as black as a photographic darkroom. He passed his hand before his eyes, seeing absolutely nothing.

The room seemed unnaturally quiet, as if it were enclosed in a soundproof bubble, cut off from the noises of passing cars and barking dogs and the other normal night sounds. A low, barely audible *errrrrrrr* broke into the silence, and he realized it was the sound of the closet door opening.

Two glowing dots appeared from the shadows surrounding the closet, hovering about two feet above the floor, their color changing from red to gold to green and then back to red.

"Get that bitch out of the house," a low, gravelly voice said.

Dave stared into the eyes that were still changing color, dumbstruck.

"Throw her out of the house," the gravelly voice said. "Make her go away. Now."

Although he was trembling and had to struggle to find his voice, Dave discovered a small reserve of courage he hadn't known was there and tapped it. "Why should I?" he asked, putting all the composure he could muster into his voice.

"If you don't, she dies," the voice said.

Suddenly the eyes—just the eyes, disembodied—leaped toward him, causing Dave to put up his arms as if to ward off a blow. The eyes swooped upward like a plane pulling out of a dive, then stopped, floating inches from his face. Staring into those eyes was like looking through two holes in the side of a furnace, peering into the red-hot flames dancing within. Dave could feel the heat. A drop of perspiration rolled down his forehead.

"Remember Ed the nurse," the voice said, and Dave thought he could feel its breath on his face, his nose wrinkling as if he'd just encountered something unspeakably fetid. And on some level he did smell something like that, even though his normal senses told him there was no odor.

"Get rid of her," the voice said. "Or it will be like Ed the nurse all over again."

And then the eyes sped away from him, shrinking into the shadows until they disappeared.

The light came back on.

The closet door was closed. The door to the hall was swinging open.

And suddenly Paula was there, hurrying over to him, her face ashen.

"Paula," Dave said. "You've got to get out of here. If you don't—"

"I heard," she said.

"Then you know—"

"No," Paula said. "It's not true."

"What's not true?"

"That I'll die."

"But—"

"I know the truth, remember? No one can lie in my presence without my knowing it."

"You mean . . ." He stopped because his brain was trying to catch up with everything he'd just heard. "You mean it's a lie . . . that they'll kill you?"

"Yes." Frowning, she sat down beside him. "Sort of."

"What do you mean, 'sort of'?"

"I mean you have to be careful about changing things around. The way it was put, it was a lie."

"If I don't make you leave, you'll die. That's how it was put."

"And those words were a lie."

Dave shook his head. "I'm getting totally confused. You mean it's safe for you to be here?"

"I don't know," Paula said. "I heard a voice telling you I'd die if you didn't get rid of me, and I knew that voice was lying to you. That's all I can say."

Dave nodded—as if it all made perfect sense.

"Dave . . ." Paula said. She was looking at him intently, her face drawn, still without color, her hands nervously fingering each other. "I was downstairs, but I heard the door close, heard voices. So I came back up as quietly as I could, listened at the door." Her eyes darted around the room for a moment, then returned to his. "Dave," she said, "what exactly were you talking to?"

"A pair of glowing eyes," he said. He told her what they'd looked like.

"I think," Paula said when he'd finished, "that whatever's supposed to happen, the reason I'm here, will happen soon."

"How do you know?"

"I . . . I just do," she said.

And then Dave realized they were holding hands again. They talked for quite a while, both of them knowing that sleep would be impossible. When Paula finally announced that she was going to get the cot, he released her reluctantly. He wanted her to sleep with him. Mainly for companionship, just so he could be within touching distance of another human being. But he made no such suggestion. Maybe the time would be right eventually. He hoped so. But he was sure Paula wasn't ready for anything like that now. It would be too much, too soon.

So when she returned with the cot, he smiled and wished her goodnight, then rolled over and closed his eyes. As soon as Paula turned out the light and got into the cot, Dave found he was aware of her breathing, her movements, the sound of the covers being adjusted. For a while, he just lay there, feeling the link between them, wondering whether she was as aware of his presence as he was of hers.

Later—he was uncertain how much later—Dave found himself staring at a moonbeam that had slipped into the room at the edge of the curtain, making a patch of yellowish light on the bed. The fog that had settled in so heavily earlier in the evening had apparently lifted. The moonlight played on his face, called him, coaxed him. *Come,* it seemed to whisper. *Come with me. See the night as only I can show it to you.*

Its pull seemed almost irresistible. Dave felt himself growing lighter, as if the shaft of pale light were one of Star Trek's tractor beams, lifting him, taking him where it would.

Come. Share the night with me.

Dave felt himself rising, riding the moonbeam, out through the window, then higher, higher, until the house was the size of a paperback book, then a matchbook, then a stamp, then a dot, then nothing at all. The lights of Castle Bay were spread out below him as if he were passing over the town in an airplane. And they, too, were shrinking, until the community vanished and Dave was in the clouds, which engulfed him with their misty arms.

And then he was falling. Falling. Faster. Faster. The earth, the town, the highways, the trees, rushing at him with the speed of a supersonic jet. At the last moment, just before Dave would have met certain disaster, he seemed to pull up, to float, and then without being certain how he got there, he was on the ground, running through the forest with a grace and ease he hadn't known possible. All his senses seemed heightened. Scents came to him in moist, pungent waves—

green growing things, needles composting themselves on the damp forest floor. And all the nuances of the forest's odors, no matter how subtle, also greeted him. A squirrel had been here, a dog there; traces of a woman's perfume still hung above a bush.

The thought of living things made him drool, and he knew the hunger was on him. Burning. Burning. Tormenting him beyond the abilities of even the most sadistic human torturer. It spread throughout his system, setting every nerve ending alight.

He caught a whiff that very nearly overwhelmed him. The hot, coppery smell of food. Salivating, the hunger like a vise squeezing his intestines, Dave dashed between the trees, the odor of food irresistible, maddening. He had to get there, had to, had to find the food, satiate the hunger, no matter that it would arise anew almost immediately.

And then he was there, at the source of the smell, and he let out a howl of pure rage, for another of his kind had been there ahead of him. The food had all been stripped from the bone, leaving not a speck, not the minutest shred. Picking up the human skeleton, he dashed it against the trees with such force that it broke apart, bones flying in all directions.

Traces of what had happened here lingered. He saw a man and a woman in a car, except the man wasn't really human. He saw him drain her blood, devour the flesh, drive away in the car. The image was almost more than he could bear, and he collapsed, clawing the soft earth, screeching out his frustration. Spotting a leg bone, he snatched it up, put it in his mouth. But it was just bone, all but tasteless, useless for satisfying his hunger. In anger he clamped his teeth down on it, biting the bone in two. He hurled the pieces into the forest.

Abruptly he smelled other food, available food. To his right. Crawling over to the spot, he began digging in the earth. His claws were efficient tools for this, and before long he had a hole two feet deep. Something moved in the bottom of the hole. He had penetrated its burrow. It squealed when he grabbed it, and then its warm, furry body

was in his mouth, its juices running out, tasting wonderful
—oh, so wonderful—and then the morsel was eaten, and
the hunger was returning, burning.

Burning.

Burning.

He got up, headed in search of more food. His nose took
him into the town, a place teeming with life. Keeping to the
shadows, he moved down alleys, slipped between buildings.
A dog poking through the contents of an overturned trash
can growled at him, staking its claim to the garbage, then
thought better of it and ran away.

The proximity of so much food was almost more than he
could bear. He sensed them in their houses, eating, talking,
sleeping, making love. He let out a cry to let the world know
of his torment. After a while, he heard voices, people talking
about the sound he'd made. There were three of them, one
armed with a gun, its deadly odor instantly obvious. Although the gun wouldn't hurt him, Dave knew that this was
a situation to avoid. The prey were to be harvested one at a
time, captured when they were alone, so as not to alarm the
others.

Though he knew this was so, the hunger made him
hesitate. Frustrated, he let out another cry of displeasure
and ran off, moving effortlessly on his taloned feet.

And the hunger burned.

Suddenly he was slipping downward, as if he were on a
playground slide, one that went on and on and on, never
reaching the ground below. But it did end abruptly, in
midair, and he was floating, surrounded by a yellow glow. It
was the moonbeam again. And then he was in his bed, the
casts weighing down his legs. Confused, he sat up, seeing
Paula on the cot, the familiar shadows of his room.

The closet door clicked, swung open. And from the depths
of the darkness that seemed to extend forever into the
enclosure, as if it had no back wall, came voices, whispering,
chanting.

You have chosen, you have chosen, they said mockingly.

His heart pounding, Dave shifted his gaze to Paula. She
was still asleep, apparently unaware of what had just

happened. The message had presumably been intended only for him.

Questions for which Dave had no answers tumbled through his head like circus acrobats gone berserk. What was it he was supposed to have chosen? Who offered him this choice? And why was he being reminded again and again that he had made it?

Nor could Dave make sense out of the dream he'd just had. In it he hadn't merely been a witness to what went on, but a participant, a . . . a what? Monster was the only word that seemed to fit. Why had he seen things through the eyes of a vile creature that had an insatiable hunger for the flesh of living things? Satisfying its need for food hadn't just been the beast's main concern; eating seemed its sole purpose for existing. Why had he been in its brain, experienced its appalling need?

Dave could still feel that hunger, the constant gut-wrenching torment of it, and he began to shiver.

What the hell's going on here? He wanted to shout that question, scream it, demand an answer. But he didn't. Dave Guthrie simply lay in bed, shivering, remembering the terrible hunger.

• 2 •

"Before I open this," Dave said the next morning, sitting at the breakfast table, "there's something I should tell you."

He was holding the *Castle Bay Crier,* still tightly rolled up and secured with a rubber band. Paula stood at the counter, making pancake batter in a stainless steel bowl. She was wearing jeans and a light-blue shirt with the tails untucked. Dressed like that, she looked like a teenager, full of innocence and enthusiasm—until she turned to face him, revealing her drawn expression and worry-filled eyes.

Fingering the rubber band that kept the *Crier*'s secrets hidden within the roll of paper, Dave said, "I had a dream . . ." He stopped, trying to find the right words. "I

217

sound like Martin Luther King, don't I? I'm afraid my dreams aren't nearly as noble as his. They're nightmares about bizarre, terrible things. The sort of dream you'd normally just sort of dismiss as craziness invented by the subconscious. And that's what I did at first. I dismissed them. Until I found out that the things I dreamed about had actually happened."

Paula had simply been standing there, mixing spoon in hand, as she listened. Now she put down the spoon and sat down at the table, facing him. "What have you dreamed?" she asked.

He told her about the fire at the commune and the man who'd died at the mobile home park. "Both things actually happened," he said. "They were in the paper."

"Has anything like this—this knowledge of events—ever happened before?" Paula asked.

Dave shook his head.

"Maybe you have psychic abilities that have been dormant until now. It would explain how you reached out to me all the way from here to Minnesota. Nothing like that's ever happened to me before. The cries for help have always been close, within a radius of a few miles."

Dave raised his hands in a gesture of helplessness. "If I have psychic abilities, they've remained latent—very latent—until now. And it started after the plane crash—when everything else began."

Paula studied him a moment, then said, "I take it you had another dream last night."

Dave told her about it, about the burning hunger that all but crushed him and that went on and on, an indescribable neverending torment.

"And you think these things might have actually happened?" Paula said. "That a woman was eaten? That monsters are roaming the city—monsters that want to devour us?"

"I'm hoping there's nothing like that in here at all," Dave said, tapping the newspaper. "But I'm afraid there will be."

He slipped the rubber band off the *Crier* and opened it,

immediately spotting a headline below the fold. It read: CITY RESIDENTS TELL OF STRANGE HAPPENINGS.

People living on the community's north side reported unusual noises last night, weird foottracks, shapes that moved through the shadows. Authorities were baffled. Chief of police Arnold Greer said someone was probably playing a practical joke, adding that the moon was full right now, which always seemed to bring out the crazies.

Dave showed the story to Paula. She said, "This could be unrelated to your dream."

"I know," he replied. "But I don't think it is."

She handed the paper back, and Dave went through the rest of it. "Nothing about any human skeletons being found," he said, "but it was in a pretty isolated spot. It might be a while before it's found."

They were both silent for a few moments; then Dave said, "What do the dreams mean? How do they tie in to all this?"

"I don't know," Paula said. "I don't know how *I* tie in."

"Why do I dream about a guy in a trailer park who dies a horrible death? Why do I dream I'm a . . . a monster of some sort? I can still feel the beast's hunger, its pain. It was . . . oh, God, it was horrible. It's like having something burning into you, causing terrible, indescribable agony that can never stop, and you have to try to satisfy it because it's driving you, controlling you." Little beads of cold perspiration had broken out on Dave's forehead. One trickled down his cheek, and he shivered.

"I wish I could explain it," Paula said. "But I'm as confused as you are."

"So all we can do is wait," Dave said.

"Yes," Paula said. "But it won't be long now. I can feel it . . . coming. I can feel that it's near—the end of all this."

Again they fell silent.

"This ability of yours to tell the truth," Dave asked, breaking the silence. "How does it work?"

"I just know," Paula said.

"But *how* do you know?"

"A lie sounds different. You know how a record sounds

when a turntable's not going at exactly the right speed? You know how a radio will get a rattly sound when it's off the station? You know how tones sound when they don't blend properly with each other? It's like all of those things rolled into one. It's unpleasant to listen to. It makes you want to cringe, like when somebody scrapes his nails across a blackboard."

"How does the truth sound?"

"Normal. Clear. But . . ." She paused, thinking. "Well, there are some truths that have an extra-special clarity about them. I don't know whether this will make any sense, but they have a sort of ringing quality to them, like the sound you get when you tap a piece of fine crystal with your fingernail. Does that make any sense?"

"Yes . . . well, I think so. What kinds of things have this quality to the way they sound?"

"Special thoughts," she said. "An honestly expressed desire to help. An honestly expressed feeling."

"Like love?"

Paula had been looking at him, but suddenly she dropped her eyes to her plate, and began cutting into her pancakes. Dave thought she'd just given him some insight into something, but he wasn't sure what. She said, "Yes, truly felt love would have that sound."

"It must be wonderful to hear that," Dave said.

"Yes," Paula replied, still not looking at him. "But you have to hear the other part too."

"The lies?"

"Yes. And there are many more of them."

"And that bothers you."

"Sometimes."

"But no one can ever deceive you. You'll never be tripped up by a used-car salesman or rip-off artists—or anyone."

"No," Paula said, but she didn't seem too happy about it.

Dave hesitated, uncertain whether to go ahead with what he had in mind. Finally he said, "Do you mind if I try something?"

"What?"

"It's sort of a test."

"Of my abilities?"

"Yes. I . . . I just want to see how it works."

"Not that you don't believe me."

"I do believe you, Paula. I do. I, well, I just want to see how it works."

She looked up at him, nodded. And Dave remembered that he could never lie to her, not and get away with it. She knew whether he was telling the truth.

"Go ahead," Paula said.

Dave took a moment to collect his thoughts, then said, "When I was a boy, my best friend was Joe Worthington. When I was a boy, my best friend was Harry Smith. When I was a boy, my best friend was Leo McQueen."

"Leo McQueen was your best friend. The other two were lies."

"Yes," Dave said. "Do you mind if I try again?"

"Go ahead." Paula took a bite of her pancakes.

"I lost my virginity to a girl named Terry. I lost my virginity to a girl named Alice. I lost my virginity to a girl named Laurie."

Paula looked a little embarrassed.

"I'm sorry," Dave said. "Maybe I should have picked another subject."

"It's all right," Paula said. "All three were lies."

"Her real name was—"

"I thought a gentleman wasn't supposed to tell."

"Grace wouldn't mind."

"How can you be so sure?"

"She went off to college and got a bunch of high-powered degrees and became a sex therapist."

Paula laughed. "Really?"

"I thought you could tell."

She nodded, chuckled. "It's a true story."

"There must have been times," Dave said gently, "when you would rather not have known the truth."

"There are times," she said after a moment's hesitation, "when knowing the truth can be painful." She paused again, then added, "But in the final analysis, it's better to know, isn't it?"

Dave wasn't sure whether she had directed the question to him or to herself. He decided to drop the subject, because the smile that had accompanied Paula's laugh a moment ago had given way to a look of melancholy. He was venturing into sensitive territory, and he really had no right to go there.

Chunk! A hunk of memory dropped into his consciousness like a door bolt being slapped home. He was in a dark place. Drifting along. Passing shapes he was unable to make out. *Choose*, a chorus of voices chanted. *Choose, choose, choose.* . . .

And then he saw the face, a huge and hideous countenance with glowing red eyes, vicious teeth, running sores. He was drifting toward it on unseen, unfelt currents, feeling a lot like the entree in a nightmarish fast-food operation. Just call Domino's Humans. We'll float one over to you within twenty minutes, or your human will be free.

The mouth opened.

Choose, choose, choose. . . .

And Dave chose. . . .

Life.

Life? The word hung there as Dave Guthrie returned from that dark and terrible place he had just visited.

Life.

He felt he'd been in that dark place—really been there. And yet there was a dreamlike quality about it that denied its reality. As if he had been there without being there. It made no sense. None. And yet he couldn't stop feeling that he had visited that nightmarish place. And that while there he had been called upon to make a momentous decision.

He'd chosen life.

Over death?

"Dave . . ." Paula was looking at him worriedly. "Is everything . . . all right? You look so . . . so troubled, withdrawn."

"I had a . . . I don't know what to call it. It seems real, like a memory, but I don't know how it could be." He told her about it.

"Did I make a choice?" Dave asked. "An evil choice?"

Paula shook her head. "I don't know. Would you make an evil choice?"

"That's the question I've been asking myself," Dave said.

• 3 •

Later that day, Paula went to the grocery store, getting her first daylight look at Castle Bay. She liked the town, liked the view of the ocean, the rustic buildings, the rocky hillsides that rose steeply at the community's western edge. Dave told her that you could see a castle in the rocks, but that it was hard to spot unless you were out in the bay. As she drove, Paula kept looking at it, but she saw nothing except gray stone dotted with the sparse vegetation that was able to cling to it.

Paula wasn't used to being around the ocean. Every time she stopped the car, she would hear the shushing of the waves. Every breath of air was filled with moisture and salt and seaweed. Gulls were everywhere. Perhaps local people took these things for granted, but to Paula they were still a marvel.

The grocery store was on Humboldt Avenue, the main drag. Paula bought a pot roast, chicken, pork chops, ground beef, potatoes, and a variety of green vegetables. Though not a gourmet like Ed Prawdzik, she could cook up a midwestern Sunday sit-down dinner with the best of them. As she wheeled her cart toward the checkout area, it occurred to her that she might be trying to impress Dave with her cooking. Am not, she thought. No way. But then the ability to delude herself had never been one of her strong points. She even knew when *she* was lying to herself.

Paula took a different route back to Dave's place, just for a change of scenery. The whole town had a weathered look about it, but not a neglected one. The weathered appearance seemed cultivated, an effort to make the town quaint. Paula didn't mind. The place was peaceful and charming, and she envied those who were able to live here.

Perhaps they need another schoolteacher.

She instantly pushed the notion from her mind. It was silly to think about the future when she hadn't even accomplished whatever she was brought here to do. There was much uncertainty ahead. And probably danger.

But she didn't want to think about that, either.

She turned onto Pacific Road, which led to Dave's house, pushed her speed up to forty-five, which was the limit. Paula believed in obeying traffic laws. She never jumped lights, failed to signal, or made rolling stops. If the speed limit was forty-five she was careful not to let the speedometer creep up to forty-six or forty-seven.

But the car was going forty-eight.

Then fifty.

Paula took her foot off the gas.

The car was going fifty-five.

She stepped on the brake, pressed lightly, then harder.

The speedometer said sixty. Sixty-five. Seventy. And the brakes had no effect. Her heart racing, Paula forgot about the brakes and just steered. The road was fairly straight, with only gentle turns. Houses and mailboxes flew past in a blur. Ahead was another car, going about forty, a red sporty model of some sort. Paula pulled out to pass it, and she was going nearly eighty. The driver honked his irritation at her recklessness.

Ahead was an oncoming van, a curve to the left. Paula gripped the wheel; all she could do was steer the car, hope for the best. She made it around the curve, the van whooshing past her in a heartbeat. She turned the key to the off position, but the engine kept running. She shifted to neutral, but the car kept accelerating. She tried the brakes again. They still had no effect. She pulled on the emergency brake. It didn't work either.

Ahead was a sharper curve, too sharp to take at ninety.

And the windshield turned black, impenetrable to light.

Paula felt the car swerve to the right, the steering wheel

pulling out of her grasp. Suddenly the wheel spun to the left, and she heard the screeching of tires. Then she was tossed upward, the seatbelt biting into her shoulder as it held her down.

• 4 •

Dave Guthrie had positioned his wheelchair in the middle of the living room, where he was sitting and thinking. He should have been in the studio working, but he had too much on his mind to work. Too many things had happened. He felt as if he'd stepped into an unbelievably bizarre dimension, where the whole basis of science and reason were upside down, where nothing was what it seemed.

And he was unable to stop thinking about the vision—recollection—he'd had earlier. A dark place. Shapes. Floating. A hideous face. Chanting.

Choose, choose, choose. . . .

Again he was overwhelmed by the certainty that he had indeed chosen something, agreed to something. Life. But in choosing life, what had he actually done? That was the sixty-four-thousand dollar question, wasn't it? He imagined himself as a contestant on a macabre version of "Jeopardy," Alex Trebec having been replaced by the hideous face, the set dark, Dave flanked on both sides by the shadowy shapes of the other contestants.

Choose, says the face.

And Dave sees that all the categories on the board are the same: "Life or Death."

Choose, says the face.

And Dave picks life.

He shook his head. The game show analogy wasn't helping. In fact, it was probably the only thing he could say with certainty about all this. It was sure as hell no game show.

The agency in Eureka had called this morning to inform

him that there was no replacement available for Ed Prawdzik. He told them Ed's Bronco was still here, parked in the drive, and the woman at the agency told him just to hang on to it until someone figured out what to do with it. Dave called the hospital again, learning only that Ed was in the intensive care unit. He'd finally pried out of the nurse he'd spoken to that Ed's condition was "guarded," whatever the hell that meant. The level of secrecy the place maintained was enough to make the CIA envious.

He was thinking about Paula, wondering where she was, when he heard her car pull into the driveway. He heard her footfalls on the wooden steps leading up to the house; then the front door opened, and Paula stepped inside.

"I think you forgot the groceries," he said. And then he realized how pale she was, how she looked on the verge of fainting. "Paula," he said, "what happened? Are you all right?"

She walked slowly over to him. "I was almost killed," she said.

"Paula, what—"

"My car was gaining speed. Nothing would slow it down. Not the brakes, not turning off the key, nothing. It just kept going faster."

"Are you hurt? Are—"

"The windshield went black, as if someone had plastered dark construction paper over it. I couldn't see."

Dave took her hand. She was shaking. "Are you okay? Are you hurt?"

"Not even my car was hurt. The wheel swung by itself, first right, then left. I . . . I was lucky. Really lucky. The car went off the road and into an area with a lot of sand dunes, just down the road. I . . . I flew up in the air, bounced down, flew up, bounced down. I'd have hit my head on the roof I don't know how many times if the seatbelt hadn't stopped me."

"Paula . . ." He didn't know what to say. If he wasn't in the damned chair, he could take her in his arms, comfort her. He felt helpless.

"The sand is loose, deep. It slowly stopped the car, safely.

A guy came by in a pickup. He had a CB, and he called a wrecker for me. I was stuck in the sand."

"Did the wrecker driver say what went wrong with your car?"

"No. He tried it, and everything worked okay. I think he thought I was crazy, some nutty woman who imagined things and couldn't handle a car very well. Anyway, he convinced me the car was safe; so I drove it. It wasn't far, so he followed me, just in case, and . . . and . . . and here I am." Her lower lip quivered, and then tears were streaming down her cheeks.

Dave reached for her, and she dropped to her knees, putting herself on his level, making it possible for him to put his arms around her. She rested her head against his chest and wept, her body shaking.

"It's okay," he said. "You got through it. You're here now. And you're not hurt."

"I . . . I was so scared," she sobbed.

"But you made it. You were stronger than they were."

"I didn't do anything but ride along. I was lucky."

"You're safe now."

"They want me to go away. They want it badly."

Dave hesitated, then said, "Are you going?"

"No."

"Paula—"

"No," she said, cutting him off. "I don't want to see you hurt. I have to stay. You need me."

She looked up, her eyes finding him. There was both terror and determination in them. "I'm supposed to be here," she said softly. "I have to be here."

"But—"

"When the voice in your room said I'd die, it was a lie."

"Death isn't the only bad thing that can happen to you," Dave said. Some things were worse than death, he thought, but he didn't say it.

"Please, Dave, I have to stay. You know I do."

"Paula—"

"No, don't Paula me."

"Are you sure you're doing the right thing?" he asked.

"I'm sure," Paula said in a voice that made her sound like a frightened little girl. And maybe that's what she was. There was certainly enough to be afraid of. The closet was full of bogeymen, the world full of monsters.

Dave squeezed her gently. He liked the feel of her warm body pressed against his. And it wasn't just because she was an attractive woman. He liked *her*. Personally. And he realized he was glad that she had come to him for comforting. He would be content to hold her, tell her it was all right forever if need be.

Suddenly she pushed away from him. "I'm sorry," she said.

Paula started to rise, but Dave took her hand, gently pulled her to him. For a moment she hesitated, her face so close to his that it was a blur, and then she let her lips meet his. For Dave it was electric, as if current was wiggling and dancing and sparking through his veins, making him tingly all over. Paula's kiss was soft and warm, and it lingered, making him feel like a bowl of melting ice cream, slowly softening, turning into a pliable custardy mass.

Abruptly Paula pulled away again. She studied him, looking uncertain, bewildered. Then she smiled and embraced him again.

CONFRONTATION

• 1 •

Officer Patrick Thorpe drove along Pacific Road, his cruiser's headlights poking into the foggy darkness. It was nice in through here, houses right on the ocean, the steady *sssssssss* of the waves to lull you to sleep at night. And the homes in this area weren't too big, which meant they were affordable. True, they were more expensive than similar homes a block or two farther from the Pacific, but they were still within reach of an ordinary working stiff if he had a working wife.

Which Thorpe didn't.

Maybe, after the baby was old enough for day care . . .

Well, it was just something he and Katie would have to talk out. They weren't going to rent forever, and maybe when the time came to buy, they could manage a small house on Pacific Road, a place by the ocean. In any case it was something to dream about, and what good was life if you didn't dream?

Thorpe spotted something off to the side of the road that set an icy hunk of terror to bobbing in his belly like a harbor buoy. It's a road kill, he told himself. Somebody's pet got hit by a car. Forget about it, he urged himself. Keep on going.

But he didn't take that advice.

He had to know for sure.

So Thorpe pulled to a stop and got out with his powerful police flashlight. The lump of fur had been a cat, a large white tom. Now it was quite dead, its body mangled and shredded. Pieces had been bitten from it. And it was dry, as if all the blood had been sucked from it. He moved the carcass with his foot. There was no red stain beneath it.

Jesus, he thought, the iciness suddenly radiating out from his gut, making him shiver.

It was like this all over town. Animals partially eaten, drained of blood. And then there was Stan Davies's Doberman pinscher, a dog so fierce and fearless no one would go near it. Something had cleaned every last speck of meat from it—the organs, everything—leaving nothing but shiny white bone. On its skull were teeth marks. Anything that could do that to that Doberman had to be one tough son of a bitch. And it wasn't just pets. Thorpe had found the carcasses of mice and raccoons and skunks and squirrels. And rats. What the hell would eat a rat? Yuk!

And he'd found more of them along Pacific Road than anywhere else in town.

Maybe he didn't want to live in this area after all.

Then he thought about the weird things that were happening all through Castle Bay—the guy getting ripped apart at the trailer park, for instance—and he wondered whether he wanted to live in this *town* anymore. Maybe it wasn't such a good place to raise the baby that Katie would be giving birth to in a couple of months. Maybe he should apply to Eureka or San Francisco. Or somewhere in Maine, which was as far from Castle Bay as you could get.

He got back into the car, not knowing how serious he was about getting out of town, but knowing for sure that something wasn't right. A chill passed through him, a long slow-moving, goose-bump-raising iciness that left him so cold he turned on the cruiser's heater, with the blower on high.

By the end of his shift he still hadn't warmed up.

•2•

In bed that night, Dave Guthrie dreamed.

He was in the jetliner, knowing it was going to crash. He tried to warn the other passengers. "Lisssssss . . ." His voice was muffled. His lips seemed leaden, barely able to move.

"Lissssssss . . ." Listen to me. Three words. Simple. Why couldn't he say them?

"Lissssssss . . ."

It was impossible. He turned to the man sitting next to him, a thin guy in a blue pinstriped suit. Knowing no words would come out, Dave tried to communicate with him in sign language, like playing charades. He tapped the guy on the arm, waved his hands.

The guy didn't look up from the magazine he was reading.

Dave tried again, tapping his arm harder this time. Still no response. Dave shook him. "Heyyyyyyy . . ."

The guy just kept on reading.

Dave yanked the magazine out of his hands, threw it into the aisle.

The guy picked up a pamphlet from the seatback in front of him, one of those promotional things the airliners always put there. Dave threw that away too. The guy started reading the card that told about how to use the oxygen if the cabin became depressurized. Dave slapped it away, then emptied out the seatback entirely, tossing the stuff into the aisle. No one seemed to notice.

The guy in the blue suit tilted his seat back and went to sleep.

The plane was going to crash in St. Louis, and Dave was unable to do a thing to prevent it. He could warn neither the pilot nor the stewardess, nor even the guy in the blue suit. The plane would crash, and the people would die.

Dave waited, and it happened.

The passengers screamed.

And then their cries were drowned out by the sound of metal being ripped apart.

Dave felt himself thrown into the air. He heard an explosion, saw a ball of flames below him, and then he was tumbling, plummeting downward. Falling. Falling.

He was in the dark place.

Choose, the voices chanted.

Behind him was a pinpoint of light. He wanted that light, and he struggled to move himself in that direction, but there was nothing here to push against. He was surrounded on all sides by nothing. And ahead was a blackness deeper than he had ever imagined. He stared into it and was filled with dread. He didn't want to go to that place. It was a bad place. He wanted the light. The light was his world, the place he belonged to, a place of sunshine and trees and the perfume of flowers. Entering the darkness meant slipping into nothingness, a total nothingness, beyond his comprehension.

You don't have to go, a voice seemed to say. *The choice is yours.*

"But what do I do?" Dave pleaded.

You choose.

"Choose what?"

Life.

"I choose life. I do, I do, I do."

Then the bargain is struck.

Dave was suddenly awake, knowing it had been a dream, but unable to shake the feeling that it had also been more than that. Not a memory exactly, but something whose reality had been distorted by his sleeping brain. Expressed symbolically, as Freud would say. The dream plane crash had been different from the actual one. Like his being in a window seat instead of sandwiched between two other passengers—not to mention his being invisible. So the other part had to be off as well, the weird after-the-crash part. But what had happened? What was the bargain he supposedly struck? With whom did he make it?

Or was the whole thing nonsense? He'd had a tough time lately knowing what was nonsense and what wasn't. The unbelievable had become the commonplace.

Dave heard a noise, a shuffling sound, and he opened his eyes.

The room was full of people.

He blinked, telling himself he was still dreaming, but he didn't feel as though he was asleep. And the people looked real, looked—

Dave broke the thought off because he'd just recognized a face. It was the freckled stewardess from that ill-fated flight. He saw other familiar faces. The fat guy in the cheap polyester suit, the girl with shiny black hair that hung to her waist, a boy who'd been wearing a jacket and tie and looking proud of himself to be dressed so nicely and traveling unsupervised on a jetliner, just like a grown-up. Dave looked into brown eyes and green eyes and blue eyes and gray eyes, at faces male and female, old and young, innocent and world-weary. They looked back at him but seemed unaware of him. They milled around, as if lost. And as Dave stared, dumbstruck, he saw something else in those faces, a deep loneliness, a sadness that seemed to overwhelm all other emotions, all other concerns.

Finding his voice, Dave said, "What do you want?"

They didn't hear him. Just like in the dream. I'm still dreaming, Dave thought. I have to be.

But he only half believed it.

Shifting his gaze to the right, he saw Paula, asleep on her cot, surrounded by the dead and totally unaware of it. "Paula," he said, "Paula." He wanted her to wake up and tell him whether she saw the same thing he did, but she continued to sleep, lost in her own dreams.

"You're dead," Dave said to the people in the room. "You're apparitions. You're not here."

They milled about, ignoring him.

"Look at me!" Dave shouted.

And they did. All of them slowly turning to face him, their eyes fixing on his. And Dave noticed a change in their expressions. Gone was the look of loneliness and purpose-lessness. It had been replaced by a grim, burning anger.

They closed in around the bed, forming a wall of people on all sides.

"You cheated," a voice accused. It took Dave a moment to locate the speaker; it was the thin man in the blue pinstriped suit.

"You cheated," the man said again.

"How?" Dave asked. "How did I cheat?"

"You made a bargain. You got out of it."

"Out of what?"

"Out of being with us," said the man in the blue suit.

"We've come for you," a woman said.

"Come for you," said a chorus of voices. "Come for you. Come for you."

"No," Dave said. "I won't go."

"We've come for you," a young voice said. The boy who'd been so proud to be traveling by himself, like a grown-up.

Hands reached for Dave.

He pulled the covers over his head, like a child hiding from the monster that lived beneath the bed. Hands pulled at them, yanked, and Dave held the covers with a death grip.

"You're ours," voices said. "You have to join us."

The covers were tugged this way and that. Hands touched him through the sheets, poked at him, tried to grab him. And still Dave held onto the covers with every ounce of strength he possessed.

"Dave!"

"No," he said. "No. Go away."

"Dave, please." It was Paula, and there was only one set of hands trying to pull back the covers now. Still, fearing a trick, Dave refused to let go.

"Dave, are you all right? I heard you screaming. I . . . I think you're having a nightmare."

Finally he eased the covers off his head enough to see into the room. The people were gone. Only Paula was there now, looking down at him with worry-filled eyes. "Oh, thank God," he said.

For several moments, she just looked down at him; then she lifted the covers and slipped in beside him. He held her, shivering, absorbing her warmth.

•3•

At 3:17 a.m. a man staggered into the emergency room at Castle Bay Community Hospital and collapsed. He was suffering from loss of blood and shock. His left arm was missing.

On closer examination, doctors discovered that it had been bitten off.

•4•

Although he didn't recall it in the morning, Dave Guthrie dreamed he was a six-legged creature with a mouth like a shark. He dreamed that he bit off a man's arm.

•5•

"I've never slept in the same bed with a man before," Paula said.

"But, as they used to say in fifties movies, nothing happened." Dave had always considered such a notion ridiculous. How could a man and woman find themselves in bed together for the first time and not make love? Now he had done it. But then terror tended to quell the sex urge.

As did the nagging fear that he had done something awful.

Dave and Paula were sitting at the kitchen table, drinking coffee. Putting down his cup, Dave said, "Is it possible to make a pact with the . . . the supernatural?"

"I've heard of making one with the devil."

Dave winced. He'd avoided using that word. "Is it possible?"

"I don't know. Do you think you've made one?"

He told her of his dream—being an invisible passenger on the ill-fated plane, then finding his bedroom full of those who'd died in the crash. And he told her about their accusations. "Did I do something bad?" he asked.

"Like what?"

He hesitated, reluctant to say out loud what he'd been thinking. "Could . . . could I have bargained the lives of the other passengers for my own?"

"You wouldn't do that." Paula said it with such confidence it cheered him for a moment. But then his doubts returned.

He said, "But is it possible?"

"I don't know. What exactly do you think happened?" She picked up her coffee cup, staring at him over the rim, her brow wrinkling. After a moment she put down the coffee without drinking any.

"I . . . I think I should have been . . . I should have died."

"Died?" Paula looked stunned. "But—"

"I might have been dead, Paula. I might have been down in some other dimension or wherever you go when you die. And I think I was offered a bargain. Let them have the others, and I could go back. I could live."

Paula shook her head. "They weren't yours to give."

"Not legitimately, but maybe I did it anyway."

"I don't think that would work. You can't bargain with what you don't have. It would be like selling the Golden Gate Bridge. Who'd buy it?"

"You're saying the forces of evil aren't that stupid."

"If they are, the forces of good don't have much to worry about." Paula frowned, searched his face. "Dave . . . is that what you think you did? Do you believe you made some kind of a pact with evil?"

"I think I made a bargain with someone."

"And you see it as a dark, sinister thing."

"The images are all dark, frightening." He smiled grimly. "Not a halo in sight."

Paula put her hand on his. "Dave," she said, looking into his eyes, "will you believe me if I tell you something? You wouldn't make a bargain like that. I know you wouldn't. I know it for certain."

"Paula, you've known me less than a week."

"But I know things others don't. Like when you're telling the truth. It speeds up the process quite a lot."

"You don't know me that well, Paula. Not well enough to say what I'd do facing death—not if my . . . my soul was already in the hands of whatever lives over there on the other side. *I* don't know myself that well."

"You're basically too good to do what you think you've done," she said. "It's a quality that's you, to your core, and it goes wherever you go—even into another life."

"Something happened after the plane crash."

"But we don't know what."

"Apparently I struck a bargain." And then an idea hit him, crashing down on him like a collapsing wall. "And," he said excitedly, "what's been done can be undone."

"But . . . how?" Paula asked, looking confused.

Backing his chair away from the table, Dave said, "Let's go into the living room."

"Why? What's there?"

"It's more or less the center of the house."

"Why is that important?"

"It seems like the right place."

"To do what?" Paula asked, following behind him as he wheeled himself out of the kitchen.

"To terminate an agreement."

· 6 ·

"Whoever I made this agreement with," Dave said, "I demand to speak to you."

They were in the living room, Paula standing beside his chair. She said, "Dave, I don't understand—"

"Stick with me," he said, cutting her off. "I don't even know whether this will work." Raising his voice, Dave said,

"Show yourself, or I renounce any agreement I made with you."

The room remained silent. Suddenly, Dave felt foolish. Here he was parked in the middle of the living room, talking to the walls and furniture.

Who're you speaking to, fellow? Oh, the monsters, huh? Oh, I see, they're invisible. Now I understand. You just stay here, guy, while I phone some nice people who will take you to a place where you can't hurt yourself.

Dave chased these thoughts from his mind. If this failed, it had to do so on its own merits, not because he'd talked himself out of it. "Present yourself, or the bargain's off!" Dave shouted.

The room was quiet. Outside the day was quiet. The only sound was the slow thudding of Dave's heart, like the measured beat of the drummer as the condemned is led to the spot where the headsman's ax will fall.

"Then I renounce any agreement I made with you," he said.

Before him the room shimmered. Paula grabbed his hand.

The walls were wiggling as if they were made of snakes imprisoned just below the paint.

A low hiss filled the air, as if the snakes had simultaneously begun to spit their venom, and a putrid stench filled the room. Paula made a retching noise, but managed to hold down the contents of her stomach.

A black spot grew out of the air, expanded into a billowing mass about five feet wide, then simply hung there, undulating, sending out wispy tentacles that dissolved once they'd reached a length of four feet or so.

"What do you want?" a raspy voice asked. It was an aged and dry sound, as dusty and brittle as leaves that had blown into a crypt over the years to lay as forgotten as the tomb's primary occupants.

Dave struggled to find his voice. "I . . . I want you to show yourself," he said. "I want to know who I struck a bargain with."

The black spot's undulations grew more rapid, like a heart beating insanely. Wisps were tossed off, dissolving as they were thrown into the room. The blackness lowered itself to the floor, where it shot out new wisps, but these didn't disappear. They formed long black limbs. A pair of red eyes appeared in the blackness, which had become a squishy-looking glob now, as if it were made of rancid pudding. New limbs shot out as the eyes began to glow. Suddenly the transformation—if that was the right term—was complete, and Dave was looking at a monster. Paula gasped. Dave could feel her trembling.

The thing before them went beyond the childhood bogey-man that lurked in the shadows, beyond nightmares. Beyond scary movies and horror novels, for those things were entertainments, frights for the tingles they provided, terrors engaged in for the sheer pleasure of getting scared.

There was nothing entertaining about what Dave saw now. Childhood's monster in the shadows was sissy by comparison. This was a gelatinous mess that kept growing limbs of various sorts only to suck them back a moment later. A clawed arm appeared, vanished. A few inches away from that spot, an octopuslike tentacle appeared, waving its suckers, and then it, too, was gone. And its eyes kept changing locations, moving higher, lower, farther apart, closer together. And the number of eyes changed, becoming three, then five, then hundreds, as if the creature's entire mass was covered with them. A moment later, it had only two eyes again, glowing red orbs the color of flames.

As Dave watched, it created hundreds of black ropey limbs around its bottom, which frantically whipped and squirmed like roots desperately trying to work their way into the floor. Like the Jell-O monster, this creature had translucent sides. Beneath its skin odd shapes were constantly moving, aligning themselves in curves and spirals and wiggly lines.

"Here I am," it said. "How do you like me?"

Dave was at a loss for words. His blood pounded in his ears, as if it were surging through him in a flash flood. Every internal warning system he possessed was screaming at him: *Run! Run! Run!*

"I thought you wanted to talk," the creature said.

"What . . . what are you?" Dave asked.

"What does it matter what you call us?" the monster answered.

"Did I make an agreement with you?"

"Of course you did. You already know that."

"Tell me the terms."

"Send the bitch away," the monster bellowed. "You were warned to get rid of her. This agreement is private, just between us."

"No," Dave said. "she stays."

The creature's substance began swirling, rising tornado-like above the floor, its whirling black eddies alive with clawing arms and legs. "This conversation is over."

"Then . . ." Dave's throat went dry, and he started again. "Then our agreement is terminated."

The root-like appendages appeared again at the creature's bottom, writhing, snapping like whips. Dave rolled his chair backward. Paula moved with him.

"You," the beast hissed, "you are nothing more than a speck of insect dung in a swamp. You will respect your agreement."

The creature abruptly grew more eyes, hundreds of them, then thousands, as if its flesh were made of them. They began to move like the lights on a theater marquee. A tentacle shot out of the monster's side, whipping through the air with a hiss, hitting Dave's face with a crack. His cheek exploded in pain as the tentacle waved about a foot from his nose. Suddenly it pulled back, and Dave thought it was going to strike him again. He put up his arm to block it, but nothing happened. Then he heard Paula scream.

The tentacle had wrapped itself around her throat. She fought with it, pounding on it with her hands, but she was unable to faze it. The tentacle lifted her off the floor. Her face was turning blue, her attempts to save herself feeble.

Powerless, unable to do anything, Dave heard himself scream. It was a distant sound, a weak, helpless, choked cry that could have come from the next house or even the next block. Then he was rolling forward, his arms putting every bit of strength he could find into moving the chair. He rolled forward, faster, his hands desperately working the wheels, pushing, pushing.

And he plowed into the monster, his casts hitting its side first. Something inside Dave cringed, knowing that a burst of pain from his mending legs was coming, but the agony never arrived.

For his feet had passed right through the side of the creature. For an instant, he simply sat there, transfixed. His feet were a good ten inches into the monster, as if he'd pushed them into a massive puddle of jelly.

Paula made a choking noise, a weak and pitiful sound. Dave pulled back on the wheels of the chair, and his feet came out of the creature as easily as they'd come out of a patch of fog. He spun the chair around, planning to do something—anything—to help Paula.

She was still being strangled by the tentacle. As he watched, it spun her like a top, wrapping more of itself around her, until she looked like a spiral of black rope. Dave grabbed the wheels of his chair, shoved them forward. He was going to grab the tentacle.

But before he got there, the tentacle twitched, and then blue sparks were flying from it, filling the room with the intense brightness of an arc welder. Unable to see, Dave shielded his eyes. The world was blue and yellow and white, sparks crackling and popping and sputtering, flying in all directions, leaving smoky trails to mark their flight paths.

Then a new sound filled the air, a noise that made Dave clasp his hands over his ears. From the walls, the floor, the foundation—if not from below the foundation, from the heart of the earth—came a bellow that shook the house.

Abruptly it was quiet.

And the sparks were gone as well.

The room was hazy with smoke. As it cleared, Dave saw Paula. She was sitting on the floor, staring at him, her eyes wide with terror and confusion. Quickly surveying the room, Dave saw no sign of the monster. He rolled his chair toward Paula, and panic appeared on her face. For a second, Dave thought she was going to scramble away from him in fear.

"Paula?" he said uncertainly.

"No," she said, shaking her head. "No, no, no."

"Paula, are you all right?"

He reached toward her, and she shrank away from him.

"Paula . . . why are you afraid of me?"

For a long moment, she just stared at him, an unreadable mixture of intense emotions filling her eyes. Finally she said, "At first, when you began talking to . . . to whatever you were talking to, what did you see?"

"The same thing you did. The monster."

"Describe it."

"It was a . . . a big glob of jelly. Arms and tentacles kept sprouting, then disappearing. It had eyes that constantly changed in number. At one point there must have been a hundred of them."

"And you talked with it."

"Of course I talked with it. You were right here."

She shook her head. "There was nothing there."

"Paula, what are you talking about?"

"There was nothing there. Not then."

"There was. It grabbed you, tried to strangle you."

"Dave, you were talking with yourself."

"What do you mean, I was talking with myself?"

"Dave, you were holding both parts of that conversation. There were two different voices, but they both came from you."

"But . . . but it attacked you. Are you going to tell me nothing happened to you?"

"That happened afterward."

"After I talked with it?"

"Yes. And after you disappeared."

Dave stared at her, his thoughts swirling. He had held a conversation with himself, then disappeared? A big cold, clammy hunk of fear was rapidly developing in his gut. He suspected it was a lot like the feeling that came over the werewolf after waking in the morning to find blood under his nails, a coppery taste in his mouth, and big, dog-like footprints leading up to the bed but not away from it.

"I . . . I disappeared?" Dave said, stunned.

"And at the same moment, the monster appeared."

"Oh, Jesus."

"It attacked me, and I thought it was going to . . . to kill me. But then there were these blue sparks . . ." Her words trailed off.

"You mean I wasn't there, trying to help as best I could?"

Paula shook her head.

"I thought I was."

Paula said nothing.

"Stay away from me," Dave said suddenly. "It's not safe for you to be around me. I'm . . . you can't trust me."

Paula searched his face. "I don't think that's true," she said.

"Paula . . ." He hesitated, not wanting to say it. "Paula, don't you see? If I was holding this conversation with myself, and then I vanished just as the monster appeared, it means I *am* the monster."

Paula was still on the floor, a few feet from Dave. She scooted over beside him, put her hand on his arm. "You're not evil, Dave. But the monster was. I could feel the evil coming off it in waves. It's a cold, wet feeling, like a chilly fog, and it makes your skin crawl. I don't feel that around you. In fact, you're just the opposite. Warm, comforting feelings come from you."

"Nice warm feelings can be deceiving."

"Not to me."

"Paula, you told me you recognized the truth when you heard it and knew when people needed help. You didn't say anything about these other things—like sensing waves of evil."

"My abilities are getting stronger. I think there are probably other things that I can do now that I couldn't do before."

Dave wasn't listening. He was seeing a ropey tentacle wrapping itself around Paula, trying to squeeze the life out of her. And he was trying to come to terms with the knowledge that the unspeakable creature from which the tentacle had sprung could, in some bizarre, incomprehensible way, be him. If so, he was a Doctor Jekyll whose nasty side had been carried to proportions so monstrous they had never even been dreamed of by Robert Louis Stevenson. Mr. Hyde, after all, was no more evil than one of today's drug dealers, while Dave Guthrie's alternate personality was something that could probably terrify the inhabitants of hell.

A shiver hit him, then another. And another. Before long he was a quivering mass of goosebumps.

Paula got a blanket, put it around him, but he continued to shiver. "I'm n-n-n-not cold," he said. "I'm afraid. Afraid of what I've become."

"I'm going to make you something warm to drink," she said. Paula was a little unsteady on her feet, but then she had a right to be. After all she'd just been attacked by a monster—a monster whose name might have been Dave Guthrie.

"Tea okay?" Paula asked.

Dave nodded as a part of him tried to send her a mental warning: *Don't come back, Paula. Go home to Minnesota where you belong. It's not safe around me, because I don't know what I've become.*

THE FINAL CONFRONTATION

• 1 •

In the kitchen, Paula put on a kettle of water to boil. Then, as she stood there, watching it, the magnitude of what had just happened hit her. Dave had been having a conversation with himself, in two different voices, as if he were two beings in one body.

And then he'd winked out.

And the monster had appeared.

She couldn't say Dave had exactly become the monster, because Dave's wheelchair had been six or seven feet from where the monster appeared. But she had no doubts that the monster would have killed her if it hadn't been for the blue sparks. She felt the tentacle wrapping around her, constricting, and suddenly her legs were too weak to support her, and she had to sit down.

The blue sparks. Dave vanishing and the monster being there as if it had been conjured by a stage magician. What did it all mean? She shuddered.

"I need help," she said to the empty room, her voice a soft, frightened whisper. "I'm the one who's supposed to help, but I can't. I don't know how." A tear slid down her cheek. "Somebody help me. I can't do this. I'm lost, and I'm afraid."

The surface of the table wavered slightly, and a dizziness washed over her. She smelled turpentine.

245

"Paula." It came from behind her, an old woman's voice, soft and gentle.

Paula turned slowly, feeling faint, the odor of turpentine still heavy in her nostrils. A woman stood there, looking at her warmly. She was elderly, gray-haired, overweight in the way old people so often were, with arms, legs, and trunk that seemed to have naturally thickened with age. Clear blue eyes looked at Paula from a wrinkled face. It was the countenance of one who had experienced much and responded to all of it with understanding and tenderness.

"Who are you?" Paula asked.

"Helen Lundquist."

"Lundquist was my mother's name."

"I'm her mother, your grandmother."

"But you died when I . . ."

"When you were a little girl, yes."

"Then how . . ."

"I'll help you understand. I would have come to you before now, but you weren't strong enough yet. I couldn't communicate with you." She smiled. "You're part of a war that's been going on for thousands of years. In its simplest form, it's good versus evil. You're on the side of good—as were many of your ancestors before you."

"You mean my . . . my psychic abilities are inherited?"

"Yes. Our family was chosen."

"You mean my mother and father could—"

"No. It never involved your father's family at all, only your mother's. It passes from mother to daughter, never to sons. Your mother, however, wasn't one of the chosen. I don't know why, but sometimes it skips a generation. Although your mother passed psychic abilities on to you, she never developed any of her own."

"Why do I have these abilities?" Paula demanded. "What am I supposed to do with them?"

"Sometimes all you're supposed to do is rescue an occasional puppy," Paula's grandmother said. "But sometimes, like now, it's harder. The battle involves the greatest forces in the universe; you have to understand that. But these powers never battle directly. If they did, there'd be nothing left. They wage war with surrogates. You've seen evil's surrogate. You're the representative of the other side."

"No, I can't be," Paula protested, overwhelmed. "I just rescue puppies and things like that. I can't defeat evil. I'm a schoolteacher. I'm—"

"Someone very special. And you'll do what you have to do."

"But I—"

"Listen to me, Paula, and I'll tell you some things you need to know. Dave Guthrie's not to blame. He was tricked. He came so close to death in that plane crash that he slipped across to the Other Side, where they could get at him. They offered him a proposition. He could go back, live again. All he had to do was say yes to their offer of life. Of course he said yes. He wanted to live.

"But it was all a lie. They had neither the power to keep him there nor the ability to return him to the world of the living. But Dave Guthrie had no way of knowing that. Having just crossed over, he was confused. He desperately wanted to live. So he said yes. But what he was agreeing to was much, much more than he knew. He'd unknowingly committed himself to bringing them back with him."

"Them?" Paula said, desperately trying to assimilate all this.

"The representatives of evil. Demons, if you will. They came with him. You see, they can't come here unless someone brings them. Willingly."

"But how did—"

"Hush," Paula's grandmother said. "All your questions will be answered. The evil ones came within him. They are part of him."

"He's possessed," Paula whispered.

"No, not possessed. They're parasites. Now be quiet and listen, Paula. They have no physical form in this world, which is another reason they need Dave Guthrie. They use him so they can eat. They crave the flesh of living creatures, especially human flesh."

"No," Paula said. "Oh, no."

"He's not Dave Guthrie when it happens. They can

secrete chemicals that change him, briefly, into one of them—one of their many forms. So when Dave Guthrie kills and eats human flesh, he's not human himself. He is unaware of doing it. He has temporarily taken on the form of a creature from the Other Side. He does not do this willingly. He fights these parasites constantly, because the things they force him to do are against his true nature. This battle goes on below the surface of his consciousness. He is unaware of it.

"This conflict within him is the reason why so many strange things have been happening. It creates strong psychic waves that can cause vivid hallucinations in the mind of the host and also in the minds of others who are attuned to them. You receive these psychic waves because you are linked to Dave Guthrie. The nurse, Ed Prawdzik, also received them, in part because they are so powerful and in part because he is psychically receptive, although he is unaware of this. That's why there were cockroaches and holes in the floor and all manner of things that seemed terribly real to Dave or Ed one moment and vanished the next.

"But this is only part of the explanation. The parasites can gather their psychic energy and use it to affect things in the physical world. That's how they made Ed Prawdzik fall off the roof, how they made a table attack you.

"They would very much like to drive you away. You are the only threat to them. Dave Guthrie's subconscious tries to resist, but it lacks the strength to succeed. You are another matter. That's why that man came after you at the motel. He's just like Dave Guthrie. He was so close to death that he slipped across to the Other Side, and when he returned, he brought them with him. But this man was naturally evil, so there was no conclift between him and the parasites. No hallucinations for him to experience or to broadcast to receptive minds in his vicinity."

"Are there others who are hosts to these . . . these parasites?"

"Oh, yes. Every time someone crosses over and then is

brought back, there is always the possibility that the parasites will come with them. You may meet them in future battles."

"If I survive this one," Paula said. She was imagining all the times people were brought back to life by doctors or paramedics or ordinary citizens who'd learned CPR—or simple mouth-to-mouth resuscitation.

"You will survive the battle, child. Have no doubts about that."

"How can you be so sure?"

"They can't harm you. Haven't you seen that? Every time they try it, something happens. A sleeping man at the motel wakes up and calls the police. Or blue sparks seem to come from nowhere to save you. Don't you see? You are the representative of a great force of the universe. That force protects you. The evil will attack you again and again, hoping to frighten you away, but it can't hurt you."

Although her thoughts were reeling, Paula was still able to recognize the truth, and her grandmother had spoken honestly. "What about Dave?" she asked. "What will happen to him?"

"They will use him, changing him into one of them so he can kill and eat his own kind until he grows old and dies. Only you can save him from this."

"How?"

"Make him see the truth. That's why you're here. Because you know the truth."

Suddenly the image of Paula's grandmother distorted, as if it were a reflection on the surface of a pond into which someone had just tossed a pebble. And then she was fading, becoming transparent.

"Wait!" Paula called. "I don't understand. I don't know what to do."

"I can't tell you what to do, Paula. But the time is now. Do it now." And then she was gone.

The teapot let out a piercing shriek, and Paula jumped. She turned off the burner, then stepped back, shaking. A huge responsibility had been placed on her, a task so awesome it overwhelmed her. Her grandmother might as well have told her to change the way the earth tilts on its axis. The assignment was so formidable she had no idea where to begin.

Abruptly Paula realized that she had to get back to Dave. If she was going to have any chance of helping him, she had to be with him. And her grandmother had said the time was now. Paula hurried into the living room, headed for the stairs, and something sprang out in front of her, blocking her path. She heard herself let out a high-pitched gasp.

A lizard was standing before her. With a face sort of like an iguana. But this lizard was standing on two legs, like a human, and its front legs were hands with long claws. It eyed her with yellow pupils rimmed in a glowing green. It opened its mouth, revealing teeth that would have made a great white shark proud.

Knowing that she had to get out of the room, get to Dave, Paula whirled, headed for the door leading outside. The reptile was much faster than she was, and it easily moved in front of her.

Paula stared at it.

It hissed at her.

The creature was only about four feet tall, but it was heavy, probably weighing a good hundred-fifty pounds or so. And its claws and teeth were wicked-looking. She did not want to challenge it.

And yet she had to. Dave needed her.

Paula took a step toward it, and it hissed again, its forked tongue flickering out of its mouth. As if to demonstrate what would happen, the creature reached behind it and drew its left claw down the wall, leaving long gouges in the plaster. Its skin was mottled yellow and brown. It had a tail with clusters of barbs on the end, like an overgrown burr, although Paula suspected its function was more like that of a mace.

The creature drooled, a slimy puddle appearing at its feet. The sickening realization came to Paula that this thing wanted to eat her. Desperately wanted to.

She reversed direction, headed for the other exit, and again the creature moved into her path. It was many times faster than she was; there was no way she could outmaneuver it. Paula stared at it, her heart beating furiously, her breath short and ragged.

The lizard eyed her hungrily.

But it made no move toward Paula. It can't hurt me, she thought. Just as her grandmother had said. The creature watched her, drooling, hunger burning in its eyes, and Paula knew that if this beast could eat her, it would have done so by now, for the desire to devour her was all but making the thing tremble with craving.

Paula's grandmother said the parasites could transform Dave into one of their kind. Did that mean that this thing before her had been Dave a moment ago? Paula shuddered at the thought. And yet maybe, if it was a transformation of Dave, maybe it still had some of Dave in it, some speck of humanity that could be reasoned with.

"Dave," she said. "Fight it. Don't let it control you."

The monster studied her uncomprehendingly, the desire to make a meal of her still burning in its eyes. Talking to it was useless, she realized, for there was nothing of Dave Guthrie in the creature. This was something evil, from an entirely different realm of existence.

Paula took a step toward it.

It hissed, flicked its tongue.

"Get out of my way," Paula said.

The creature emitted a sound that was part growl, part shriek.

Paula continued to advance on it. "Move," she said. "You have no choice. You can't hurt me, and you don't have the power to hold me here."

The floor in front of her opened up. Her foot was poised over a bottomless pit from which steam and smoke rose. And dimly, as if from miles and miles away, she could hear screams of unendurable torment.

"It's not there," Paula said. "The floor is there. This is just the bad guys playing with my mind."

She took a step.

Her foot landed solidly on the floor.

The image of a pit vanished, and Paula was again confronted by the creature. She was within three feet of it now. It stared at her with hate-filled eyes, trembling, drooling, not giving way. If the good guys are on my side, I need them now, Paula thought. She reached out to touch the lizard, which opened its mouth as if to bite off her hand. Paula hesitated, then forced herself to continue reaching toward the lizard.

Blue sparks flew from her fingers an instant before they would have made contact with the creature's head.

The lizard made a hissing, whining noise, then vanished.

Paula dashed up the stairs and into the bedroom. Sitting in his wheelchair, Dave studied her. "You forgot the tea," he said.

Paula was relieved. She hadn't known whether she'd find Dave or . . . or something else. "Never mind that," she said. "I know what this is all about, and I think I know what you have to do. It was all lies. You were tricked."

"Paula, I don't have any idea what you're talking—"

"The plane crash. You'd crossed over to the Other Side. For a few seconds you were dead. You were in their world."

"Whose world?"

"The parasites'." She explained what her grandmother had told her.

When she finished, Dave was staring at her, wide-eyed. "It's not true," he said. "I wouldn't . . . I'm not a cannibal."

"You don't do it, Dave. When it happens, you're transformed into one of them. It's not you. There's nothing of you in the monsters."

"Oh, God," he said. Then he frowned. "Paula, maybe it isn't so. I mean . . . well, you said it was a vision of your dead grandmother. Couldn't you—"

"Have imagined it? I don't think so. Don't forget that I can recognize the truth. The image *was* that of my grandmother, and the things she said had the ring of truth."

Dave was still wrapped in the blanket. As Paula talked to

him, he grew paler. He looked like someone who was about to succumb to a long illness. Paula took his hand.

"Renounce the agreement," she said. "Don't just threaten to renounce it like you did before, but actually do it. You brought them into this world, and only you can send them back."

Dave just stared at her, his eyes full of confusion.

"Do it, Dave. Renounce the agreement. I'll be right here. I'll tell you if what you hear is the truth."

He drew in a slow breath. "Will you be all right? Remember what happened last time."

"I told you. They can't hurt me."

"Are you sure?"

"My grandmother was telling the truth. I'm sure."

For a moment Dave's eyes held hers; then he shifted his gaze to the center of the room. "I renounce the agreement," he said.

The room seemed totally silent. Outside waves hissed onto the beach, but that was in another world.

"I terminate the agreement," Dave said forcefully. "It's null and void. No more. Over. You got it? Now get out of my body and go back where you came from."

For several moments the only sound was the whisper of the waves spilling onto the beach. Then Dave said, "The agreement cannot be broken." But the voice was not his. It was deep and rumbling and powerful, nothing at all like Dave's voice. "The bargain is forever," it said. And then it laughed.

•2•

As Dave watched, the room suddenly shimmered as if it were filled with thousands of wiggly heat waves. The black spot appeared, the eyes began to glow in its center, but this time it did not change into a monster. "The bargain is forever," a deep rumbling voice said.

253

Paula was saying something, but the words were garbled, as if played backward at the wrong speed on a phonograph. She was looking at him anxiously, urgently.

"What?" he said. "I can't understand."

Again her lips moved, making incomprehensible noises.

"Forget her," the black spot said. "Look at me." It hung there, the eyes staring at him, making him feel as though they were somehow touching him with that look, making his flesh hot, itchy.

"The agreement's off," Dave said. "Go away."

"You don't know about the hunger," it said. "Ohhhhhhhhh, the hunger! Imagine this, you chunk of dung. Imagine that you can never die. And that you can never leave the place you're in. And that you are hungry to the point of desperation—desperation beyond anything you've ever known. A craving worse than anything suffered by a heroin addict. A total, consuming need that can never be satisfied because you are trapped forever in a place with no food. Imagine that. Immmmmmagine it. Immmmmaaaagine the huuuuuunger!" There was desperation in the voice, a haunting, burning need.

"Are you from . . . from hell?" Dave asked.

"Your word, not ours."

"But is that where you're from?"

"Not exactly."

"Then *where* are you from?" Dave wondered why he was asking these questions. Was it really necessary that he understand? What was the point? He was here to end the agreement—once and for all.

"The dark place."

"You'll have to go back," Dave said. "I'm terminating the agreement."

The dark spot convulsed, twisted in on itself, pulled itself inside out, shrank, expanded, grew two arms, then two legs, then a head. For an instant it was a human shadow; then a man appeared, popping into existance as if someone had switched him on like a light bulb.

He moved to the bed, sat down on it with a jaunty bounce. Dressed in brown tweed, he had on one of those caps

Irishmen wore. His shirt and eyes were green, his face lightly freckled. Grinning at Dave sardonically, the man looked like an oversize leprechaun.

"Dude, dude, dude," he said, his voice holding just a hint of a Southern twang. "What am I going to do with you?"

It took Dave a moment to collect his thoughts. He said, "What's this, some sort of good guy–bad guy routine? First I get the monster to end all monsters; then I get the smiling man?"

The man's grin broadened. "Either way, dude, I'm the same guy."

"Either way," Dave said, "the bargain's off."

The man shook his head resignedly, as if he were having a hard time trying to get through to an obstinate child. "Can't do that, dude."

"Yeah, I can. I just did."

"But it don't mean nothing, dude. Bargain's made, it stays made. There ain't no out clause. Get it?"

Paula tugged on his hand. She was shaking her head vigorously.

"You're lying," Dave said.

"Lying?" The man looked shocked, as if to say, You would accuse me of a thing like that? "There's nothing to lie about. We have a straightforward agreement—which, I might add, you made to save your own ass."

"No, you're lying about something."

"Dude, you been listening to that woman, haven't you? Says she can tell the truth from lies, sort of a lie detector with tits. She's putting you on, dude. She can't tell shit."

"Then why have you been so anxious to get rid of her?"

"Because she's on the other side. She's with the opposition."

"So am I."

Slowly shaking his head, the man looked at Dave sadly. "You just don't understand, do you? If you break the agreement, you're dead."

Paula was saying something, but her words were still garbled. Looking frustrated, she frantically shook her head.

"Why should I believe you?" Dave asked.

"Hey, think about it, dude. We agreed to give you back your life in exchange for certain considerations. You go back on your part; we go back on ours."

"I'm already here."

"Dude, dude, dude. Who do you think you're dealing with here, the ladies' afternoon tea society? We'll *take* you."

"How do I know you can do that?"

"You are a hard man to convince," the man said. "We can do it all right. And you're ours now, because you bargained with us. And we would be very displeased with you. Think that over a moment. You know what it would be like for you. Actually, don't bother to think it over. There's no way you can conceive of it."

Dave said nothing. He didn't like the way this conversation was going. Icy tendrils of fear were wrapping themselves around his vital organs.

"And then there's Paula," the man said. "You two had a real nice time the other night, didn't you? All cozy and nice, fallin' in love. You back out on us, and you'll never see her again. It's bye-bye, Paula. No more nice nights in bed, no life together, learning all about each other, going places together. You can have that. Or you can have what you get from us when we're annoyed with you." He grinned happily. "Either way you belong to us. The way that works is up to you."

Dave thought about that, recalling last night with Paula, knowing that their love would grow, that it could easily work out for them to spend their lives together. Dave considered that, considered the alternative. How could he leave Paula? How could he?

Again he heard her distorted voice, but when he looked at her she was just a blur, a barely discernable shape wrapped in foggy shadows.

She seemed to be getting dimmer, fading away from him. And suddenly he was filled with confusion. What if Paula had been wrong? What if it was this man who was telling the truth? What if he was already beyond hope? He envisioned himself being whisked away to a dark, terrible place inhabited by the monsters, theirs forever, to do with as they pleased.

Paula wasn't infallible. No one was. She could be mistaken. And where did that leave him? His thoughts were in turmoil, as if his brain had divided into warring factions intent on destroying each other.

Out of the confusion came a single, powerful thought. He had to trust Paula, had to know in his heart that the words she'd heard had truly been lies.

Dave screamed, "I don't believe that I can't renounce the agreement! And I renounce it right now! It's null and void! You hear me? It's over! It's over!"

The man vanished.

The black spot disappeared.

Suddenly air was being sucked into the place the blackness had occupied. The room seemed caught in a windstorm, the gale whipping Dave's hair, making the blankets flap.

A pillow flew into the spot.

Then some loose items from the dresser—a handkerchief, a bottle of deodorant, Dave's wallet.

Then a blanket.

Then Dave's shoes.

His clothing was flapping now.

His chair was being rolled slowly toward the opening.

Faster.

Faster.

Dave tried to stop it, but it kept moving toward the spot.

Dave felt himself being lifted from the chair.

Pulled toward the blackness.

Floating toward the blackness.

THE TRUTH BE KNOWN

• 1 •

Dave floated toward the blackness.

He tried to resist, fought with every ounce of will he could muster to reverse his movement, to fight the force pulling him forward, but his efforts had no effect, for there was nothing to push against, no grip to wriggle out of. And the blackness grew larger, surrounded him, claimed him.

Suddenly a coldness wrapped itself around him, penetrating to his physical center, then going beyond that to his very soul. It was total coldness, off the scale of any man-made measuring device, beyond the ability of his brain to comprehend. A spot in deep space, trillions of light years from the nearest sun, had more warmth than the place Dave Guthrie was in now.

And yet he was not frozen, for he was no longer a physical being. He was neither walking nor floating, for these terms didn't apply here. This was a place of nothing. No up. No down. No top. No bottom. No light. Not even darkness. All that existed here was the cold. And the emptiness. Dave was experiencing loneliness as he had never known it could be. It was the isolation of being reduced to thoughts, existing solely as observations, notions. Disconnected. Hanging there. In the middle of a nowhere Dave never could have conceived of, for it was made up of nothing, nothing at all.

Welcome to the afterlife, a voice seemed to say. Dave

recognized it as the voice of the oversize leprechaun who'd sat on his bed. He clung to the sound, even though it really wasn't noise per se. It was a break in the nothingness, the acknowledgment that he had *something*, no matter how horrible, for company—at least for a moment.

Don't go away, Dave thought. Please don't. Please.

You can wander here forever, the voice seemed to say.

No, please.

Many have come here before you, dude. Many more will come in time. You'll all be here together, but you'll never meet, never be aware of each other.

I don't like this place.

Dude, dude, dude. You still don't get it, do you? You're not supposed to like it. This is a place of punishment. Eternal punishment.

But . . . I don't belong here.

You don't, huh?

No, I'm not a bad person. What did I do to deserve this?

You bargained with me.

I . . . but . . .

If it was possible to have a sinking feeling in this place, Dave was experiencing one now. He'd made a deal with the devil—or the devil's representative. And this was hell. This was where you went after you did something like that. It was nonsense, at best a bit of mythology, and yet at this moment, Dave Guthrie believed it completely.

Despair, total and consuming, descended on him, crushing him like the weight of a building. He saw loneliness, emptiness, stretching out in front of him forever, his sole companions his own thoughts, which would only serve to remind him of how miserable he was. He wanted to die, wanted it desperately, but then he realized that this was death. Neither a razor blade to the wrists nor an overdose of pills nor a gun to the temple would get you out of this.

No, Dave thought. No, no, no, no.

Oh, please. Oh, please. Oh, please.

And then he saw Paula, the image appearing as if someone had switched on a TV set. He missed her terribly, and a longing spread throughout him that promptly became an unbearable ache. Oh, to have Paula again, take her in his arms, kiss her, talk to her . . .

She was lying on the bed, crying, and Dave seemed to sense all her feelings. She was crying because she missed him as much as he missed her. Sobbing, she got up, her face a mask of misery. Dave moved with her, like a camera being dollied to follow the action. Paula went into the bathroom, took out a bottle of pills, studied the label a moment. No, Dave thought, don't!

Paula uncapped the bottle, put it to her lips.

No! Dave screamed mentally. Don't! No!

Paula tipped the bottle, which was full, its entire contents slipping into her mouth.

No! Don't do it, Paula! "No, no, no!"

His last words were real. Actual sound. And he was experiencing sensations. Air currents moving around him, the weight of his body in a chair—the wheelchair. Dave was back in his bedroom. There was no sign of Paula.

The man was still sitting on the bed. He said, "You renounce the agreement, that's what you get, dude. The agreement's all that's keeping you alive. And if you die now, after bargaining with the bad guys . . ." The man grinned, a maniacal smile that had absolutely no warmth in it.

Dave shuddered. Could he stand that place—for eternity? And was the image he saw true? Would Paula miss him so much she'd commit suicide? And then, despite all the good things she'd done in her life, would she be swept away to a place of total emptiness and loneliness like the one he'd just seen?

Dave was sitting on the razor's edge of indecision, and he felt as though it would surely slice him in half.

Keep your part of the bargain. Live. Have Paula.

Renounce the agreement because it's evil and horrible and should never have been made, and then what happens to you, to Paula?

And there were other ingredients to the mix, things he didn't know. He'd dreamed of people dying at the hands of hungry monsters. Monsters he'd apparently invited here.

Monsters that lived within him. Was he responsible for those deaths? Would they continue if he allowed the agreement to stand? How much blood would be on his hands? And would Paula want to be with someone who could be party to such a monstrous agreement?

And then it occurred to Dave that the focus of the discussion had shifted. Not too long ago he was being told that he could not break the agreement, and now he was being told that awful things would happen to him if he did. Where was the truth? And where was Paula? Without her he had no idea what to believe.

And then he remembered that she had told him what was true. He tried to recall her words, but they were vague, distorted memories that floated just beyond his grasp.

"Decision time," the man said.

"I don't know what to do," Dave said.

"No more time," the man said, rising. "I'm taking you with me if you renounce the agreement. Decide. Now."

Dave's thoughts were a confused jumble. The man—if he was a man—was coming on like a high-pressure salesman. Take the deal now or I'll withdraw the offer.

"What do you mean by take me back?" Dave asked.

"What the hell do you think I mean, dude?"

And that answered that, didn't it? He was saying that Dave was on his way to the Other Side if the agreement was nullified. Instantly. Immediate death for his physical self . . . and something unimaginable for his spiritual self.

"Time's up," the man said. "Choose."

I can't, Dave thought.

"Decision time, dude." The words were forceful, compelling.

Can't . . .

"Paula or death. Pick one. Now."

No, can't . . . can't.

"Last chance for us to forgive you. Last chance to be with Paula. Last chance to avoid what's in store if you anger us."

Dave was frozen, unable to open his mouth, unable to think.

"Time's up, dude."

Suddenly blue sparks filled his field of vision. And then he saw Paula, a dreamlike Paula who seemed to have no substance. She stood before him, her body engulfed in blue energy, which arced from her fingers to her knees, from her toes to her elbows.

"It's lies, Dave. All of it. Everything."

Her voice was in his head, and Dave realized he was psychically linked with her. The dream-like Paula before him began to dissolve, but Dave could still feel her in his mind.

"You're not theirs, Dave. You never were. And you can break the agreement because it was made using lies and trickery."

The man let out a roar that Dave heard both in his ears and with his brain itself, as if it had been transmitted directly into the core of his mind. Abruptly the man was gone, replaced by a black spot again, which hovered about ten feet from Dave.

"Choose," a raspy voice said. "Choose now."

"I renounce the agreement," Dave said.

"Then you are ours."

The black spot expanded, rushed at Dave, surrounding him, claiming him. And Paula was slipping from his mind like a distant station on a car radio. He received one last message, and then she was gone. He thought the message was, *The truth shall make you free.*

•2•

Paula was still holding Dave's hand. At first, when he'd started conducting a conversation with himself, she'd found herself cut off from him, unable to warn him about the parasites' lies. Then she'd called on her special abilities, which seemed to be gaining strength by the moment, and reaching into Dave's mind, Paula established a link.

But now that link was severed.

Dave had been taken to a place she could not go, not even

psychically. Gathering all her strength, she sent him one last message and hoped it got through. *The truth shall make you free.*

Then his hand was yanked from hers, and Dave vanished, leaving Paula to stare at his empty wheelchair.

•3•

Dave streaked through the darkness like a bullet, strange sensations flooding his mind. He was in a place of no air, for he could feel nothing as he zipped along. And he could see nothing but darkness, and yet he knew he was moving at an incredible speed.

At the same time he was traveling only a tiny distance, small enough to bridge in a single step. It made no sense, this perceived speed taking him somewhere he was already within touching distance of. It came to him that he was traveling between adjacent worlds, a journey that was short in some respects and incredibly long in others, which was why his senses were providing him with such contradictory input.

Suddenly he was there, in the place he'd dreamed—or recalled. The place with the shadowy creatures all around him, the place in which he floated toward the hideous face.

Choose, voices seemed to say.

Choose what? he asked without using his mouth or vocal cords.

Choose life or choose death.

Abruptly there were fires all around, their flames erupting out of the darkness with no apparent source, foul-smelling blazes whose flames seared his nasal passages, made his eyes water. And they illuminated his surroundings. The shadowy shapes were people, some of them bloody, some with limbs bent at impossible angles. And Dave recognized them. These were the others from the plane crash. All dead. All part of this place now.

He heard them moaning, giving voice to their despair. They were here now, in the land of the dead. Forever.

You're the lucky one. You have a choice.

What choice? Dave asked.

You can choose life.

Why? Why me?

You come from an isolated place, one we can inhabit without creating too much of a stir in your world.

I don't understand.

We must be invited, or we cannot come.

And if I don't invite you?

The head appeared before him. He was floating toward it, slowly, unstoppably. The mouth opening to receive him.

You will be our host, and we will let you live.

No.

Then you are ours. Forever.

No, please.

Choose.

What will you do in my world?

Be free of this one. We do not wish to be confined here any more than you do.

But what will you do?

Live as we have always lived. We wish only freedom. To live with you in peace.

Dave thought of people around the world whose struggles to be free he had applauded. The students in Beijing. East Germans who fled to the West. Blacks in South Africa. The oppressed in Chile. These beings were different, of course, but didn't they have the right to be free too—just like those Chinese students?

And on a more personal level, Dave Guthrie did not want to be in this place. With every fiber of his being, he did not want to be here. He wanted life, his house in California, his job as an illustrator, Jackie.

Jackie?

What about Paula?

And then Dave realized he was seeing this as it had happened the first time, before he even knew Paula Bjornson existed. He had been given the choice. Stay here forever or choose life. He had chosen life.

And he opened his mouth to say the words again, and then he closed it, for he did not need to speak here, only to direct thoughts. He had chosen life the first time, and he would choose it again. He was offering freedom to the beings of this place, and he was avoiding death. What other decision could there be?

It's lies, Dave. All of it. Everything.

Paula's voice.

He was getting closer and closer to the horrible mouth, the pointed teeth about to turn him into raw ground meat.

Choose. Choose.

Again Dave was on the verge of making the only decision that made any sense. Choosing life. The alternative was what awaited him in the hideous mouth. He struggled to force himself away from the teeth, the bloody lips, but it was impossible. Unseen forces propelled him forward, into this cavern of death.

All right, Dave said/thought/transmitted. I choose. I choose. The odor of death, rotting things, swirled in his nostrils, making his nose wrinkle, his stomach churn.

And then he sensed that there was another presence here—or other presences—and that they wanted him to reject the offer of life. But how could he do that? Choose death, this place? Over life?

And yet he also knew that he was being given a second chance. He was back where he had been after the crash, doing it again. And this time he could do it differently. Maybe this second chance was coming because he'd renounced the bargain he'd made the first time. His thoughts danced like water droplets on a hot griddle, boiling and popping into nonexistence almost as soon as they formed.

The truth shall make you free.

But he wasn't sure what the truth was anymore. The things Paula told him seemed distant, dream-like, while this place was very real, very threatening.

Lies. All of it. Everything.

But what if Paula was wrong? Making the wrong decision could mean staying in this horrible place forever. How could he risk that?

Dave was almost in the mouth now, close enough to be inhaled like a speck of dust.

Suddenly it occurred to him that if he did stay here, the parasites would be stuck here too. By sacrificing himself he could save his world from the horrors they would inflict upon it.

As Dave entered the mouth, it started closing. He saw pieces of putrid flesh wedged between the teeth.

Dave fought for the courage to choose death.

There was no time for further consideration, because the mouth was almost closed, rows of wicked teeth on each side of him like meshing picket fences. A flick of the tongue, and he would be in those teeth, just another chunk of mangled flesh.

I choose to reject your offer of life, Dave said/thought.

Then you are ours. Forever.

The tongue began to undulate, ready to steer the Dave Guthrie morsel to the proper spot for masticating, and again he heard Paula's words. *The truth shall make you free.*

Dave said, No, it's a lie. I'm not yours. I reject your offer. The others died in the crash, but I didn't. I was never yours to begin with. You lied about that. You lied about only wanting to live with us in peace.

You are ours.

Dredging up every ounce of strength and determination he possessed, Dave Guthrie said: GO FUCK YOURSELF!

The tongue undulated.

The teeth meshed.

And suddenly Dave Guthrie wasn't in the mouth anymore. Not even in the dark place, because lights—red and yellow and white and blue—were passing him in a blur. Again he had the sensation of hurtling through distance while traveling only a short way. And then he was back on his bedroom floor, looking up at Paula.

"Dave," she said, "I—" Her words broke off, and a startled look appeared on her face.

He followed the direction of her stare. At the door of his

closet was a big black hole, like the entrance to a cave, and things—indistinct shapes—were being sucked into it as if it were a vacuum cleaner gathering dirt particles. He thought he detected things hairy and things lizard-like, monsters of all varieties, but they were all but a blur, and he couldn't be sure exactly what he was seeing.

"You can see it too, can't you?" Dave said.

"I'm linked with you, so I see what you see. I wish I could have done it before now."

A sound filled the room, like the dying wail of an old-type police siren as it spun to a stop. But this sound was steady, the moan of suction from another world taking back its own. And beneath that, Dave realized, was another wail, this one higher-pitched, more desperate. It had to be the cry of the creatures who'd come here to satisfy their hunger and would dine no more. Maddening, unrelenting hunger. Dave shuddered at the thought.

And then the room was quiet, although the hole by the closet door remained. A man stepped in front of the opening. It was the man Dave had seen before, the one who called him—

"Dude, I don't know what I'm going to do with you."

"There's nothing you can do with me," Dave said. "The deal's off. Go back where you belong."

"You got any idea what perpetual, gnawing, gut-wrenching hunger's like, dude?"

Dave didn't reply.

"It's awful," the man said. "That's what you've condemned us to."

"Not me," Dave said. "You were condemned long before you met me."

"But you set us free, dude. Now you've gone back on the agreement."

"It was an agreement solicited under false pretenses."

"A little distortion in a good cause. Nothing to get upset about. But you, dude, you couldn't live with it, could you? You just had to send us back where we have a horrible craving that can never be satisfied. You got any idea what that's like, dude?"

"It's over," Dave said. "Go away."

"Oh, I'm going, dude. But not just yet. I've got one piece of unfinished business.

His tweed coat disappeared, along with his cap. For an instant he just seemed blurry, and then he was changed. Dave gasped. He was looking at the same head that had been on the verge of devouring him. Except that now it was a normal-size head on a normal-size body. The pale body of a corpse, dressed in ragged jeans, a faded plaid shirt. A maggot crawled out of one of the sores on the face, wriggled down the cheek. The creature brushed it off, stepped on it with a bare foot that was composed of rotting flesh that hung in wet strings.

"One more meal before I go," the creature hissed, and it flew at Dave, grabbing him with hands that were more bones than flesh, locking on his throat, squeezing. As Dave's flow of air was cut off, the mouth, the horrible, rancid-smelling bloody mouth came at his face. Opening. Ready to tear off a hunk of Dave's cheek.

Suddenly electricity was crackling and dancing before Dave's eyes. Blue sparks. Paula had inserted her hand between Dave's cheek and the monster. Instantly skeletal fingers released his throat, and the creature leaped back, howling and hissing its rage. Abruptly it changed into a scorpionlike monster the size of a large dog, waving and snapping its claws. In the next instant, it was a shaggy creature that could have been a yeti, and then it was a fanged reptile with a barbed tail. Emitting a steady screech of frustration, it kept changing, becoming a many-legged thing with huge mandibles, a quivering mass of oozing sores, a three-headed cobra. And as it changed, it began to drift toward the closet door, as if being slowly reeled in by some unseen fisherman.

The changes were coming so rapidly now the creature had become a blur from which an occasional claw or talon appeared only to disappear in almost the same instant. And then it was gone, sucked back into the place from which it had come. The opening between its world and this one shrank until it was a marble-sized dot of blackness, hesitated, then vanished.

Dave was still sitting on the floor. Suddenly Paula was hugging him. "I . . . I thought I'd lost you," she said. "You disappeared. The link was broken."

"There were several moments there where I thought I was lost," Dave replied, returning her hug. They rocked slowly back and forth a few moments, just holding each other, happy to be alive and together. Finally Dave broke the silence. "How'd you do that?" he asked.

"Do what?"

"The blue sparks."

"I don't consciously do anything. It just happens."

Dave shook his head. "All those women out there, and I had to fall in love with one who makes blue sparks."

They hugged again, and then Paula began to cry. For a long time they just stayed on the bedroom floor, holding each other.

EPILOGUE

• 1 •

"Are you sure this is wise?" Paula asked as she climbed out of bed. Her sheer green gown trailing behind her, she quickly crossed the room, got her robe from the closet, and slipped it on.

"Is what wise?" Dave asked, swinging his legs over the edge of the bed. He stared at them as though he'd never seen them before. The last of his two casts to come off had been removed a couple of weeks ago. His legs felt strange, almost weightless, and they were still extremely white. He needed to get outside in shorts or swimming trunks and tan them up.

"Seeing each other," Paula said.

"We've been living together for months. How can we not see each other?"

"But it's supposed to be bad luck."

"Because it's our wedding day?"

"Yes," she said.

"Silly old superstition," Dave said. "Anyone who'd believe in that would believe in goblins and demons and who knows what." He'd said it, hoping it would be humorous, but as his words died away, a tension seemed to fill the room. His eyes were drawn to the closet door. Nothing there now but Paula in her robe, looking lovely even first thing in the morning.

"Sorry," Dave said. "I guess there are some things I shouldn't joke about."

Paula came over and sat down beside him on the bed. "I guess we have to try to joke about it," she said.

"We shouldn't trivialize it," Dave said.

"No, not to trivialize it. To cope with it. I mean, to most people, what happened to us is impossible. We can't even talk about it. No one would believe us. But we still have to deal with it. It's over with, done with—except for the psychological aftereffects. Maybe joking about it can help us there. I think it's better than just pretending it never happened."

Dave put his arm around her. "You're right. But then you usually are. The only thing that makes me doubt your judgment is your somewhat questionable taste in men."

"My taste in men is excellent, I'll have you know."

He nibbled her ear playfully. "I'm just glad you have the taste you do."

"None of that," she said. "You have to wait until after we're married."

"You can say that after last night?"

"But this is our wedding day. On our wedding day you have to wait until after the ceremony."

"I haven't even said 'I do' yet, and already she's making rules."

"Want to change your mind? There's still time."

"No way, lady."

She snuggled close, slipping her arm around him.

A few silent moments passed; then Dave said, "I still can't get over the fact that the whole thing was based on a lie. I was hovering near death, and I momentarily slipped into their territory, but that was all. No matter what I said, they couldn't have prevented my return to the world of the living."

"Lying is what they do."

"The father of lies . . ." Dave said, letting the thought trail off.

"Yes," Paula said.

"Legends, myths, stories, the Bible, other such books . . . are they true?"

"There are elements of fact in many myths and legends," Paula said.

"And there are many things we don't know," Dave said.

"Yes."

"Is this an ongoing thing then?" Dave asked. "Do other people hovering near death have the same experience? Are the monsters just waiting for another opportunity to tell their lies, get invited into this world?"

"That's what my grandmother said."

"Wow," Dave replied.

A silence settled over the room, began to lengthen, and Paula said, "What's for breakfast?"

"You're asking me?"

"You don't expect me to cook on my wedding day, do you?" Paula asked.

"It's my wedding day too, you know."

"Oh yeah, it is, isn't it?"

"You mean you were going to get married by yourself?" Dave asked.

She punched him playfully on the arm. "Actually, I'm leading up to a suggestion."

"Which is?"

"Let's skip this cooking and washing up afterward stuff and eat at the pancake house. Whaddaya say?"

"Deal," Dave said. He sprang up, enjoying the bounce in his healed legs. "Last one in the bathroom has to pick up the check."

She grabbed his arm, pulling him back down beside her. "One question first," she said.

"Yes, I did rob all those banks and deflower all those tender young women."

"No, you didn't. You can't lie to me, you know." She frowned. "Which is my point. This is your last chance to back out."

"Never."

"But you'll never be able to tell me a lie—not even a little white one to protect my feelings. Are you sure you know what that's going to be like?"

"I've been living with it for the past few months, haven't I?"

"Yes, but—"

Dave sprang up, pulling his arms free. Then he dashed for the bathroom, yelling, "You're going to have to pay for breakfast."

Paula dashed into the hall, catching him just as he reached the bathroom. Suddenly they were all tangled up, and then they were on the floor, giggling uncontrollably.

"I can take years and years and years of this," Dave said.

"Me too," Paula replied.

•2•

As she dressed, Paula recalled the second time her grandmother had appeared to her. It had happened a few weeks ago in a dream.

"You did well, child," the old woman had said.

"I did very little."

"But it was enough."

Paula hesitated, then said, "He wants me to marry him."

"Yes, I know."

"What should I do?"

"Why do you have doubts?"

"Because I'm not like other women. My power is still growing. I can feel it."

"That's as it should be."

"But it could be horrible for Dave to be married to someone like me."

"You'll know all his secrets. He can never tell even a white lie to you."

"What worries me even more than that is the future. Will I be called on again?"

"It's quite likely that you will," the old woman had said.

"How can I subject Dave to that—or our children if we have them."

"What does Dave say?"

"He says he loves me and that's all that matters."

"I think he's right."

"But . . . Grandma, I'm not sure I should ever marry anyone. Because of . . . of the way I am. What kind of a mother would I be? I'm not normal. My life will never be normal."

"You'll be a good mother. And you must have children, don't you see? You must have a daughter and pass on your abilities to her. It's the destiny of your family. It will always be so."

"You mean it's my duty," Paula said softly.

"Is it so unpleasant to have this duty, child?"

"Marrying Dave and raising his children? No, it's the kind of a duty I'd love, the kind of life I never thought I'd have."

"Put your worries aside and be happy, child."

And Paula had said she would.

"In time we'll talk again," her grandmother said. "But not right away."

And the old woman had faded away.

• 3 •

Before leaving for the office of Judge Zane T. Liggenmeyer, who was going to marry them, Dave phoned the hospital to check on Ed Prawdzik. Ed, the nurse replied, was still in a coma, as he had been since the accident. Maybe he would come out thirty seconds from now, maybe tomorrow, maybe next year, maybe never. It was what Dave had expected to hear, so he didn't let the news spoil his and Paula's special day.

They were married at 1:43 P.M.

They went home and spent the remainder of the afternoon making love.

The next morning they boarded a commuter flight bound for San Francisco, where they changed to a jet bound for England, where they would spend their honeymoon.

•4•

Ed Prawdzik floated in a place of darkness, a place with neither up nor down nor right nor left. And as he floated, voices seemed to call to him.

Choose.

And he knew what his options were. Life. Or this place.

Fire flared from nowhere, and Ed saw shadowy shapes chained to posts. Other shapes were torturing them, doing unspeakable things. Ed closed his eyes, and yet the vision would not go away. Nor would the screams—terrible cries of agony—that reverberated within his head.

Stop it, he thought. Oh, please stop it.

Choose.

I can't, Ed thought. I can't.

Go back to Andrea, be happy. Or stay here and be ours.
Choose!
CHOOSE!

•5•

In the ICU at Castle Bay General Hospital, subtle changes were noted by the instruments keeping track of Ed Prawdzik's life signs.

Then Ed's eyes fluttered open.

FROM THE BESTSELLING AUTHOR OF
SECRETS OF THE MORNING

TWILIGHT'S CHILD

V.C. ANDREWS™

The V. C. Andrews series continues
with the next mesmerizing chapter in
the Cutler series—TWILIGHT'S CHILD.

At long last Dawn is happy. She's
found her daughter Christy and she and
Jimmy have finally married. The future
is theirs. Yet Dawn's happiness is as
short lived as the dark clouds that have
always hovered above Cutler's Cove.

Dawn's happiness is threatened by her
sister Clara Sue's insane jealously, her
brother Philip's mad love for her and
the return of Michael Sutton her old
love—who may destroy her new world.

TWILIGHT'S CHILD

**COMING FROM
POCKET BOOKS
IN FEBRUARY 1992**

POCKET
B O O K S

194-01

Innocent People Caught
In the Grip Of
TERROR!

These thrilling novels—where deranged minds create sinister schemes, placing victims in mortal danger and striking horror in their hearts—will keep you in white-knuckled suspense!

- ☐ **BLOOD LEGACY** by Prudence Foster 67412/$3.95
- ☐ **THE CARTOONIST** by Sean Costello 67859/$3.95
- ☐ **DEADLY AFFECTIONS** by Billie Sue Mosiman 67874/$4.50
- ☐ **GHOST STORY** by Peter Straub 68563/$5.95
- ☐ **DARK LULLABY** by Jessica Palmer 70309/$4.95
- ☐ **WINTER SCREAM** by Chris Curry & Lisa Dean 68433/$4.95
- ☐ **GOAT DANCE** by Douglas Clegg 66425/$4.50
- ☐ **NIGHT THIRST** by Patrick Whalen 70654/$4.95
- ☐ **BLOOD LEGACY** by Prudence Foster 67412/$3.95
- ☐ **THE HACKER** by Chet Day 67611/$3.95
- ☐ **INTO THE PIT** by Warner Lee 66358/$3.95
- ☐ **IT'S LOOSE** by Warner Lee 67252/$3.95
- ☐ **THE PRIORY** by Margaret Wasser 66355/$3.95
- ☐ **SCARECROW** by Richie Tankersley Cusick 69020/$4.50
- ☐ **SATAN'S SERENADE** by Brent Monahan 67628/$3.95
- ☐ **BLAKE HOUSE** by Adrian Savage 67250/$3.95
- ☐ **THE DEVIL'S ADVOCATE**
  by Andrew Neiderman 68912/$3.95
- ☐ **DARK FATHER** by Tom Piccirilli 67401/$3.95
- ☐ **BREEDER** by Douglas Clegg 67277/$4.95
- ☐ **WITCH HUNT** by Devin O'Branagan 68455/$4.50
- ☐ **WITCH** by Katrina Alexis 67627/$4.50
- ☐ **CAPTAIN QUAD** by Sean Costello 70224/$4.95

Simon & Schuster, Mail Order Dept. TER
200 Old Tappan Rd., Old Tappan, N.J. 07675

POCKET
B O O K S

Please send me the books I have checked above. I am enclosing $_____ (please add 75¢ to cover postage and handling for each order. Please add appropriate local sales tax). Send check or money order—no cash or C.O.D.'s please. Allow up to six weeks for delivery. For purchases over $10.00 you may use VISA: card number, expiration date and customer signature must be included.

Name _____

Address _____

City _____ State/Zip _____

VISA Card No. _____ Exp. Date _____

Signature _____ 351-22